# COMMON LANGUAGE FOR PSYCHOTHERAPY PROCEDURES
## The first 80

Isaac Marks, Editor
Lucio Sibilia & Stefania Borgo, Co-Editors

www.commonlanguagepsychotherapy.org

First edition, 2010

Copyright (C) 2010 Centro per la Ricerca in Psicoterapia (CRP).
Piazza O. Marucchi n.5 - 00162 Rome (Italy)
Email: *info@crpitalia.eu*
*http://www.crpitalia.eu*

Permission is granted to copy and distribute this document under the terms of the GNU Free Documentation License, Version 1.3 or any later version published by the Free Software Foundation, with no Front-Cover Texts and no Back-Cover Texts. Invariant Sections are: "Sponsoring organisations", "Acknowledgements", "Task Force members", "Authors of accepted entries", and "Introduction". A copy of the licence is included in the section entitled "GNU Free Documentation License" at:
http://www.gnu.org/copyleft/fdl.html

Printed by: Books on Demand GmbH, 22848 Norderstedt, Germany

ISBN: 978-88-86290-02-9

# Contents

Sponsoring organisations ............................................................. 6
Task Force members .................................................................. 8
Authors of accepted entries ........................................................ 9
Introduction .............................................................................. 17

## Procedures:

Acceptance, promoting of ......................................................... 19
Anger management ................................................................... 21
Applied relaxation ..................................................................... 24
Assertiveness (assertive, assertion) training .............................. 27
Attention training ..................................................................... 29
Becoming the other .................................................................. 31
Behavioral activation ................................................................ 34
Cognitive defusion .................................................................... 37
Cognitive restructuring ............................................................. 39
Community reinforcement approach ......................................... 41
Compassion-focused therapy .................................................... 43
Computer-aided vicarious exposure .......................................... 46
Coping cat treatment ................................................................ 48
Countertransference, use of ..................................................... 51
Danger ideation reduction therapy ........................................... 53
Decisional balance .................................................................... 55
Dialectical behaviour therapy ................................................... 57
Dream interpretation ................................................................ 60
Empathy dots, use of ................................................................ 63
Evoked response arousal plus sensitization .............................. 65
Experiment ............................................................................... 67
Exposure, interoceptive (to internal cues) ................................ 69
Exposure, live (in-vivo, live desensitization) ............................. 71
Expressed empathy .................................................................. 73
Expressive writing therapy ....................................................... 75
Family focused grief therapy .................................................... 77
Family work for schizophrenia .................................................. 80
Fixed-role therapy .................................................................... 83

Free association.....................................................................................................85
Guided mourning..................................................................................................87
Habit reversal.......................................................................................................89
Harm reduction ....................................................................................................92
Imagery rehearsal therapy of nightmares............................................................94
Imagery rescripting therapy..................................................................................96
Imago relationship therapy...................................................................................99
Inflated responsibility, reducing..........................................................................102
Internalized-other interviewing...........................................................................104
Internet-based therapy.......................................................................................107
Interpersonal psychotherapy .............................................................................109
Interpreting defenses against unpleasant feelings.............................................112
Life-review (reminiscence) therapy....................................................................114
Linking current, past and transference relationships ........................................116
Mentalizing, promotion of...................................................................................118
Metacognitive therapy .......................................................................................121
Metaphor, use of................................................................................................123
Method of levels ................................................................................................125
Mindfulness training...........................................................................................128
Morita therapy....................................................................................................131
Motivational enhancement therapy ...................................................................134
Motivational interviewing ...................................................................................136
Narrative exposure.............................................................................................138
Nidotherapy........................................................................................................140
Problem-solving therapy ....................................................................................141
Prolonged exposure counterconditioning..........................................................143
Prolonged-grief therapy......................................................................................145
Promoting resilience in young children..............................................................148
Puppet play preparing children for surgery........................................................151
Reciprocal role procedures, describing & changing..........................................154
Repairing rupture...............................................................................................157
Repertory grid technique....................................................................................159
Ritual (response) prevention..............................................................................161
Schema focussed emotive behavior therapy ....................................................163
Self as context...................................................................................................166
Self-control skills training ..................................................................................168
Self-praise training.............................................................................................171

Sibling fighting-reduction training.................................................................173
Skills-directed therapy ................................................................................175
Socratic questioning....................................................................................177
Solution-focused questioning / brief therapy..............................................179
Speech restructuring...................................................................................181
Stimulus control of worry............................................................................183
Task concentration training ........................................................................185
Time-boundary setting and interpreting......................................................188
Time-in management..................................................................................190
Token economy...........................................................................................193
Transference interpretation.........................................................................195
Triple P – positive parenting program.........................................................199
Two-chair technique....................................................................................202
Validation of feelings...................................................................................205
Values exploration and construction...........................................................207
Well-being therapy .....................................................................................209

## Sponsoring organisations

Association for Behavioral and Cognitive Therapies
www.abct.org

European Association for Behavioural and Cognitive Therapies
eabct.glimworm.com

American Psychoanalytic Association
www.apsa.org

Asian Psychological Association
www.cdu.edu.au/apsya

Australian Psychological Society
www.psychology.org.au

British Association for Counselling & Psychotherapy
www.bacp.co.uk

Centro per la Ricerca in Psicoterapia
www.crpitalia.eu

Royal College of Psychiatrists
www.rcpsych.ac.uk

Sociedad Mexicana de Psicología
www.sociedadmexicanadepsicologia.org

Society for Psychotherapy Research
www.psychotherapyresearch.org

Society for the Exploration of Psychotherapy Integration
sepiweb.org

World Psychiatric Association
www.wpanet.org

## Acknowledgements

This volume has been made possible thanks to the collaborative work of the clp Task Force members and of the 95 authors of the 80 entries listed below.

## Task Force members

Co-ordinating Editors
**Isaac Marks**, Institute of Psychiatry, King's College London, UK
**Lucio Sibilia,** Dept. of Clinical Sciences, Università di Roma Sapienza, Italy
**Stefania Borgo,** Dept. of Education, Università di Roma Sapienza, Italy

Deputy Co-ordinating Editor
**Miguel A Fullana,** Dept. of Psychiatry, Autonomous University of Barcelona, Bellaterra, Catalunya, Spain

Administrator
**Lorena Fernández de la Cruz,** Dept. of Psychiatry, Autonomous University of Barcelona, Bellaterra, Catalunya, Spain

*Association of Behavior and Cognitive Therapy (ABCT)*
**Marvin Goldfried,** Dept. of Psychology Stony Brook University, Stony Brook, NY, USA
**Michelle G Newman**, Dept. of Psychology, Pennsylvania State University, USA
**George Stricker,** Argosy University, Washington DC, USA

*Australian Psychology Society* (APS)
**Kate Moore,** Faculty of Education, Health and Science, Charles Darwin University, Darwin, Australia

*European Association of Behaviour and Cognitive Therapy (EABCT)*
**Pim Cuijpers**, Dept. of Clinical Psychology, VU University Amsterdam, The Netherlands
**Mehmet Sungur,** Psychiatry Dept. of Marmara University Hospital, Istanbul, Turkey

Psychodynamic Editor
**Jeremy Holmes,** Dept. of Clinical Psychology, Washington Singer Building, University of Exeter, UK

Dynamic website creator and manager
**Marco Benard,** Dept. of Clinical Psychology, VU University Amsterdam, The Netherlands

Book-on-Demand Editor
**Dimitra Kakaraki,** Centro per la Ricerca in Psicoterapia, Roma, Italy

Classification Consultant
**Miquel Tortella**, Dept.of Psychology, University of Balearic Islands, Palma, Majorca, Spain

## Authors of accepted entries

**ALLEN, Jon G**
*Mentalizing, promotion of*

**ALPERS, Georg W**
*Exposure, live (in-vivo, live desensitization)*
*Internet-based therapy*

**ANGUS, Lynne**
*Expressed empathy*

**ARKOWITZ, Hal**
*Experiment*
*Motivational interviewing*

**ATHANASSIADOU, Eftychia**
*Puppet play preparing children for surgery*

**BAILEY, Bridget**
*Interpersonal psychotherapy*

**BARLOW, David H**
*Exposure, interoceptive (to internal cues)*

**BARRETT, Paula**
*Promoting resilience (social/emotional competence) in young children*

**BASDEN, Shawnee L**
*Exposure, interoceptive (to internal cues)*

**BATEMAN, Anthony W**
*Mentalizing, promotion of*

**BLACKLEDGE, John T**
*Acceptance, promoting of*
*Cognitive defusion*
*Self as context*
*Values exploration and construction*

**BÖGELS, Susan**
*Task concentration training*

**BOHLMEIJER, Ernst**
*Life-review (reminiscence) therapy*

**BORGO, Stefania**
*Assertiveness (Assertive, Assertion) training*
*Cognitive restructuring*

**BORKOVEC, Thomas D**
*Stimulus control of worry*

**CAREY, Tim**
*Method of levels*

**CHASSON, Gregory S**
*Habit reversal*

**CHRISTOGIORGIOS, Stelios**
*Puppet play preparing children for surgery*

**D'ZURILLA, Thomas J**
*Problem-solving therapy*

**DISKIN, Katherine M**
*Decisional balance*
*Motivational enhancement therapy*

**DOBSON, Keith S**
*Socratic questioning*

**ELBERT, Thomas**
*Narrative exposure*

**ESPOSITO, Rosario**
*Validation of feelings*

**FAVA, Giovanni**
*Well-being therapy*

**FISHER, Peter**
*Applied relaxation*

**FOLENSBEE, Rowland**
*Stimulus control of worry*

**FONAGY, Peter**
*Mentalizing, promotion of*

**GILBERT, Paul**
*Compassion-focused therapy*

**GREENBERG, Leslie S**
*Two-chair dialogue*

**HARRIS, Tirril**
*Transference interpretation*

**HERPERTZ-DAHLMANN, Beate**
*Metacognitive therapy*

**HODGINS, David C**
*Decisional balance*
*Motivational enhancement therapy*

**HOFFMAN, Leon**
*Free association*
*Interpreting defenses against unpleasant feelings*

**HOLMES, Jeremy**
*Countertransference, use of*
*Linking current, past and transference relationships (triangle of person)*
*Metaphor, use of*
*Time-boundary setting and interpreting*

**HOPKO, Derek R**
*Behavioral activation*

**JONES, Mairwen**
*Danger ideation reduction therapy*

**KENDALL, Philip C**
*Coping cat treatment*

**KERKHOF, Ad JFM**
*Community reinforcement approach*

**KHANNA, Muniya**
*Coping cat treatment*

**KISSANE, David William**
 Family focused grief therapy

**KOLAITIS, Gerasimos**
 Puppet play preparing children for surgery

**KIRKBY, Ken**
 Computer-aided vicarious exposure

**LEFF, Julian**
 Family work for schizophrenia

**LEJUEZ, Carl W**
 Behavioral activation

**LISON, Sam**
 Imago relationship therapy

**LOGAN, Diane E**
 Harm reduction

**LOVELL, Karina**
 Empathy dots, use of

**MANSELL, Warren**
 Method of levels

**MACAULAY, Helen**
 Expressed empathy

**MARKS, Isaac**
 Assertiveness (Assertive, Assertion) Training
 Cognitive restructuring
 Token economy

**MARLATT, Alan**
 Harm reduction

**McKAY, Dean**
 Ritual (response) prevention

**MENZIES, Ross**
 Speech restructuring

**MONTANGERO, Jacques**
*Dream interpretation*

**NAKAMURA, Kei**
*Morita therapy*

**NEUNER, Frank**
*Narrative exposure*

**NEZU, Arthur M**
*Problem-solving therapy*

**NEZU, Christine M**
*Problem-solving therapy*

**NOVACO, Raymond W**
*Anger management*

**ONSLOW, Mark**
*Speech restructuring*

**PAHL, Kristine**
*Promoting resilience (social/emotional competence) in young children*

**PARKES, Colin Murray**
*Guided mourning*
*Prolonged-grief therapy*

**PAUNOVIC, Nenad**
*Prolonged exposure counterconditioning*

**PENNEBAKER, James W**
*Expressive writing therapy*

**PILECKI, Brian**
*Ritual (response) prevention*

**POSTMA, Kirstine**
*Solution-focused questioning / brief therapy*

**RADOMSKY, Adam S**
*Inflated responsibility, reducing*

**RAO, Nasa Sanjay Kumar**
*Solution-focused questioning / brief therapy*

**RENWICK, Stanley J**
*Anger management*

**RICHARDS, David**
*Empathy dots, use of*

**RONEN, Tammie**
*Skills-directed therapy*
*Self-control skills training*

**ROOZEN, Hendrik G**
*Community reinforcement approach*

**ROSENBAUM, Michael**
*Skills-directed therapy*
*Self-control skills training*

**RUBEN, Douglas H**
*Evoked response arousal plus sensitization*
*Self-praise training*
*Sibling fighting-reduction training*
*Time-in management*

**RYLE, Anthony**
*Reciprocal role procedures; describing & changing*

**SAFRAN, Jeremy D**
*Repairing rupture*

**SANDERS, Matthew R**
*Triple P – Positive Parenting Program*

**SCHAUER, Maggie**
*Narrative exposure*

**SCHNEIDER, Sylvie**
*Metacognitive therapy*

**SIBILIA, Lucio**
*Assertiveness (Assertive, Assertion) Training*
*Cognitive restructuring*

*Imagery rehearsal therapy of nightmares*

**SIMONS, Michael**
*Metacognitive therapy*

**SMITH, Alistair**
*Mindfulness training*

**SMUCKER, Mervin R**
*Imagery rescripting therapy*

**SNYDER, Maryhelen**
*Becoming the other*

**STANTON, Maggie**
*Dialectical behavior therapy*

**TAYLOR, C Barr**
*Internet-based therapy*

**TOMM, Karl**
*Internalized-other interviewing*

**TSIANTIS, John**
*Puppet play preparing children for surgery*

**TYRER, Peter**
*Nidotherapy*

**WELLS, Adrian**
*Attention training (AT)*

**WHITE, Kamila S**
*Exposure, interoceptive (to internal cues)*

**WILHELM, Sabine**
*Habit reversal*

**WINTER, David**
*Fixed-role therapy*
*Repertory grid technique*

**WINZELBERG, Andrew J**
*Internet-based therapy*

**ZORN, Peter**
*Schema focussed emotive behavior therapy*

## Introduction

Common Language for Psychotherapy (clp) project hopes to develop a general lexicon of psychotherapy procedures. Having no common language can confuse clinicians and patients, hamper communication, and impede research. It is frequently hard to know exactly what therapists do just from the names of their procedures and their orientation. There may be no clear connection between what therapists do and the reasons given for doing it. Different terms are sometimes used to describe the same or very similar procedures (e.g. "brainstorming" at p.141 and "free association" at p.85) and the same term for different procedures (e.g. "experiment" at p.67).

The lack of a common language also impedes research. Though there is ample evidence that certain problems improve with particular psychotherapy `packages', those packages may have a variety of names for varying combinations of procedures. This obscures which procedure/s within the packages produce the improvement. The Babel of babble about what therapists do prompted the European and the North American Associations of Behavioural and Cognitive Therapy to set up a Task Force to work towards a common language for psychotherapy (clp) procedures that is internationally accepted. Many more psychotherapy associations representing diverse approaches have added their sponsorship. The emergence of shared plain terms can reduce confusion and speed the evolution of psychotherapy into a science. Progress towards a common language to describe psychotherapy procedures is seen in the expanding website: www.commonlanguagepsychotherapy.org.

In this CLP website therapists portray how they use particular procedures in everyday language shorn of theory, and clarify what they do with brief real case illustrations. Therapists submit website entries describing a procedure in response to personal or clp-website invitations. Their entry/ies describe operationally what they do with clients, regardless of any background theory. Each entry submitted is edited interactively between the Task Force and the Author to ensure it follows the common clp template. Each entry gives an empirical fly-on-the-wall view of what the therapist does to apply a procedure, including a practical case illustration, and avoids theory as far as possible.

This reference volume is the fruit of the work of the clp Task Force and the authors of the entries. It shows the first 80 entries for procedures to appear on the clp web-site. They represent many therapy approaches. Their 95 authors are from Australia, Canada, France, Germany, Greece, Israel, Italy, Japan, Netherlands, Sweden, Switzerland and the UK and USA. More authors of entries are in train. Their contributions and those of further therapists will be included in a later expanded volume.

All therapists are invited to join this ongoing attempt to describe most psychotherapy procedures in a way which anyone can understand.

*Isaac Marks*
*Lucio Sibilia*
*Stefania Borgo*

London, August 2010

# ACCEPTANCE, PROMOTING OF

John T BLACKLEDGE, Morehead State University, Kentucky 40351, USA; ph +1 606-783-2982; & Association for Contextual Behavioral Science Board of Directors

**Definition:** Training a willingness to experience thoughts, feelings, and bodily sensations without trying to avoid or change them.

**Elements:** Discuss costs in the client's life of non-acceptance e.g. from harmful avoidance such as procrastination or drinking. Encourage contact with the present both within (e.g. ask someone reluctant to feel anxiety during pursuit of a valued relationship to allow each sensation felt when frightened to remain as it is and regard thoughts about those feelings as just thoughts or words) and without (be mindful of and accept external cues encountered while pursuing a value that elicits anxiety). Clients are encouraged to practice acceptance when distressing experiences impede engagement in valued action.

**Related procedures:** *Exposure, mindfulness.*

**Application:** In individual or group ACT (acceptance and commitment therapy).

**1st use?** Hayes (1994) in ACT. Is also promoted in other therapies and in meditation and religious practices.

**References:**
1. Hayes SC (1994). Content, context, and the types of psychological acceptance. In SC Hayes, NS Jacobson, VM Follette, MJ Dougher (Eds.), *Acceptance and change: Content and context in psychotherapy* (pp. 13-32). Reno, NV: Context Press.
2. Hayes SC, Wilson KW, Gifford EV, Follette VM, Strosahl K (1996). Experiential avoidance and behavioral disorders: A functional dimensional approach to diagnosis and treatment. *Journal of Consulting and Clinical Psychology, 64*, 1152-1168.
3. Hayes SC, Strosahl KD, Wilson KG (1999). *Acceptance and commitment therapy: An experiential approach to behavior change.* New York: Guilford.
4. Luoma JB, Hayes SC, Walser RD (2007). *Learning ACT: An Acceptance and commitment therapy skills-training manual for therapists.* Oakland, CA: New Harbinger.

**Case illustration 1:** (Blackledge unpublished)

Jill: "I can't think about this anymore - it just makes me too anxious". Therapist: "I know this is important to you, so let's see if we can just ease into this experience one piece at a time. *Physically, where in your body do you feel this anxiety?*" Jill: "My shoulders are tense... my stomach feels nauseous". *"Let's focus just on that shoulder tension. Imagine you have a red felt-tip pen and are coloring in the exact area where that shoulder tension is and its borders... Now, notice what quality that tension has. Is it a dull pain, a sharp pain, a tightness?... Is there anything about that muscle tension... - that you can't have? If so, can you let go of that resistance and instead let that muscle tension be there, on its own terms?"* Jill assents to fully allow the tension to be there.

Therapist moves onto other aspects of her experience of anxiety, one at a time.

**Case illustration 2:** (Blackledge unpublished)

Bill: "I'm so ashamed of what I've done, I don't know if I can face her". Therapist:"*Your relationship with Joy is very important to you - and you and I know that to maintain it you'll need to face her, and you'll probably feel ashamed when you do so. With that goal in mind, are you willing to stay with your sense of shame in here, right now?"* Bill (after long pause): "Yeah, I'll try...". Therapist (empathically):*"Tell me about that shame you're feeling now. What thoughts come with it?... Where does that feeling sit in your body - what sensations go with it?... When a piece of that experience - a thought, a feeling, a sensation - shows up that you're unwilling to have, let me know, and we'll work through it."*

# ANGER MANAGEMENT

Raymond W NOVACO & Stanley J RENWICK, Department of Psychology & Social Behavior, University of California, Irvine, CA 92697-7085; ph +1-949-824-7206

**Definition:** A structured treatment to foster self-regulation of anger and aggressive behaviour.

**Elements:** Clients are taught to become alert to triggers and signs of their anger. Anger management tries to reduce anger frequency, intensity, duration, and mode of expression in three key areas:
1. Cognitive restructuring of clients' attentional focus, thinking styles, fixed ways of perceiving aversive events, and rumination.
2. Reducing general tension, arousal to provocation, and impulsive reactions by training controlled breathing, deep muscle relaxation, and use of tranquil imagery.
3. Training behavioural coping (e.g. diplomacy, strategic withdrawal, and respectful assertiveness) to handle provoking situations constructively and promote problem solving.

Cognitive, arousal reduction and behavioural skills are fostered through therapist-guided progressive exposure to simulated anger-provocations in imagined and role play scenarios. People with angry dispositions, particularly in forensic settings, often require preliminary raising of readiness for anger management by fostering recognition of the costs of recurrent anger, by learning and practising self-monitoring and relaxation skills, and by making it safe to talk about anger.

**Related Procedures:** *Cognitive restructuring, exposure, mindfulness, motivational interviewing, problem-solving, relaxation training, role play, schema-focused therapy, social skills training, stress immunization (inoculation).*

**Application:** Individually and in groups, for adolescents and adults, in community and institutional settings. Depth and length of sessions vary with client needs.

**1st use:** Novaco (1975).

**References:**
1. Cavell TA, Malcolm KT (2007). *Anger, aggression, and interventions for interpersonal violence.* Mahwah, NJ: Erlbaum.
2. Novaco RW (1975). *Anger control: The development and evaluation of an experimental treatment.* Lexington, MA: DC Heath.

3. Novaco RW, Chemtob CM (2002). Anger and combat-related posttraumatic stress disorder. *Journal of Traumatic Stress*, 15, 123-132.
4. Renwick S, Black L, Ramm M, Novaco RW (1997). Anger treatment with forensic hospital patients. *Legal and Criminological Psychology*, 2, 103-116.

**Case illustration:** (Novaco & Renwick, unpublished)

Sandy, a soldier aged 26, was admitted to hospital after attempting suicide by overdose. He was angry, irritable, slept poorly, and drank excessive alcohol. Outbursts caused social isolation and frightened his family. Anger had been lifelong, and alternated with depression. He blamed recurrent "road rages" on `bad driving by miscreants', whom he pursued and confronted. Those "road rage" episodes had begun three years earlier, after two driving accidents in a combat zone where he'd been the commanding officer but not the driver. The accidents left him disabled with pain and discomfort. He was judged unfit for service. Social withdrawal led to self styled "paranoid" rumination with high arousal and sensitivity. There was no post traumatic stress disorder. He'd been physically abused as a child.

Sandy had anger management in individual one-hour sessions twice-weekly over six months. Keeping an anger diary helped him detect thinking, feeling, and action aspects of his anger reactions. He was helped to spot and replace antagonistic thinking with more constructive thoughts. For example, he believed that his trouble in getting medical care and military-unit support was because they felt embarrassed by and wanted to discharge him. On uncovering this belief, the therapist encouraged Sandy to question its validity and see realistic alternatives, such as errors in administration and care pathways -- i.e., a flawed system rather than a conspiracy. His "paranoid" world view was challenged supportively and changed from seeing "conspiracy" to seeing "fallibility" or "incompetence". In parallel, the therapist helped Sandy to detect anger at its onset (e.g. when provoked by an official letter or pain from his injuries). Early detection of anger signs prevented anger intensifying and escalating into conflict with others. Slow breathing, calming self-instructions, and shifting attention to something benign served to reduce angry feelings on the spot. Arousal-reduction skills were enhanced by training in muscle relaxation and using tranquil imagery. Recurrent critical problems were reviewed to help him adopt alternative constructive ways to deal with them. In a stress-inoculation procedure the therapist reviewed with Sandy past anger-evoking situations and re-exposed him to them, progressing gradually from low-anger to high-anger ones. Sandy did the re-exposures in imagined and role-play scenarios, such as difficult contacts with administrators about his continuing medical-care needs. The therapist showed and rehearsed with Sandy how to elicit the help he needed and to set aside his hostile manner that alienated people.

During anger management work, Sandy's anger outbursts became less frequent and intense. This, in turn, helped him to sleep better, drink less alcohol, and improve his family life. Despite continuing pain and disability, he became more positive and self-confident.

# APPLIED RELAXATION

**Peter FISHER**, Department of Clinical Psychology, University of Liverpool, Whelan Building, Brownlow Hill, Liverpool, L69 3GB, UK; ph +44 151 794 5279

**Definition:** Learning to relax rapidly as soon as signs of anxiety are recognised.

**Elements:** The therapist teaches the client to watch for early signs of anxiety (worrying thoughts, somatic symptoms e.g. palpitations, abdominal discomfort, muscle tension) as cues to immediately start *progressive muscle relaxation*. This involves repeatedly tensing-then releasing a succession of muscle groups across the whole body, starting with hands & fingers, forearms, biceps, shoulders, etc. For 15-30 minutes the client tenses each muscle group for 5 seconds, then relaxes it for 10-15 seconds, and is asked to practise this as daily homework. Later, the client practises the same tensing-releasing with larger muscle groups such as the whole arm. This is followed by *release-only* sessions and homework in which the client focuses on relaxing to release the tension from each muscle group from the head down to the feet. Next, in *cue-controlled relaxation*, clients link release-only relaxation to breathing. As they breathe in they are told to think 'in' and as they breathe out to think 'relax' and release tension at the same time, and to practise this daily and achieve a relaxed state in 2-3 minutes. Eventually, in *rapid relaxation*, the therapist asks the client to take a few deep breaths, think `relax' before exhaling slowly, and aim to become relaxed in less than 30 seconds.

Application training follows. Clients are taught to achieve a relaxed state during daily activities e.g. walking, shopping, and to apply and practise rapid relaxation during exposure to feared situations until these are no longer frightening. They are encouraged to scan their bodies for signs of anxiety and do rapid relaxation whenever they feel anxiety/muscle tension, and to continue practising rapid relaxation after therapy has ended.

**Related procedures:** *Progressive muscle relaxation, systematic desensitisation, imaginal exposure, live (in vivo) exposure, breathing retraining, modeling.*

**Application:** With individuals, sometimes in groups, for panic, phobia and general anxiety, and medical conditions worsened by anxiety/muscle tension.

**1st use?** Jacobson (1938) developed progressive relaxation and advocated its use in real-life stressful situations.

References:
1. Jacobson E (1938). *Progressive Relaxation*. Chicago, IL: University of Chicago Press.
2. Ost L-G (1987). Applied relaxation: Description of a coping technique and review of controlled studies. *Behaviour Research and Therapy*, 25, 397-409.

**Case illustration:**

Maggie, a teacher age 45, had since her late teens worried about many things, especially about being under-prepared for her classes. She became anxious on leaving for work and for a few minutes just before starting a class, and couldn't give pupils her full attention. She had butterflies in her stomach and palpitations and couldn't relax.

Maggie had 12 sessions of applied relaxation. She rated anxiety and mood weekly, initially rating moderate-to-severe anxiety and mild depression. She was taught to recognise early signs of anxiety and to relax rapidly on noticing these. On a self monitoring form she noted early signs of anxiety in everyday situations. She began progressive muscle relaxation by tensing-then-releasing many small muscle groups e.g. toes, feet, calves, and later her whole leg. Next she practised release-only relaxation by breathing slowly and normally with calm, regular breaths and noticing her growing relaxation. She was then asked to relax each small muscle group in turn, interspersed with instructions to keep her breathing calm and controlled. She was given an audiotape of this session to listen to during release-only relaxation homework. Differential relaxation followed starting with cue-controlled relaxation to relax while using only those muscles needed for a particular activity e.g. *'look out of the window while relaxing every muscle except those needed to turn your head', 'cross your legs using only the muscles necessary and keep all your other muscles relaxed'*.

Differential relaxation training in everyday situations began by walking round the therapist's office while relaxing facial muscles. Maggie then practised relaxing every muscle except those required during tasks such as reading or eating. Next she shortened cue-controlled relaxation to achieve rapid relaxation. The therapist modelled this for Maggie and guided her through taking one deep breath and then slowly exhaling while visualising the word `relax'. She practised this in session and as homework in many situations e.g. walking her dog, playing board games with her children, shopping, then at school. To overcome self-consciousness that teachers or pupils would notice her doing relaxation, to check that she was relaxing appropriately the therapist asked Maggie to demonstrate rapid relaxation to him in session and then accompanied her to a real supermarket and modelled rapid-relaxation there to show it was inconspicuous. Maggie also looked at a video of her practising rapid relaxation in the therapist's office to see that her class was unlikely to notice her doing rapid relaxation. By 3-month follow-up she had no panics, worried far less about school and teaching, was not depressed, and managed occasional anxiety just before classes and at other times by applying rapid relaxation.

# ASSERTIVENESS (ASSERTIVE, ASSERTION) TRAINING

**Isaac MARKS**, 43 Dulwich Common, London SE217EU, UK; ph+44 208 2994130; **Lucio SIBILIA**, Dipartimento di Scienze Cliniche, Università Sapienza di Roma & Centro per la Ricerca in Psicoterapia, Roma, Italy; ph +39 06 86320838; **Stefania BORGO**, Università Sapienza di Roma & Centro per la Ricerca in Psicoterapia, Roma, Italy; ph +39 06 86320838.

**Definition:** A form of *social skills training* to carry out culturally / context-appropriate assertive behaviors that the client lacks e.g. initiating, continuing and/or stopping social contact; responding to requests, demands and/or annoying behaviors; expressing feelings; exercising own rights while respecting other people's rights.

**Elements:** Targets the behavioral, cognitive, and emotive components of assertion e.g. what to say, how to say it, tone, body language. Involves *role play*, *modeling*, *feedback* of *videotaped practice*, *homework* of increasingly difficult social tasks, praise of progress (*reinforcement*, *reward*, *contingency management*). Includes:
- *Problem-solving* by helping clients to: define their problem social behaviour and break it down into manageable bits to be learned one by one; find alternative (adaptive) forms of social interaction; *self-observe* to *achieve perspective* (*distancing*).
- *Exposure* to feared social situations and *behavioural experiments* to challenge the negative thoughts, self-talk and imagery evoked by those situations.
- *Rehearsal* of new social behaviour in the treatment session and in *homework* in imagination and in real life (involves *exposure* and *behavioural experiments* if behaviour/situations are feared), followed by *reward*.
- *Cognitive restructuring* to change socially maladaptive thoughts to more adaptive ones.

**Related procedures:** *Social skills training* to remedy social skills deficits (not excesses as in *anger management*) and of *rational emotive therapy* in its education in personal rights.

**1st use?** Salter A (1949) *Conditioned Reflex Therapy*, Capricorn Books, NY used `Assertiveness Training' to describe how to increase clients' social skills and reduce social anxiety.

**References:**
Marks IM (1986). *Behavioural Psychotherapy. Maudsley Pocketbook of Clinical Management*. John Wright, Bristol.

**Case illustration:** (Marks et al 1986)
Pat had long feared and avoided eating with people, and always been shy and reserved with a limited social life. With her therapist she set medium-term targets of eating a meal with three other friends and also at her boyfriend's home with his family (*goal setting*). She described a detailed imagined scene of having a meal with her boyfriend (*imaginal [fantasy] exposure*) and the therapist *prompt*ed Pat's flow of talk when she flagged (*guided fantasy/imagery*). She then actually had a meal with herboy friend (*live [real, in vivo] exposure*); Pat also *role play*ed asserting herself appropriately. In `playlets' her therapist pretended to be a shop assistant and Pat acted the part of a customer returning defective goods. This was *videotaped* and played back to her (*feedback*). She was taught what to say as a disgruntled customer (*assertion*), and they played the same parts again and switched roles with Pat as the salesperson (*reverse role play*). They also acted asking the way in the street from a stranger and refusing to carry out an unreasonable request from a colleague. The therapist first *modelled* what to do and then asked Pat to do the same thing (*rehearsal*). Pat then lunched with an acquaintance (*live [real, in vivo]* exposure). Pat now joined five other socially phobic patients for a day-long group session (*social skills training*). The therapist outlined the program. They played contact party games to encourage mixing, like having one of their number break out of a circle... etc... made by the others, and without using hands transfer an orange held under the neck to another patient. These warm-up exercises led into *role play* of increasingly difficult social situations (*exposure*). Toward evening the group split into subgroups to shop for ingredients for a meal to cook together (*social skills training, confidence building*). They chatted to one another and then ate together. After initial unease they enjoyed themselves and planned to meet one another after the group's conclusion. Pat had further sessions with the therapist alone. By six-month follow-up she was dining regularly with her fiance and his family and in selected restaurants with him and occasionally with a larger group of friends.

# ATTENTION TRAINING (AT)

**Adrian WELLS,** University of Manchester, Division of Clinical Psychology, Rawnsley Building, MRI, Manchester, M13 9WL, UK; ph +44 161 276 5399

**Definition:** AT involves attending to several kinds of sounds coming at the same time from different places for about 11 minutes at a time without trying to improve symptoms or perform particular tasks.

**Elements:** The therapist tells patients their disorder is maintained by patterns of thinking that dwell on symptoms, traumas and social problems, so Attention Training (AT) can help them control and react flexibly to those patterns. If during AT practice unpleasant feelings/thoughts/ memories or bodily sensations arise, patients should simply see these as noise and continue attending to them without trying to get distracted from or analyse those or make themselves feel better. Instead AT helps them suspend any response of worry, rumination or attention to threat. Before starting AT, patients are asked to rate self-focus on a scale from -3 (entirely externally focused) to +3 (entirely self-focused) and try to reduce self-focus by 2 points by the end of the AT-practice session.

In attention training the therapist presents 5-7 sounds simultaneously and asks the patient to:

1. for 5 minutes, attend <u>selectively</u> to each of those sounds in turn, first identifying it and then attending intensively to it e.g. *"focus intensely on each (specified in turn) of 6 sounds which you can hear in the near distance on your right hand side"*;

2. for the next 5 minutes, <u>switch</u> attention <u>rapidly</u> from one sound to a different sound at another location e.g. *"switch your attention quickly from each of those 6 sounds to another of those sounds"*;

3. for the next minute, <u>divide</u> attention by <u>simultaneously</u> focusing on as many different sounds and locations as possible e.g. *"For 1 minute focus at the same time on as many as possible of the 6 sounds that you can hear together* (pause). *Now, expand your attention and count how many sounds you can hear at the same time"*.

At the end of the session the therapist says *"As homework until your next session, once or twice a day when you're **not** feeling anxious, practise 5' of <u>selective</u> AT, then 5' of <u>rapidly-switching</u> AT, then 1' of <u>divided</u> AT. Keep a diary of the number of times you practise AT'.*

**Related procedures:** *Meditation, task-focusing* in sport psychology, *test-anxiety,* and *pain management, task concentration training.*

**Application:** AT is used to attain flexible control over runaway worry, rumination and focusing on threat that might worsen depression and anxiety. AT may be used alone or during some applications of metacognitive therapy.

**1st use?** Wells A (1990).

**References:**
1. Wells A (1990). Panic disorder in association with relaxation induced anxiety: An attention training approach to treatment. *Behavior Therapy, 21*, 273-280.
2. Wells A, White J, Carter K (1997). Attention training: Effects on anxiety and beliefs in panic and social phobia. *Clinical Psychology and Psychotherapy, 4*, 226-232.
3. Papageorgiou C, Wells A (1998). Effects of attention training in hypochondriasis: An experimental case series. *Psychological Medicine, 28*, 193-200.
4. Papageorgiou C, Wells A (2000). Treatment of recurrent major depression with attention training. *Cognitive and Behavioral Practice, 7*, 407- 418.

**Case illustration:** (Wells, unpublished)

Mary had been depressed for nine months - her second depressive episode. She had negative thoughts e.g. "I'm a failure, a depressive, defective; I'll never recover; Why do people seem happier than me?". The therapist said those thoughts could be made easier to interrupt by practising attention training (AT) in each therapy session and as homework. This could help her gain flexible non-repetitive thinking. At the start of each session Mary did 11 minutes of AT (5' <u>selective</u>, then 5' <u>rapidly-switching</u>, then 1' <u>divided</u> <u>AT</u>) followed by metacognitive therapy. The therapist asked Mary to listen to a combination of sounds such as a ticking clock, a radio tuned between stations, a metronome, tapping with a pencil, and other sounds coming from outside. He also asked Mary to do AT practice at home twice a day listening to several sounds at the same time which varied in loudness and location, including an AT recording he gave her of sounds such as church bells, running water, birdsong, traffic, and a clock.

After 8 sessions of attention training and other aspects of metacognitive therapy Mary became less depressed and remained improved to 6-month follow-up.

# BECOMING THE OTHER

**Maryhelen SNYDER**, 9672 Farmside Place Vienna, VA 22182, USA, ph +1 703 759 3168

**Definition:** Teaching clients to dialogue empathically with another person, speaking 'in that person's shoes' expressing that person's view and experience.

**Elements:** The therapist asks: *'If you'd like to learn to listen deeply, could you describe an emotionally important memory (up to 3 minutes)?'*. The client tells this. The therapist may say: *'If it's OK, I'd like to speak now as though I'm you,... trying to enter your world and feel what you feel. I won't interpret or analyze but may use words you didn't when I try to speak as you. I'm not actually you, so please interrupt if what I say doesn't fit exactly for you'*.
The therapist guides the client to:
- *'Listen carefully in order to experience another person's feelings, values, intentions, and growing edges'*.
- *'While listening, set aside analysis, judgment, your perspective; instead, welcome the other's experience into your consciousness'*.
- *'As you practice "becoming", allow yourself to deepen what the other person has said... to be moved'*.
- *'If you're interrupted (even by a facial expression that something doesn't fit), you can say, "I didn't get that quite right, did I? Can you help me?"* (or *"Let me try again")*.'
- *'When you stop, you can ask "Does that feel right? Is there anything you'd like to correct, or add?"* '
    Clients & couples practice 'becoming' the other person within and between sessions, starting with minor, and later major, conflict areas. At follow-up couples who're 'blocking' can have booster sessions.

**Related procedures:** Active listening, expressed empathy, internalized-other interviewing, two-chair dialogue.

**Application:** In individual, couple, and family therapy, and in training and supervision.

**1st use?** Of 'Becoming', Snyder (1995).

**References:**
1. Scuka R (2005). *Relationship enhancement therapy: Healing through deep empathy and intimate dialogue.* New York: Routledge.
2. Snyder M (1995). "Becoming": A method for expanding systemic thinking

and deepening empathic accuracy. *Family Process*, 34, 241-253.
3. Snyder M (2009). Becoming each other: A single case example of relational consciousness in couple therapy. *Clinical Social Work Journal*, 37, 190-199.

**Case Illustration 1:** (Snyder unpublished)
Ron and Janet attended their 4th weekly session where each spoke to the other from their own experience, listened attentively as though inside the other's skin, and accepting corrections with grace and without argument. Janet told Ron her differing view about their argument the previous night, without being mean or critical. Ron's face reddened with rigid neck tendons, protruding veins, and clenched jaw.

Trying to empathize with clenched teeth without feeling attuned to the speaker doesn't usually work, so the therapist asked Ron if he'd like the therapist to answer empathically and then allow him to express his feelings. Ron replied "I might speak as you showed us in our last session" (see Elements above. Clients can learn empathic skill after just once speaking "in the shoes" of another person. Ron spoke as Janet while looking at her: "Last night when we talked I wanted so much to have you understand why I don't feel heard by you, but I couldn't explain it right. It was one more time when I didn't feel I was getting what I felt across to you," and relaxed as he did this. Janet cried and said through tears, "You understood me better than I understood myself." Ron added, "Until now I could never get why you felt as you did." They listened while "becoming the other" to dialogue *with* rather than *against* each other.

**Case Illustration 2:** (Snyder 2009)
After couple therapy with several therapists, before starting with Mel Snyder Jean and Adam decided to divorce once their daughter finished high school the next year. Jean saw Mel practising `becoming' as a visiting presenter, practised `becoming' as an intern, and invited Adam to learn `becoming' with Mel to help them understand each other. By their 8th 2-hour couple session with Mel they had practised "becoming each other" at home, and wanted coaching.
Jean: (turning to Adam) `You say you're a "creature of habits" which sometimes seem more important to you than I am so I'd like to understand more what you mean.
Mel: `Is it OK if I become you, Jean, and ask Adam about that somewhat differently?' (Jean assents. *Mel moves a chair beside Jean to also face Adam*).
`I long for more closeness with you. ...Your habits - watching TV, reading the newspaper, being alone when you get home - seem to take you away from me. I miss you. Might being a "creature of habit" be about fear? I want more of you. I get lonely. (Adam's body relaxes; Jean appears moved).
Mel: (to Jean) *Does that feel right? Is there anything you want to change or*

*add?*
Jean: Yeh, that's right. I feel vulnerable. I want to add something. (To Adam) Saturday morning we usually each do our own thing, but last Saturday I broke the mold and it felt scary. Instead of going to Starbuck's - a habit of mine
Adam: (smiling) Ding.
Jean: (laughing)... `I thought "I'll see if Adam will come with me to our second house to work on the garden." Your saying "yes" meant a lot because gardening is my thing. You came and seemed to enjoy it.'
Adam: `Can I be you?' (Jean nods). `I want us to be closer. I get lonely when you withdraw into the comfort of TV or newspapers. I wonder if you're afraid. Saturday, when I risked asking you to come with me and you did and we had a good time, made me happy.
Jean: (nodding assent through this) Yip
Adam: Mel's modeling getting to your pain about this was very helpful.
Jean: Yeh, I could feel the shift... .

  6 months after ending therapy Jean and Adam still often `became each other' when they felt disconnected.

# BEHAVIORAL ACTIVATION

**Carl W LEJUEZ,** Center for Addictions, Personality, and Emotion Research (CAPER), University of Maryland-College Park, ph +1 301. 405.5932 / fax 314.9566; **Derek R HOPKO**, University of Tennessee-Knoxville, ph +1 865.974.3368/fax 3330

**Definition:** A structured way of training patients to gradually increase pleasant, personally rewarding behaviors in order to improve thoughts, mood, and overall quality of life.

**Elements:** Behavioral activation typically takes 8-15 sessions. In early sessions the therapist explains how depressive behavior weakens efforts to engage in rewarding activities and worsens already-depressed mood, and that increasing pleasant activities that fit within their values and life goals can improve mood. The therapist encourages the patient to record current activities every day and then to select weekly behavioral goals concerning relationships, education, employment, hobbies, exercise, and spirituality. Collaboratively they construct a hierarchy of 15 activities ranging from "easiest to do" to "hardest to do". The therapist and patient together then work out weekly goals for how often and how long the patient will engage in each valued pleasant activity. Every day the patient rates progress up this activity hierarchy on a Behavioral Checkout Form, and in each weekly session reviews this with the therapist on a Master Activity Log, sets goals for the next week depending on success or difficulty with goals in the last week, and works out weekly rewards for meeting weekly goals. In some forms of behavioural activation, therapists particularly encourage hitherto-avoided pleasant activities, do social skills training to help the patient engage in social activities, and teach mental rehearsal of such activities. The therapist may also teach the patient how to cope with depressive thoughts by distraction and/or mindfulness to accept negative thoughts or feelings without judgement when distraction is ineffective.

**Related procedures:** *Goal setting, contingency management, exposure therapy, successive approximation, homework, diary keeping.*

**Application:** Done individually or in groups for people with depression when it is the sole concern as well as when depression is comorbid with anxiety, substance use or personality disorders and/or obesity, HIV or cancer.

**1st use?** Lewinsohn (1973).

**References:**
1. Lewinsohn PM, Graf M (1973). Pleasant activities and depression. *Journal of Consulting and Clinical Psychology, 41*, 261-268.
2. Lejuez CW, Hopko DR, LePage J, Hopko SD, McNeil DW (2001). Brief behavioral activation treatment for depression. *Cognitive & Behavioral Practice, 8*, 164-175.
3. Martell CR, Addis ME, Jacobson NS (2001). *Depression in context: Strategies for guided action.* New York: WW Norton.
4. Hopko DR, Lejuez CW, Ruggiero KJ, Eifert GH (2003). Contemporary behavioral activation treatment for depression: Procedures principles, and process. *Clinical Psychology Review, 23*, 699-717.

**Case illustration:** (Lejuez & Hopko, unpublished)

Phyllis age 30 had had recurrent depression since age 13. After high school she became an administrative assistant for 12 years. In early sessions she was asked to record her daily activities. This showed that though she went to work regularly and busied herself with fairly unenjoyable activities like completing errands for others and housework, she did few things she valued like being with friends and family and exercising. After Phyllis and her therapist assessed her short- and long-term life goals and discussed the treatment rationale, she constructed an activity hierarchy from fairly easy tasks such as organizing her home and phoning friends to harder goals such as regular exercise, dating, spending more time with friends and family, and taking steps to find a more fulfilling job. At each session the therapist reviewed Phyllis's Behavioral Checkout Form, praised her for goals she'd achieved in the past week including phoning her sister one night, cooking for a sit-down family dinner on 3 nights, and taking a 20-minute walk after dinner on 2 of the nights, and encouraged her to pick a reward for herself in the next week - she chose buying a book recommended by a friend she was spending more time with. Once she 'mastered' particular goals at her ideal frequency and duration for 3 weeks in a row she stopped monitoring them. She and her therapist discussed whichever chosen goals she hadn't met in the past week, problem-solving these to address obstacles and modifying goals as needed and setting those for the next week. For example, her goal of starting yoga classes by going to a studio and finding out membership details felt overwhelming, so she limited the next week's goal to making a list of nearby studios and phoning for a consultation time, with later goals to go to the studio and enrol in a class, and attend each week.

Over her 12 one-hour sessions, Phyllis increased her rewarding activities until she achieved her ideal goal for each of her less- and moderately-difficult activities like those above and waking up 30 minutes earlier each morning to spend time with her family and to feel less rushed at the start of her day, and met most of her difficult goals including weekly attendance at a yoga class, reconnecting with a friend she had stopped speaking to because of an argument, and starting a search for a new, more rewarding job. By termination and 3-month follow up, without having explicitly discussed her negative thoughts or social and assertiveness skills, her depressive thoughts and mood had improved and she had become more independent and assertive.

## COGNITIVE DEFUSION

**John T BLACKLEDGE,** Morehead State University, Kentucky 40351, USA; ph +1 606-783-2982; & Association for Contextual Behavioral Science Board of Directors

**Definition:** Reducing distress from thoughts by training people to focus on their process of thinking rather than its content or meaning.

**Elements:** Cognitive defusion diverts attention away from the *content* or meaning of words and sentences toward the *process* of forming words and stringing them into sentences by concentrating on their sound, pattern, rhythm, frequency, and individual letters or words. Defusion temporarily disrupts the usual meaning of thoughts or spoken/written words even though their form or content may stay the same.

**Related procedures:** *Self as context, mindfulness, meditation, metacognitive awareness, semantic satiation.*

**Application:** In individual or group ACT (acceptance and commitment therapy) and other therapies and religious practices.

**1st use?** As an ACT term, by Hayes & Strosahl (2004) who initially called it 'deliteralization', and in other therapies and religious practices.

**References:**
1. Blackledge JT (2007). Disrupting verbal processes: Cognitive defusion in acceptance and commitment therapy and other mindfulness-based psychotherapies. *The Psychological Record, 57,* 555-576.
2. Hayes SC, Strosahl KD (2004). *A practical guide to acceptance and commitment therapy.* New York: Springer.
3. Hayes SC, Strosahl KD, Wilson KG (1999). *Acceptance and commitment therapy: An experiential approach to behavior change.* New York: Guilford.
4. Wilson KG & Murrell AR (2004). Values work in acceptance and commitment therapy: Setting a course for behavioral treatment (pp. 120-151). In S Hayes, V Follette, M Linehan (Eds.), *Mindfulness and acceptance: Expanding the cognitive-behavioral tradition.* New York: Guilford.

**Case Illustration 1:** (Blackledge, unpublished)
　　　　Jim struggled with his feeling that he was a "bad father" for often having been unsupportive of his children, especially as he now felt they mattered very much to him. To help Jim experience the thought "I'm a bad father" as 'just a thought rather than a thought defining him, a repetitive defusion

exercise was conducted. *Therapist: "I'd like to try something a little odd just to show you how thoughts like 'bad father' work. Let's start it with words that are less compelling. Say the word 'milk' once, and notice what shows up."* [Client says 'milk' and says he imagines a clear glass of white, cold milk.] *"Now, let's say the word 'milk' out loud, over and over, fairly quickly, for at least a minute".* [Therapist and client repeat "milk-milk-milk milk-milk...] *"At the end of that exercise, what did you feel as you kept saying 'milk'?"* Jim: "Nothing... just this weird sound and a weird physical sensation in my throat". *Therapist: "What if this is all words are? What if they're just arbitrary sounds, just noises you make? And when you look at them in a different way, they're exposed for that?"* Jim: "It certainly seems that way with 'milk'!" Jim then agreed to and completed the same exercise with the words "bad father". At first saying this was extremely distressing, but after he and the therapist had together repeated "bad father" on and on for over a minute, Jim said: "The words just kind of fell apart. They 'lost their power' over me. The thought just pulls me in less now."

**Case Illustration 2:** (Blackledge, unpublished)

Jill believed she was a "bad person" because of how she'd sometimes treated people. The thought was problematic, in part because it often kept her from engaging with others in a deep and meaningful way. With her consent, the therapist tried a defusion exercise to 'mess up rules of the language game' and help her view this thought differently. Together, Jill and the therapist spoke the words "I am a bad person" out loud very slowly, spending 4-5 seconds on each syllable: *"IIIIIIII...ammmmmmmmm... ..aaaaaaaaaaaaaa... baaaaaaaadddd... ... ... ...perrrrrrrrrrrrrrrrrr... ... ... ...sonnnnnnnnnnnnnnnnnnnn."*
Jill then said the words seemed strange, 'fishy, less substantial, just sounds'. The therapist suggested *'carry those sounds with you'* the next time she had an opportunity to get closer to her partner.

# COGNITIVE RESTRUCTURING

**Isaac MARKS**, 43 Dulwich Common, London SE217EU, UK; ph+44 208 2994130; **Lucio SIBILIA**, Dipartimento di Scienze Cliniche, Università Sapienza di Roma & Centro per la Ricerca in Psicoterapia, Roma, Italy; ph +39 06 86320838; **Stefania BORGO**, Università Sapienza di Roma & Centro per la Ricerca in Psicoterapia, Roma, Italy; ph +39 06 86320838.

**Definition:** Methods that encourage clients to identify dysfunctional sets of thoughts and beliefs relating to their problem, and to challenge the validity of those in order to produce and use more adaptive alternatives.

**Elements:** Helps clients to identify and challenge maladaptive thoughts (e.g. *absolute / all-or-none / dichotomous / black-and white / catastrophising / over-generalising thinking*) and beliefs concerning the problem through interviews and *daily thought diaries*. May include:
- *Socratic questioning* to weigh evidence for/against each thought and belief
- *Downward arrow (what if?) technique* and *probabilistic reasoning* to challenge maladaptive thoughts and beliefs
- *Behavioural experiments* to *challenge* maladaptive beliefs
- *Distancing/giving perspective* to generate alternative adaptive thoughts and beliefs.

**Related procedures:** *Rational emotional therapy, self-instructional training, problem-solving.*

**Application:** Usually taught individually rather than in groups.

**1st use?** Concept first used by Alexander JM (1928).

**References:**
1. Alexander JM (1928). *Thought control in everyday life*. Funk & Wagnalls, New York.
2. Beck AT (1967). *Depression: Causes and treatment*. University of Pennsylvania Press, Philadelphia.
3. Ellis A (1969). A cognitive approach to behaviour therapy. *Internat. J.Psychother*, 8, 896-900.
4. Lovell K (1999). Exposure and cognitive restructuring alone and combined for PTSD. PhD dissertation, University of London.

**Case illustration:** (Lovell 1999)
      A man of 26 with PTSD for 2 years after being assaulted, injured and scarred was asked to keep *daily diaries* of thoughts to record negative

thoughts and beliefs. They related to fear of being re-assaulted. When asked, he rated his belief in the probability of being re-assaulted as 80% *(monitoring)*. This belief was challenged by *probabilistic reasoning* - he was asked to calculate how often he'd been out with friends in the years before the assault and to estimate the probability of a future assault. The self-rated difference between his initially perceived (80%) and the probable (now rated as 10%) risk led him to *identify his thinking error* of over-estimation of danger. He *reframed* his belief as the alternative `My chances of being attacked are no more than other people's', and rated his reframed belief in it as 90%. Soon after this he began to go out with friends and then alone.

He also identified shaming thoughts and beliefs (*diary keeping*) e.g. `I'm a coward as I cried after the attack; men don't cry'. He rated their validity as 85%. When challenged to provide evidence for and against such thoughts, he recalled that his father had been upset after the assault and had cried when visiting him in hospital, but his father was not a coward. He also recalled that he and his friends had wept at a funeral, which was appropriate and not a sign of cowardice. He then reframed his thought to: `Crying is appropriate in stressful situations'.

He *recorded a negative overgeneralising thought*: `People with scars are thought to be criminals, so others seeing my scar will think I'm a criminal'. He rated this thought as 85% valid. He was asked to list the hair colour, height etc of criminals and to compare these features with his own. Mismatch of the two lists led him to rerate his belief that others would consider him a criminal as 40%. For *homework* he listened to the audiotape of the session and was required to think of people he knew with scars and how much he believed them to be criminals, and to spot his thinking error. At the next session, he said he realised he knew many scarred people but did not think them as criminals. He generated an *alternative response*: `Acting suspiciously and having a past criminal record suggest criminality, not a scar'. He rated his belief in this reframed thought as 100%. He *labelled his thinking error* as mind-reading (false attribution). The PTSD had reduced markedly after 10 sessions and even more so 1 year later.

# COMMUNITY REINFORCEMENT APPROACH (CRA)

**Hendrik G ROOZEN**, GGZ Bouman Mental Health Care, Thorbechelaan 63, Spijkenisse, Netherlands & **Ad JFM KERKHOF**, Department of Clinical Psychology, Vrije Universiteit, Van der Boechorststraat 1, 1081 BT Amsterdam

**Definition:** In the community reinforcement approach (CRA) the therapist helps the patient to identify and engage in rewarding social and other activities in the community that compete with rewards from substance use, and persuades the patient to recruit a 'significant other' to aid adoption of a healthier lifestyle.

**Elements:** The therapist trains patients' skills by role-playing with them how to refuse drugs and alcohol, communicate positively and appropriately assertively, and how to behave in job interviews, and encourages them to find and engage in pleasant hobbies and other non-substance related pursuits, and to enlist a trusted relative or friend for help in carrying out the CRA.

**Application:** Both individually and/or in groups and in different settings such as in- or outpatient settings, often supported by a relative or friend and combined with medication.

**Related procedures:** *Behavioral activation, contingency management, reinforcement, token economy, Morita therapy, motivational interviewing, nidotherapy, stimulus control, successive approximation; role play, social skills training; homework, diary keeping, problem-solving.*

**1st Use?** Hunt GM, Azrin NH (1973).

**References:**
1. Budney AJ, Higgins ST (1998). *National Institute on Drug Abuse therapy manuals for drug addiction: Manual 2. A community reinforcement approach: treating cocaine addiction.* (NIH Publication No. 98-4309). Rockville, MD: U.S. Department of Health and Human Services.
2. Hunt GM, Azrin NH (1973). Community reinforcement approach to alcoholism. *Behaviour Research & Therapy*, 11, 91-104.
3. Meyers RJ, Smith JE (1995). *Clinical guide to alcohol treatment: Community Reinforcement Approach.* New York, NY, USA: Guilford Press.
4. Roozen HG, van den Brink W, Kerkhof AJFM (1997). Toepassing van naltrexon/clonidine bij een biopsychosociale behandeling (CRA) van opiaatafhankelijken. In Buisman WR, Casselman J, Noorlander EA, Schippers GM, de Zwart WM (Eds.). *Handboek Verslaving (B4250, 1-24).* Houten: Bohn Stafleu Van Loghum (in Dutch).

**Case illustration:** (adapted from Roozen et al 1997)
Mary, aged 29, sought outpatient help to withdraw and then abstain from heroin especially and from cocaine and from methadone maintenance. A boyfriend had introduced her to drugs 9 years earlier. They broke up after a couple of years, after which she lived on her own. Recently she had stayed with her parents. She had been heroin-dependent for 8 years and on substitute methadone 40mg daily for 5 years. She had had no meaningful job for some years and currently only had substance-using friends.

When the outpatient community reinforcement approach (CRA) began, Mary and her mother agreed with the therapist that mother would help Mary throughout treatment. Both attended weekly outpatient sessions over 6 months. Over 30 days Mary reduced cocaine and heroin use from daily to infrequently and took prescribed methadone more regularly; her methadone dose was increased slightly and stabilized. She then had opioid detoxification over 72 hours to stabilise abstinence from heroin and methadone.

She had naltrexone (opioid-antagonist) induction followed by naltrexone 25mgs daily throughout the CRA to prevent relapse. After detoxification Mary felt depressed and spent most of her time in bed at her parents' home for three weeks, during which she reported one cocaine relapse. She completed happiness scales to evolve treatment goals with her therapist and mother. Mary targeted and was encouraged to do potentially rewarding activities such as: shop, visit family with mother, meet a non-drug-using old school friend, start fitness exercises and classes including stationary cycling (spinning) at a gym, and find a job. Mother helped Mary take her naltrexone and do homework assignments. Outpatient staff took urine specimens and did urinalysis. Mary, her mother and the therapist discussed and completed functional analysis forms showing that relief from depression was transient after substance use and alternative longer-term relaxation came from healthy pro-social behaviors, and Mary kept a `goals of counselling' diary.

Completing the forms aided Mary's growing stimulus control by gradually avoiding drug-related situations and spending more time in pleasant activities, as above, incompatible with drug use. In rehearsals with mother and therapist in outpatients andat home visits Mary improved communication with mother. Mary also rehearsed job- interviews with her therapist. After 1-month abstinence verified by urinalyses, Mary found a nearby factory job and her mood improved rapidly. After 10 months of abstinence she discontinued naltrexone and the CRA, feeling confident she would stay abstinent. Mary kept her job, went on vacation with new friends, and engaged in frequent sports and other fitness activities such as spinning and jogging. She made new friends, and planned to start adult education classes to get a better job later.

At 6 months follow-up she reported sustained abstinence.

# COMPASSION-FOCUSED THERAPY

**Paul GILBERT,** Mental Health Research Unit, Kingsway Hosp, DerbyDE22 3LZ, UK; ph +44 1332 623579

**Definition:** Teaching people how to feel compassionate to themselves and others during therapy and at other times.

**Elements:** Compassion involves empathy - being able to understand one's own and other people's feelings - and being caring, accepting and kindly tolerant of distress in self and others. Compassion-focused therapy teaches clients that, because of how our brains have evolved, anxiety, anger and depression are natural experiences which are 'not our fault'. Clients are helped to explore how early experiences (e.g. neglect, abuse or other threatening experiences) may relate to ongoing fears (e.g. of rejection, abuse), safety strategies (e.g. social avoidance or submissive behaviour), and unintended consequences such as social rejection or other mental health problems. When people feel threatened and self-critical with strong bodily feelings, they can learn to slow their breathing and refocus attention on imagining a compassionate place, becoming a compassionate person, and/or imagining someone compassionate talking to them. For example, someone who thinks s/he is useless and a failure can be taught to think kinder thoughts (e.g. 'I've actually achieved... in my life', 'friends often seek my support', 'these thoughts come only when I'm depressed and so aren't real'). Clients are helped to practise exercises to detect self-criticism and then refocus compassionately by creating and practising feelings and thoughts that are kind, supportive and encouraging, and noticing mindfully how this helps them. Some people take to this within a few sessions, and others within 10 or more sessions to work through resistance to positive feelings.

**Related Procedures:** *Acceptance, anger management, cognitive restructuring, imagery practice, meditation, mindfulness, validation of feelings, well-being therapy.*

**Application:** During individual and group therapy for any clients, especially if they feel much shame and self-criticism.

**1st Use?** Gilbert & Procter (2006), compassionate imagery in Buddhist practice for 2500 years.

**References:**
1. Gilbert P (2009). *The Compassionate Mind.* London: Constable-Robinson. Oaklands CA.: New Harbinger.

2. Gilbert P (2009). An Introduction to compassion focused therapy. *Advances in Psychiatric Treatment*, 15, 199-208.
3. Gilbert P, Procter S (2006). Compassionate mind training for people with high shame and self-criticism: A pilot study of a group therapy approach. *Clinical Psychology and Psychotherapy*, 13, 353-379.
4. Laithwaite H, Gumley A, O'Hanlon M, Collins P, Doyle P, Abraham L, Porter S (2009). Recovery after psychosis (RAP): A compassion focused programme for individuals residing in high security settings. *Behav & Cogn Psychotherapy*. 37, 511-526.

**Case Illustration:**
For many years Jane had had occasional depression with suicidal attempts. As a child she had tried to appease her critical mother to win affection. Jane had shame memories about being bullied at school and mother's criticism. Conflicts and setbacks triggered self-criticism -"I've messed up again, people don't like me, I should deal with this better". The therapist explained.*"We have three types of feeling -anxiety and anger when threatened, enjoyment and wanting to do things, and, third, contentment, peaceful wellbeing and feeling soothed. Soothing feelings help us manage other feelings, and come when we feel people are being kind and helpful. Criticism from others or ourselves makes us anxious, whereas kindness and helpfulness soothes us"*. Jane remained reluctant to develop kind compassionate-self practice because she thought compassion is "going soft, letting one's guard down, being self-indulgent; I don't deserve it, I should be tougher, not compassionate".

The therapist said "*Such reluctance is common. Let's go one step at a time. We don't want to take your guard down. You're free to keep that if you want, to ignore compassion if you think you don't deserve it at the end of therapy, but you might find it useful to explore how to feel compassion and how it works for you*". This encouraged Jane to start practising and desensitising to her fear of feeling affiliative by exercises such as: *To develop your compassionate self, sit comfortably and focus on your breathing. Now imagine you're a deeply compassionate person. Think of your personal qualities and create a kind expression*". After doing this repeatedly (like methodacting practice) Jane could go into compassionate-self mode to practise compassion to her anxiety and anger. She would imagine herself as a compassionate person, think of what was making her anxious, and become compassionate to her anxious self, and what she'd like to say or do to her anxious self to be helpful to it. She was taught the links between thinking, feeling and behaviour, and to monitor self-criticism and become mindful of it by slowing her breathing: "*Bring self-critical thoughts to mind and notice what happens to your body and feelings* (pause for 30 seconds). *Now let those thoughts fade, breathe more slowly, and imagine someone talking to youin a kind, understanding way*". Helping Jane notice how criticism and kindness feel different was important. The therapist also asked Jane to engage in one compassionate behaviour towards herself each day and notice how she feels with this behaviour. She completed compassion- focused therapy in 25 sessions.

# COMPUTER-AIDED VICARIOUS EXPOSURE (CAVE)

**Ken KIRKBY**, Psychiatry Department, University of Tasmania, 28 Campbell St, Hobart 7001, Australia; ph +613 6226 4885, +61 419 120041

**Definition:** A computer game to teach users exposure therapy as they direct a supposedly phobic screen figure to approach and remain in avoided feared situations shown on the screen until that figure's fear score drops.

**Elements:** By pointing and clicking with CAVE's computer mouse, users steer a 'phobic' screen figure through avoided discomforting scenes (e.g. spider phobic nearing a spider, agoraphobic leaving home, claustrophobic entering a lift, OCD washer touching garden soil) as that figure's supposed anxiety thermometer score rises with each approach and then falls as the figure remains in the situation. The game gives and displays to users points for moving the figure towards exposure scenes, the aim being to score 2000 points. All mouse human-computer interactions are recorded for process analysis.

**Related procedures:** *Vicarious/symbolic/live/in vivo modelling of exposure, vicarious/etc mastery* (high initial fear falls as exposure continues), *coping, computer-aided self-help.*

**Application:** Used individually to date in research trials.

**1st Use?** First CAVE software: Kirkby et al (1992).

**References:**
1. Clark A, Kirkby KC, Daniels BA, Marks IM (1998). A pilot study of CAVE for obsessive-compulsive disorder. *Australian and New Zealand Journal of Psychiatry*, 32, 268-275.
2. Gilroy LJ, Kirkby KC, Daniels BA, Menzies RG, Montgomery IM (2003). Long term follow-up of CAVE vs live graded exposure in the treatment of spider phobia. *Behavior Therapy*, 34, 65-76.
3. Kirkby KC, Daniels BA, Watson PJ (1992). An interactive computerised teaching program for self exposure therapy of avoidant behaviour in phobic disorders. 4th World Congress on Behaviour Therapy, 4 July 1992, Gold Coast, Queensland, Australia; Abstracts, Australian Academic Press, Queensland, pp 73.

**Case illustration:** (Kirkby, unpublished)
Jill aged 45 had been phobic of spiders since childhood. After outpatient assessment she had three 45-minute sessions of CAVE at 2-week in-

tervals. At Session 1 she met a researcher who remained to answer queries. She sat at the computer to complete CAVE's 5-minute explanatory introduction on the screen which showed navigation techniques for its animation scenes. The researcher left the room. Over 45 minutes by trial and error Jill learned the effects of directing CAVE's screen figure to do various things, eg approaching a spider in a room (= exposure), leaving that room (= avoidance), staying in another room (= neutral). Jill saw the anxiety thermometer on the screen display the screen figure's anxiety which was high on first exposure to the screen spider and then gradually fell with accumulating exposure. The aim of the game was to score 2000 points gained, for example, by moving the screen figure to repeatedly or persistently touch a perspex container with a large live spider inside. She learned by doing how to achieve the target score by exposing the screen figure to the phobic scenes and observing how this reduced anxiety over time.

After 3 CAVE sessions Jill looked closely at a container with a large spider in it, and held this partial improvement to follow-up some years later.

# COPING CAT TREATMENT

**Philip C KENDALL & Muniya KHANNA**, Child & Adolescent Anxiety Disorders Clinic, Department of Psychology, Temple University, 1701 N. 13th Street, Philadelphia, PA 19129, USA; ph +1 215 746 5704 / fax 3311

**Definition:** The therapist helps anxious children to recognize signs of anxiety, to relax, and to modify anxious self-talk and thinking, followed by self-monitored exposure tasks in and out-of session to help them better manage their thoughts, feelings and behavior when anxious.

**Elements:** The therapist and youth together create a personalized FEAR plan (e.g. Case Illustration below) to use in anxiety-evoking situations. Its steps include answers to: *F*eeling frightened?; *E*xpecting bad things to happen?; *A*ctions and Attitudes that can help?; *R*esults and Rewards. The child memorizes these coping steps by their acronym FEAR and then practises them during planned exposure tasks to feared situations in session and as homework. Exposure tasks are graded from imagined slightly-frightening situations to moderate and then very frightening real ones. Though done in a supportive environment, the tasks should challenge and evoke anxiety. With this graded exposure children habituate to and apply coping strategies in anxiety-evoking situations and develop a sense of mastery rather than anxious expectations.

**Application:** In 16 individual or group sessions over 16 weeks for children aged 7-13, helped by a workbook whose exercises parallel therapy sessions to aid involvement and skill acquisition. Also done in 6 computer-guided and 6 therapist-guided sessions over 12 weeks using *Camp Cope-A-Lot: The Coping Cat CD Rom*.

**Related procedures:** *Graded exposure, role play, cognitive restructuring, problem- solving.*

**1st Use?** Kendall PC (1994) to convert taunts that frightened children are "scaredy cats" into a coping version.

**References:**
1. Kendall PC (1994). Treating anxiety disorders in children: Results of a randomized clinical trial. *Journal of Consulting and Clinical Psychology*; 62, 100-110.
2. Kendall PC, Hedtke K (2006). *Cognitive-behavioral therapy for anxious children: Therapist manual (3rd ed.)*. Ardmore, PA: Workbook Publishing.
3. Kendall PC, Khanna MS (2008). *Camp Cope-A-Lot: The Coping Cat CD*

*Rom*-available too as *Coach's Manual* CD (2008) and *Go-to-Gadget* workbook CD (2008). Ardmore, PA: Workbook Publishing Inc.
4. Kendall PC, Hudson JH, Choudhury MS, Webb A, Pimentel SS (2005). Cognitive- behavior treatment for childhood anxiety disorders. In ED Hibbs & PS Jensen (Eds.), *Psychosocial Treatments for Child and Adolescent Disorders: Empirically Based Strategies for Private Practice*, 2nd Edition. American Psychological Association.

**Case illustration:** (Kendall et al 2005)
Sample FEAR plan from session 9 for Bill aged 10 who feared giving a class presentation and getting lost when going to new places.
*F*eeling frightened? "Well, I have butterflies in my stomach and my palms are sweaty."
*E*xpecting bad things to happen? "I'll mess up"; "The other kids may make fun of me"; "I'm going to look stupid and they'll laugh at me."
*A*ctions and Attitudes that can help: "I can practice beforehand to make sure I know what I'm going to say"; "I didn't mess up the last time I gave a report and the teacher said I did a good job"; "Even if I mess up, it's not a big deal anyway because everybody messes up sometime"; "I can laugh too."
*R*esults and Reward: "I was nervous in the beginning but I felt okay by the end"; Nobody laughed"; "I think I did a pretty good job and I tried really hard"; "My reward is to go to the movies with Mom and Dad this weekend".
Typical use of the FEAR plan: In session 7 Bill and the therapist prepared for an exposure task (walk around a shopping mall for 10 minutes alone while the therapist waits outside) to challenge Bill's fears that he'll get lost in new places.
*Therapist*: Are you feeling nervous now?
Bill: I don't know. Not really.
*Therapist*: How would you know when you were starting to get nervous?
Bill: My heart would start beating faster.
*Therapist*: (recalling Bill's common complaint) What about your breathing?
Bill: I might start breathing faster.
*Therapist*: And what would you be thinking to yourself?
Bill: I might get lost or I don't know where I am.
*Therapist*: And what are some things you could do if you start getting nervous?
Bill: I could take deep breaths and say everything is going to be OK, there are tons of adults here.
*Therapist*: That's good, but what if you were unsure where you were or got lost?
Bill: I could ask somebody.
*Therapist*: Yes, you could ask somebody. Might it be a good idea to ask one of the guards or policemen? How are you feeling? Are you ready to give it a

try?

The therapist and Bill agreed on several side-trips that Bill would do alone between then and the next session within the mall, varying in distance, duration, and familiarity. Bill wrote his exposure experience (including his FEAR Plan) into his workbook. During one trip, Bill had to ask a guard for directions in order to feel comfortable doing this in future, if needed.

# COUNTERTRANSFERENCE, USE OF

**Jeremy HOLMES,** Department of Clinical Psychology, Washington Singer Building, University of Exeter EX4 4QG

**Definition:** The therapist's use of his/her persistent or brief emotional responses to the patient (countertransference) - as clues to the patient's past and present emotions.

**Elements:** a) The therapist senses and identifies his/her own feeling towards the patient, b) verbalises this internally (e.g. *'I'm feeling sad'*), c) offers this to the patient as a possible emotional resonance (*'I wonder if you're feeling sad right now'*) usually without referring explicitly to the therapist's own feelings, and d) suggests this feeling may reflect recurrent themes in the patient's life (*'perhaps you usually avoid feeling the pain of sadness'*).

**Related procedures:** *Transference interpretation.*

**Application:** Psychoanalytic and psychodynamic therapy with individuals, groups and couples.

**1st Use?** Freud S (1910).

**References:**
1. Bateman A & Holmes J. (1995). *Introduction to Psychoanalysis* pp109-117.London: Routledge.
2. Freud S (1910). Future prospects of psychoanalysis Standard Edition 11 (Eleven) pp. 145. London: Hogarth Press.
3. Gabbard G (1995). Countertransference: the emerging common ground *Int J.Psychoanalysis*, 76, 475-85.
4. Gabbard G. (2005). In (Eds). G Gabbard, J Beck & J Holmes *Oxford Textbook of Psychotherapy* pp. 8 Oxford: OUP.

**Case Illustrations** (Holmes, unpublished)
1. *Using countertransference as a clue to a patient's repressed rage* Alexandra's husband had chronic depression and killed himself while she, mother of a 3-year-old son, was pregnant with her second child. She sought help to come to terms with the suicide and find stability to raise her children as a widow. During early sessions she poured out sadness and grief at what had happened, guilt about a row with her husband on the day of his death, and expressions of her lost love for him. The therapist was initially very moved by this but, as sessions continued, despite understanding the suicide risk in depression, felt outraged at what the husband had done to his wife

and family, and intuited that anger was conspicuously absent in Alexandra's narrative. Sensing that she had repressed these feelings, partly to present a positive image of her husband to her children, the therapist tentatively suggested in Session 4 that in addition to her feeling of loss and sadness she might be enraged at her husband for abandoning her. She dismissed this initially out of hand, but at the next session said she had woken in the night feeling overwhelming fury at her husband for what he had done. Expressing this seemed to reduce her guilt and enable her to realise that at moments when she felt unable to talk to her son about his father it was because her anger prevented her from seeing the positive side of his dad which her son was seeking.

2. *Using countertransference as a clue to the patient's early and current relationship difficulties*

Peter, an unmarried loner, was an information technology specialist seeking help for chronic low self-esteem and feeling inadequate. He had recently been cautioned at work and told that, despite technical competence, unless he 'examined his attitude', dismissal was likely. He often felt that his excellent suggestions for reorganising his department were ignored, and after months of resentment had a 'blazing row' with his boss about this. An only child, he described a loveless upbringing which emphasised order and achievement rather than fun. The therapist repeatedly suggested that Peter's anger with his boss might relate to similar anger towards his parents, but Peter ignored this or dismissed it as absurd – "I come from a totally normal family". At session 12, the therapist used his countertransference sense of a lack of progress in therapy to point out how Peter tended to pass over his comments and suggested that perhaps Peter felt he had never been really *heard* or taken seriously by his parents, who knew in advance 'what was best' for him, and that similar feelings might explain his interpersonal difficulties at work. At this Peter dissolved into tears, for the first time in therapy, complaining bitterly that his true feelings seemed of no consequence to anyone. Later he saw that 'not being heard' worked both ways and that his few girlfriends had left him when he had tried to impose his ideas of how things should be rather than responding to their wishes.

## DANGER IDEATION REDUCTION THERAPY (DIRT)

**Mairwen JONES,** University of Sydney, POBox 170 East St, Lidcombe, NSW 1825, Australia

**Definition:** Cognitive-restructuring and attention focussing aiming to decrease danger-related expectancies concerning contamination and disease in obsessive-compulsive washers.

**Elements:** DIRT tries to change unrealistic thoughts about illness to realistic ones by: *cognitive restructuring* with *probability*-of-illness *estimation* before and after *giving* detailed *corrective information* concerning the immune system, disease rates, and usual risks people take without becoming ill, shows filmed interviews with cleaners etc who touch dirt and brief reports about scientific contamination experiments; daily *attention* exercises without thoughts intruding by normal breathing (neither slow nor rapid) while focusing on a series of numbers while breathing in and focusing on the word 'relax' while breathing out - no instructions are given about fear of or exposure to contamination.

**Related procedures:** *Attention focussing (training), cognitive restructuring, diary-keeping, homework, probability estimation, rational emotive therapy.*

**Application:** Taught individually or in groups to obsessive-compulsive washers.

**1st Use?** Jones MK, Menzies RG (1997). Danger Ideation Reduction Therapy (DIRT): preliminary findings with three obsessive-compulsive washers. *Behaviour Research and Therapy*, 35, 955-960.

**Reference:**
Hoekstra R (1989). Treatment of OCD with rational-emotive therapy. Paper (describing probability-of-catastrophe-estimation task) to 1st World Congress of Cognitive Therapy, Oxford: 28 June-2 July, 1989.

**Case illustration:**
   Over 6 years, for fear of contamination Mary aged 34 had avoided using public transport or toilets, shaking anyone's hand, touching garbage or raw meat, and contact with pets and pet owners. She showered 6 times a day and washed her hands with antiseptic for 5 mins after touching anything 'contaminated' and before handling food. Her therapist said incorrect beliefs about contamination caused the problem and asked her to *keep a diary (homework)* of thoughts and beliefs about dirt and illness.

Mary felt 99% certain that touching her garbage bin would cause vomiting and diarrhoea. With her therapist she analysed the steps for this to occur (bacteria on the bin, transfer to her hand, entering her body, immune failure) and estimated the probability for each step. Multiplied together these yielded an illness probability of .014% compared to her initial estimate of 99%. She was asked to apply such *probability estimation* to one new situation a week. Mary was shown a 10-min film of a healthy cleaner who often touched pets' hair while cleaning homes, used gloves only to prevent hand irritation from bleach, and on finishing washed only briefly with any soap available.

Discussion noted that pet- and pet-shop owners, vets and cleaners were not unduly ill (*giving corrective information*). The therapist gave Mary a 1-page microbiology report that undue washing can cause skin cracks allowing in infection, and a 2-page report of an experimenter who with one hand touched a cat, scoop for a cat litter tray, and garbage bin, after which no pathogens grew from that hand or the other, control, hand. Mary was helped to challenge excessive risk estimates for tasks, and asked her to read and copy the summary daily for 15 min to make her thoughts realistic (*cognitive restructuring*).

From early on Mary was asked to practise *attention focussing (training)* for two 10-minute sessions daily with eyes closed: during her 1st breath in she had to focus on the number `1' and during her 1st breath out to say `relax', during her 2nd breath in to focus on `2' and during her 2nd breath out to say `relax', and so on until on her 10th breath in she focussed on `10' and during her 10th breath out said `relax'. She repeated this 10-breath cycle over and over for 10 minutes and was asked to, between sessions, practise these 10-min focusing-*homework* sessions twice a day in gradually noisier environments with her eyes open.

After 12 one-hour individual DIRT sessions weekly and at 6-month follow-up Mary's contamination fears and washing reduced markedly. Without fear she took the bus to shops, used public toilets and touched garbage bins, and stroked pets which friends brought to her home.

## DECISIONAL BALANCE

**Katherine M DISKIN**, Mental Health Services, CFB Esquimalt, Victoria, British Columbia, Canada; ph +1 250 363 4411 & **David C HODGINS**, Department of Psychology, University of Calgary, Calgary, Alberta, Canada; ph +1 403 220 3371

**Definition:** A decisional-balance exercise is an elaborated form of "pros-and-cons" review that is often used in deciding whether to change behaviour. It provides an opportunity to examine both the negative and positive aspects of a behaviour, acknowledge ambivalence, and allow clients to feel understood rather than judged.

**Elements:** Decisional balance can be done in written form or in conversation at any point in therapy which seems appropriate. The clinician shapes the process through questions, summaries and selective emphasis. Like a pros-and-cons discussion, the therapist usually starts by exploring "good things" and then "not-so-good things" about the status quo, and finally asks clients to consider what might be "good and also not-so- good" if they ever decided to change their behaviour. The client and the therapist can thus weigh both the positive aspects and the potential difficulties of behaviour change, and how drawbacks could be addressed.

**Related Procedures:** *Motivational interviewing, motivational enhancement therapy, pros-and-cons review.*

**Application:** When indicated during any session of motivational interviewing or motivational enhancement therapy or when addressing potential behaviour change, e.g. when discussing reducing addiction or other harmful behaviours, leaving an abusive relationship, starting an exercise program, returning to school.

**1st Use?** Janis & Mann (1977), elaborated by Miller & Rollnick (1991).

**References:**
1. Janis IL, Mann L (1977). *Decision-making: A psychological analysis of conflict, choice, and commitment.* New York: Free Press.
2. Miller WR, Rollnick S (1991, 1st ed. & 2002, 2nd ed.). *Motivational interviewing: Preparing people to change addictive behaviour.* New York: Guilford. http://motivationalinterview.org/clinical/decisionalbalance.pdf

**Case illustration:** (Diskin unpublished)
During therapy session 3 Gina and her therapist agreed that exercise

could probably help her low mood yet Gina hadn't managed to start. The therapist then shaped a decisional-balance discussion which lasted 11 minutes:

    **(1. Staying unchanged - not exercising: A. Good things)**
T. *So tell me what's good about not exercising?*
G. I just don't have the energy; it's hard to get started... I don't have the time either - I drag myself around on weekends to do my chores
T. *You sound pretty tired and overwhelmed already. What else?*
G. Well, I'm out of shape, fat, a mess...I hate having to start
    **(B. Not-so-good things)**
T. *I see it's really hard to get going ...on the other hand, ... tell me what you dislike about not exercising?*
G. It's funny, but when I was working out I had more energy, and felt stronger, less tired
T. *Anything else?*
G. I'm gaining tons of weight, hate looking like this. I used to be really fit when I was running.
    **(2. Changing - starting to exercise:    A. Not-so-good things)**
T. *Imagine you did decide to start. What would be hard, get in the way?*
G. I'm in terrible shape. I'd hate feeling so weak.... but already feel that way.
T. *What else would be hard?*
G. I don't like to run on my own. I'd have to phone someone and feel such a slob.
T. *So it would be hard to call old running friends because they'd look down on you?*
G. Yeah, ...except Jen called a few times to ask if I want to run. She was injured and wants to start.
T. *You mentioned time as a problem.*
G. Yeah, but I used to run before work, it wasn't that bad once I started...
    **(B. Good things)**
T. *So if you did start and kept it up, what would that be like?*
G. Well, I'd stop feeling a slob. ...could lose weight, wear some of the clothes I had to put away.
T. *Anything else?*
G. I'd have more energy – I used to be able to run in the morning, work all day and go out at night. Now I'm barely making it to work... I like feeling strong...
T. *It felt good physically. Do you remember what your mood was like when you were exercising?*
G. Yeah, I felt a lot better and spent less time alone watching TV. I did more non- running things, volunteer work.

    After completing this exercise the therapist and Gina reviewed it, Gina gradually began exercising, and her mood improved during her remaining 7 sessions over 2 months.

# DIALECTICAL BEHAVIOUR THERAPY (DBT)

**Maggie STANTON,** Psychology Services, 59 Romsey Rd, Winchester, Hants, SO22 5DE, UK; ph +44 1962 825600

**Definition:** DBT for borderline personality disorder with suicidal and other impulsive and high-risk behaviours includes skills training, exposure, cognitive modification and contingency management balanced with acceptance by validation and mindfulness.

**Elements:** In a pre-treatment phase of 4-6 weekly individual sessions, a therapist identifies client goals, orients the client to DBT, shapes commitment to its goals, and develops a target hierarchy of the order in which to address problem behaviours. If the client completes pre-treatment and agrees to DBT, the client enters Stage 1 which encompasses five functions:
1. Enhance capabilities: Clients learn skills, usually in a group, in four modules: mindfulness; distress tolerance; emotion regulation; and interpersonal effectiveness.
2. Improve motivation: In individual sessions, the therapist analyses cues for problem behaviours and reduces obstacles to more skilful behaviour by exposure, cognitive modification and contingency management.
3. Generalization: Clients can usually phone outside office hours for skills coaching.
4. Structure the environment to reward progress e.g. by offering an opportunity to extend treatment. With adolescent clients a therapist may meet their parents to advise contingency management of the target behaviours.
5. Enhance therapist skills and motivation by supervising the therapist team in a weekly meeting.

**Related procedures:** *Cognitive restructuring, contingency management, diary-keeping, exposure, mindfulness, problem-solving, role-play, social skills training.*

**Application:** After 4-6 weeks of pre-treatment individual sessions a team of ≥4 therapists gives weekly individual and group sessions plus phone coaching usually over a year. DBT was developed for suicidal people with borderline personality disorder. Adaptations are appearing for other disorders.

**1st use?** Linehan M (1987).

**References:**
1. Linehan MM (1987). Dialectical behavior therapy: A cognitive behavioral approach to parasuicide. *Journal of Personality Disorders*, 1, 328-333.

2. Linehan MM (1993). *Skills Training Manual for treating Borderline Personality Disorder*. Guilford Press, New York & London.
3. Linehan MM (2006). Two-year randomized controlled trial and follow-up of dialectical behavior therapy vs therapy by experts for suicidal behaviours and borderline personality disorder. *Archives of General Psychiatry*; 63, 757-766.

**Case illustration:** (Stanton M, unpublished)

Julia, 32, had for 15 years repeatedly overdosed, cut her arms, misused alcohol, and been hospitalised. DBT began after a serious over-dose. During 6 individual pre- treatment sessions, Julia identified goals of having a boyfriend and a job. With her therapist, Julia developed a hierarchy of target behaviors, which were: *life threatening* (overdosing, suicide planning/actions, cutting herself, self-harming urges), *therapy interfering* (missing therapy sessions), and *quality-of-life interfering* (not applying for jobs, drinking >8 units of alcohol/week or >4 units/day).

Julia attended an open weekly 2.5-hour skills-training group with 6-8 other clients and 2 therapists. She recorded on a diary card self-harming behaviour, suicide ideas, alcohol intake, and DBT skills used. In week 1, she recorded trying mindfulness on 3 days, self-harming 5 times, and daily self-harming and suicidal urges. In weekly 1-hour individual sessions Julia chain-analysed her top target behaviour ('cut my arm on Tuesday evening') for links among thoughts, feelings and actions in order to develop more constructive behaviour for each link. The therapist, by cognitive restructuring, contingency management, skills coaching and exposure, encouraged Julia to role-play each new behavior in session. For example, Julia had argued with a friend, felt disliked by her, became angry, and drank a bottle of wine to blot this out. When that did not work, she cut her arm. The therapist validated that distress is natural after arguing with a friend, and role-played with Julia skills to talk to her friend without arguing while being mindful of her judgments. She calmed herself by deep, slow breathing and practised thinking kindly about her friend's perspective. This reduced her anger and self-harming urges.

Over the first 2 months Julia noticed that self-harming and drinking alcohol reduced distress. She became aware of her feelings, their triggers, and reasons for them. She could decide when to act on them or do something different.

Julia's frequent brief phone calls to her therapist for skills coaching diminished as her skills came automatically. She attended therapy regularly by arranging her own mobile-phone prompts. She chain-analysed target behaviours and devised helpful solutions. For example, on feeling strong self-harming urges and examining links in the chain Julia realised she felt sad because a friend was moving away and imagined this was her own fault. Julia recognised it was natural to feel sad, mindfully noticed her thoughts without involvement in them, challenged thoughts of being responsible by noting her friend was moving to be near her ill mother, and resolved to keep in email contact with her friend.

Julia began volunteer work in a plant nursery and was offered paid work. After a year of weekly outpatient individual and group sessions and telephone coaching, she began monthly 1-hour advanced-group meetings with one therapist and 4-5 DBT `graduates' for mutual support in maintaining skills. She could come as long as she kept using her skills and has attended 6 such meetings so far.

# DREAM INTERPRETATION

**Jacques MONTANGERO,** 76, ch. de la Miche – F-74930 Esery, France; ph +33 450 31 86 83

**Definition:** Attributing to the content of a dream a meaning related to the dreamer's concerns, aspirations, behaviour, or life episodes.

**Elements:** Dream interpretation starts with elements of the dream report and leads to new ideas associated with these that the client considers relevant.
    Psychoanalytic dream interpretation concerns clients' *free associations* to dream content, which the analyst relates to psychoanalytic *metaphors* e.g. oblong objects may represent a penis, and to *topics* such as transference, sexuality, and early child-parent relationships. In Hill's dream interpretation the client is asked to describe the dream in detail and to re-experience associated feelings. Next the client is asked `What could your dream mean?`, and after this interpretation is asked how s/he would like to change the dream and corresponding aspects of waking life.
    Montangero's cognitive-behavioural dream interpretation has <u>three steps</u>.
1. `Please `<u>describe</u>` your dream again with everything you saw, or felt was present but didn't see, concerning its setting, action, characters and feelings'.` 2. `Now say what `<u>memory</u>` comes to mind about elements of your dream, not necessarily as they were in the dream, e.g. about a blue car you saw'.` 3. Next, can you <u>reformulate</u> your dream in <u>more general terms</u>, describing it sentence by sentence with your meaning of each element (e.g. instead of `my neighbour` - `an uninteresting housewife') or its encompassing category (e.g. instead of `going down stairs' - `changing level') or its function (e.g. instead of `the door` - `something giving access). I may make suggestions, but only you can decide what is relevant'. A doctor reformulated his dream of `Two "gangs" competing in a flower market by spraying flowers to refresh them` as `Two groups competing in their task to cure'. Reformulation helps clients interpret how their dream applies to their experience - the doctor said it applied to two groups of doctors each claiming superiority for their competing type of treatment. Such interpretations suggest helpful topics to discuss e.g. feelings or ways of relating not mentioned before (e.g. guilt, or avoidance of intimacy with a partner).
    Interpretations may also raise awareness of distorted thinking, e.g. a depressed young man dreamt about people who were either omnipotent (devils, his rich influential landlady) or hopeless (someone homeless, prisoners). Discussion of this made him aware that he judged people unrealistically in all-or-nothing terms (either complete winners or total losers). Dream

interpretations may also raise awareness of a 'schema' - a belief underlying distorted thoughts, e.g. commenting on her dream of feeling terribly embarrassed when her boss came late to care for a client, a young woman said she could never do that: `I must do everything for other people, and immediately, otherwise they won't love me'. Finally, dream interpretation allows the therapist to underline a client's resources e.g. a woman dreamed she was driving and was stopped by a barrier that she managed to lift up, but further on her car stuck in the mud and she had to get out and walk to go on. She interpreted her dream pessimistically: "It shows my life is full of difficulties". The therapist pointed out that her dream also showed she knew she could go on in spite of obstacles.

**Related procedures:** *Psychodynamic interpretation of slips of the tongue, cognitive restructuring, free association, reframing.*

**Application:** Psychoanalytic and psychodynamic therapy, occasionally in cognitive-behaviour therapy - usually individual.

**1st use?** Freud S (1900).

**References:**
1. Freud S (1900). *The interpretation of dreams.* 1965 New York: Basic Books.
2. Hill CE, Rochlen AB (2002). The Hill cognitive experiential model of dream interpretation. *Journal of Cognitive Psychotherapy*, 16, 75-89.
3. Montangero J (2007). *Comprendre ses rêves pour mieux se connaître (*Understanding one's dream in order to improve self-knowledge*).* Paris: Odile Jacob.

**Case illustration** in cognitive-behaviour therapy: (Montangero 2007)
Charles came for help with his gambling dependency. In session 6 he reported dreaming of seeing a chamois (wild mountain goat) rubbing its horns against a tree trunk, but they were deer antlers, not chamois horns. Asked to *fully describe* what he saw, felt and thought during the dream, he said the rubbing helped the chamois get rid of the antlers. Asked what *memories* came to mind about a chamois and then a deer, Charles said he remembered seeing chamois during his experience of great freedom when hiking in the mountains before he married. He also remembered a friend telling stories of hunting deer, and of deer rubbing their antlers until they lose them even though the rubbing is painful.

Charles *reformulated* the dream report *in more general terms* as: "A symbol of freedom (the chamois) tries to get rid of (rubs), a feature of victims (deer are victims of hunters)." He immediately added his interpretation: "This applies well to me now, to my effort to get rid of my gambling dependency."

His interpretation steered therapy toward reinforcing Charles's desire for freedom. Charles was asked to list every aspect that freedom could take for him, then every way in which gambling restricted his freedom, and was encouraged to feel free to make changes in his life. He got another, more interesting, job, and resumed hiking accompanied by his wife. This gave him a new sense of control over his life that he was keen to keep by not gambling again. The dream interpretation also led him to address painful aspects of not gambling and of being in therapy, which Charles had denied until then.

# EMPATHY DOTS, USE OF

**David RICHARDS,** School of Psychology, University of Exeter, Room 118, Washington Singer Building, Perry Road, Exeter, EX4 4QG, UK; ph +44 1392 724615 & **Karina LOVELL,** School of Nursing, Midwifery & Social Work, University of Manchester, University Place, Oxford Road, Manchester, UK, M13 9PL, UK; ph +44 161 306 7853

**Definition:** Empathy dots are marks which a high-volume mental health worker puts into the margin of a pre-printed or hand written psychotherapy interview schedule that is about to be followed during an appointment - seeing the dots reminds the worker to say something warmly empathic and/or understanding at intervals within the interview.

**Elements:** Just before seeing a patient the mental health worker puts simple dots at intervals down the right-hand margin of their assessment-, treatment-, and follow-up interview schedules. Each dot is a reminder that regular empathic statements convey understanding and improve patient satisfaction in therapy. For example, *"that must be very difficult for you"*, *"I can see your anxiety is causing you distress"*. As therapists navigate through the questions in their interview schedule they see the empathy dots at intervals. These remind workers that as well as covering the required specific factors in the interview, they must also express empathy. Such reminders are extremely useful when therapists treat large numbers of patients with typical individual caseloads of 45- 60 patients.

**Related procedures:** *Expressing verbal empathy, reward.*

**Application:** When using therapy-interview schedules in high-volume clinical environments.

**1st use?** Richards & Whyte (2008).

**References:**
1. Richards DA, Whyte M (2008). *Reach Out: National Programme Educator Materials to Support the Delivery of Training for Practitioners Delivering Low intensity Interventions.* London, Rethink.

**Case illustration:** (Lovell, unpublished)
 (This - unlike in other clp-website entries – details a therapist's procedure with many patients, not just one). `I run a guided-self help clinic 1 day a week in a deprived area. On an average day I complete about 4 30-minute assessments and 17 15-minute follow-up appointments, which means I see

about 21 patients a day. I give low-intensity help to people with common mental health problems which are often severe and enduring and complicated by a risk of suicide and a wealth of social problems, so I must also liaise with many other agencies. I'm kept very busy. Though I enjoy the work I sometimes feel frustrated. Gathering information in patient-centred interviews to obtain a shared understanding, agree goals and offer the right guidance/support means I must think carefully about every question I ask so that I maximise the value of my limited time with each patient. Working under such pressure can make one risk forgetting to engage patients by warm empathy, particularly when one is seeing the 20th patient of the day and still has 10 phone calls to make to other agencies.

`I know I can't always feel warm empathy but can try to express it by my facial, body and verbal language. Just before I see each patient I spend a few seconds reminding myself that `this person is trying to cope, ... is honest, ... is responsive'. To ensure that I show warm empathy I put and look for prominent 'empathy dots' in the right-hand margin of my interview schedule (I usually increase the number of dots as the day goes on!). The dots remind me to check that I've expressed empathy, warmth and understanding to enhance engagement and partnering with the patient.' For example, "Life seems to be pretty tough for you at the moment", "I can see how your feelings of depression are stopping you doing what you want to do right now".

# EVOKED RESPONSE AROUSAL PLUS SENSITIZATION

Douglas H RUBEN, Best Impressions International, 4211 Okemos Road, Suite 22, Okemos, Michigan 48864, USA; ph +1 517-347-0944

**Definition:** A way to eliminate chronically ritualistic, violent child tantrums that are self-injurious or dangerous to others. Staff ask an admired peer/s to watch the tantrums from unpredictable times after their start. When the tantrum ends, staff ask the child who had the tantrum to say sorry to the observing peer/s.

**Elements:** Staff pre-select at least 3 children whom the aggressive child admires - looks for, is aware of their presence, imitates their gestures, postures, speech or other behaviours, and is never violent in their presence. When the child has a tantrum, staff remove surrounding objects as if s/he has a major fit and wait for it to pass while placing an admired peer at a safe distance away but still within clear sight. After the outburst ends, staff ask the violent child to look at and say sorry to the admired peer. The violent child may well refuse and looks uncomfortable on seeing the admired peer, and even more so if more admired peers are added as observers at later times. The violent child then tends to postpone and interrupt the tantrum ritual, which then attenuates and stops.

**Related procedures:** *Differential reinforcement of incompatible or low-rate behaviours, avoidance conditioning, sensory extinction, shame aversion, covert sensitisation.*

**Application:** For children individually (not in groups) who can stand around others and mingle, and are age 6 or older; in schools, residential and group-transition homes, psychiatric institutions, and correctional youth centers.

**1st Use?** As a concept, Asmus et al (1999).

**References:**
1. Asmus JM, Wacker DP, Harding J, Berg WK, Derby KM, Kocis E (1999). Evaluation of antecedent stimulus parameters for the treatment of escape-maintained aberrant behavior. *Journal of Applied Behavior Analysis*, 32, 495-513
2. Ruben DH (1999). Why traditional behavior modification fails with urban children. In NR Macciomei & DH Ruben (Eds.) *Behavior Management in the Public Schools: An Urban Approach,* p19-27. Wesport, CT: Praeger Press.
3. Ruben DH (2003). Aggressive tantrum elimination using evoked response arousal plus sensitization in preschool developmentally disabled. *Behavioral*

*Systems Monograph*, 2, 1-6.

**Case illustration:** (Ruben, unpublished)

Becky, a girl of 9 with autism, attended a special education classroom for developmentally disabled children. With no or minimal warning, she exploded several times a day in a cascade of behaviors harming herself and others. She beat her chest, hit her face, fell on the floor, might knock down nearby furniture, and struck peers who were in her way. Staff pre-selected 3 peers she admired, around whom she never showed tantrums. During Becky's first tantrum of the day, staff asked a pre-selected peer to stand several feet away and watch the tantrum from where Becky could see her. When the aggressive burst ended, the teacher asked Becky to say 'I'm sorry' to the observing peer. Becky refused, got upset and ran to another part of the room. At a different interval after the start of Becky's next tantrum that day, the same peer watched her again until the tantrum ended. When it ended, the teacher again asked Becky to say sorry to the observing peer. Becky refused. A second admired peer was recruited as a tantrum-observer and the teacher asked Becky to apologize to both peers after her outburst ended. Again Becky refused. By the 3rd or 4th consecutive day of tantrums with the admired peers coming in unpredictably to watch Becky, Becky did something different. Before she started her first tantrum of the day, Becky began to look around the room 2-3 times to see if admired peers were present. If they were not, she started her tantrum and after 30-60 seconds stopped abruptly and again looked around for admired peers. If they remained absent she resumed her tantrum for up to a minute, and again looked round. By days 5 or 6, Becky delayed starting her tantrums until later in the day. They become briefer and less self-injurious, and she stopped mild outbursts within 30 seconds. Within 2 weeks her ritual violent tantrums stopped entirely, and she only made occasional angry or obscene verbal remarks in a low voice over the next 3 months.

# EXPERIMENT

**Hal ARKOWITZ,** Department of Psychology, Arizona University, Tucson, Arizona 85721 USA; ph +15203254837

**Definition:** An activity a client carries out during or between therapy sessions in order to test an idea about thoughts/feelings or to discover or become aware of new therapeutic information.

**Elements:** In discussion with the therapist, the client designs new activities (experiments) to try during or between sessions. The activities may test hypotheses in any area. They usually concern: in anxiety, over-estimations of danger; in depression, overly negative views of the self, world, and future. Interpersonal experiments concern how the client or others might react to his/her new behavior. Awareness experiments may include discovering how s/he responds to a new situation about which s/he has no preconceptions.

**Related procedures:** *Assignments*; *homework, cognitive restructuring, exposure, programmed practice, empty-chair technique, two-chair technique, guided discovery/fantasy/imagery, psychodrama, rehearsal, role-play, shaping, successive approximation.*

**Application:** Usually in individual therapy, sometimes with couples or groups.

**1st use?** 'Experiment' first denoted exercises to increase awareness and growth (Perls et al., 1951), and later denoted hypothesis-testing (Beck et al. 1979).

**References:**
1. Arkowitz H (2003). An integrative approach to psychotherapy based on common processes of change. In F Kaslow (Ed.) *Comprehensive Handbook of Psychotherapy, Vol. 4, Integrative and Eclectic Therapies*, J Lebow (Ed.), (pp.317-337). New York: John Wiley and Sons.
2. Beck AT, Rush JA, Shaw BR, Emery G (1979). *Cognitive therapy for depression.* New York: Guilford Publications.
3. Perls FS, Hefferline RF, Goodman P (1951). *Gestalt therapy: Excitement and growth in the human personality.* New York: The Julian Press.
4. Greenberg, L.S., Rice, L.N., & Elliott, R. (1993). *Facilitating emotional change: The moment-by moment process.* New York: Guilford.

**Case Illustrations**
1. Hypothesis-testing experiment (Arkowitz 2003)
    A young woman with panic and agoraphobia tested her idea that if

she tried to get to a shopping mall she would panic so she wouldn't even get out of the car. She was to report her feelings while anticipating all stages towards entering a mall as far as she could get *(imaginal exposure)*. Her husband drove her to the mall *(live exposure)* and remained in the car in the parking lot while she stood just inside the mall entrance for 10 minutes and found that anticipating entering the mall made her more anxious than actually being in the mall *(homework; cognitive restructuring; live exposure; programmed practice; shaping; successive approximation)*. After standing at the entrance for a few minutes she became far less anxious than she had anticipated, which encouraged her to do more. In subsequent days, she was able to enter the mall and spend time shopping there. Had she been too anxious to actually go to the mall, she would have examined her feelings when thinking of trying to do so.

2. Proposed hypothesis-testing experiment (Arkowitz 2003)

A young man with a flying phobia sought psychotherapy saying he wanted to join his wife on some of her trips. In the therapist's office he did imaginal exposure but resisted doing live exposure, even as minimal as a proposed experiment to drive to the airport with the therapist and see what he felt while sitting in the car watching planes take off *(homework; cognitive restructuring; exposure; programmed practice; shaping, successive approximation)*. He thought this would not make him particularly anxious, and finally admitted his unhappiness in the marriage and reluctance to spend more time with his wife than he had to. After discussing this. he and his wife sought marriage counseling.

3. Awareness experiment (Arkowitz 2003)

A woman sought help for depression and guilt 2 months after she had inadvertently caused a car accident in which a driver (Steve) died. His family blamed her for his death even though she was not at fault; they banned her from attending Steve's funeral, making it harder for her to mourn his death. In therapy session 6 she seemed to speak to him directly and agreed to a two-chair experiment in which she spoke as herself and as Steve at various times *(empty-chair technique; guided discovery / fantasy / imagery; psychodrama; rehearsal; role-play)*. This experiment took part of each of the next 5 sessions. The therapist suggested that she switch roles as needed and say how she felt (e.g. "Tell `Steve' how that makes you feel"). At first, she was apologetic and guilt-ridden, and `Steve' was angry, aggressive, and critical of her. Then she said she was sorry for what happened but it wasn't her fault and she wanted him to stop harassing her. Her exchange became more heated with her often asking "What do you want from me?" `Steve' surprised her by saying he wanted her to have a `ritual' for him, and she began to cry. In the next week she went to his grave in the evening, bringing a candle which she lit and placed on the headstone while she read a poem she had written for the occasion. These events seemed central to her eventual recovery.

# EXPOSURE, INTEROCEPTIVE (TO INTERNAL CUES)

Kamila S WHITE, Shawnee L BASDEN, David H BARLOW, Center For Anxiety & Related Disorders, Boston University; 648 Beacon Street, Boston, MA, 02215, USA

**Definition:** Interoceptive exposure involves repeated engagement in tasks which reproduce the full experience of distressing emotions such as panic/anxiety and associated somatic sensations. It is commonly combined with situational exposure, cognitive restructuring, and psychoeducation in the treatment of panic/agoraphobic and other anxiety disorders.

**Elements:** Patients repeatedly induce emotion-evoking internal cues and sensations until those no longer feel threatening. For panic/anxiety such exercises can include spinning in a chair, breathing through a straw, vigorously exercising, and tensing muscles throughout the body.

**Related Procedures:** *Vicarious/live/in vivo exposure, carbon-dioxide (CO2) challenge tasks, mindfulness training.*

**1st Use?** Wolpe J (1958).

**References:**
1. Barlow DH, Craske MG (2000). *Mastery of your anxiety and panic (MAP-3): Client workbook for anxiety and panic (3rd ed.)* San Antonio, TX. Graywind/Psychological Corporation.
2. Ito LM, Noshirvani H, Basoglu M, Marks IM (1996). Does exposure to internal cues enhance exposure to external cues in agoraphobia with panic: A pilot controlled study of self-exposure. *Psychotherapy & Psychosomatics*, 65, 24-28.
3. White KS, Barlow DH (2002). Panic disorder and agoraphobia. In Barlow DH *Anxiety and its disorders:The nature and treatment of anxiety and panic* (2nd ed) New York: Guilford Press.
4. Wolpe J (1958). *Psychotherapy by reciprocal inhibition.* Stanford, CA: Stanford University Press.

**Case illustration:**
Ellie first panicked at age 14 on a school trip. She suddenly felt palpitations, shortness of breath, a sense of choking, and dizziness; these lasted 10 minutes. She feared she might choke to death or embarrass herself by fainting, so she avoided caffeine, spicy foods, social activities, and sports. She sought treatment 4 months after her first panic. The therapist explained that panic disorder is maintained by avoidance of not only public places such

as theaters and social events but also of other things which bring on panic-like sensations, e.g. caffeine, exercise (palpitations), hot showers (hot flushes), spicy foods (stomach discomfort), scary movies, skipping meals, wearing a scarf (sense of choking), sexual arousal. After completing tests to identify her feared sensations e.g. spinning in a chair for 60 seconds, breathing through a straw for 2 minutes, Ellie was asked to do interoceptive exposure exercises by engaging repeatedly in hitherto avoided activities like those above until she felt no fear. During the exercises she was instructed to focus fully on experiencing the sensations induced, to become a passive observer doing nothing to reduce frightening feelings, to just patiently try to get used to them by the end of the session. For homework she was asked to do similar exercises daily 3 consecutive times. For each exercise she was told to wait for ensuing unpleasant sensations to subside, and then to repeat the procedure again. She completed interoceptive exercises of spinning in a chair for 1 minute, running in place for 1 minute, shaking her head from side to side for 30 seconds. As these became easier they were made more challenging, often by pairing them with exposure to more frightening external situations e.g. having caffeinated drinks at a mall, wearing a scarf to a social event. After 14 sessions Ellie no longer avoided frightening sensations and was instead seeking them out.

# EXPOSURE, LIVE (IN-VIVO, LIVE DESENSITIZATION)

Georg W. ALPERS, Universitaet Wuerzburg, Biologische Psychologie, Klinische Psychologie und Psychotherapie, Marcusstrasse 9-11, 97070 Wuerzburg, Germany; ph +49 931-312840/2

**Definition:** Systematic repeated exposure to real live situations that cause distress until the resultant discomfort subsides.

**Elements:** Patients are asked to work out whichever cues usually evoke undue fear from the least to the most frightening. They are then persuaded to gradually expose themselves to those real situations repeatedly, usually for up to an hour or more at a time, to experience ensuing feelings and thoughts to the full without escape, to continue exposure until the discomfort starts to subside, and to do exposure homework preferably daily or as often as possible. If patients so wish, they can start with intense exposure to very frightening situations. Exposure may be with or without a therapist and/or guided by appropriate self-help books or computer systems.

**Related procedures:** *Exposure, habituation, extinction, confrontation, contact desensitization, systematic desensitization (done with relaxation), graded modelling, guided mastery (participation), programmed practice, cue-controlled relaxation, applied relaxation, imaginal (fantasy) desensitization, flooding (intense exposure – implosion if imagined), interoceptive exposure, arugamama in Morita therapy, behavioral experiment, paradoxical intention, narrative exposure, prolonged exposure counterconditioning, virtual reality exposure, CAVE (computer-aided vicarious exposure), rehearsal relief, cognitive restructuring, homework.*

**1st Use?** Garfield et al. (1967).

**References:**
1. Alpers GW, Wilhelm FH, Roth WT (2005). Psychophysiological assessment during exposure in driving phobic patients. *Journal of Abnormal Psychology*, 114, 126-139.
2. Garfield ZH, Darwin PL, Singer BA, McBrearty JF (1967). Effect of "in vivo" training on experimental desensitization of a phobia. *Psychological Reports*, 20, 515- 519.
3. Malleson N (1959). Panic and phobia: a possible method of treatment. *Lancet*, 31, 225-227.
4. Watson JP, Gaind R, Marks IM (1971). Prolonged exposure: a rapid treatment for phobias. *British Medical Journal*, 1, 13-15.

**Case illustration:**
Jen age 35 consulted a therapist for her severely handicapping and inexplicable fear of spiders. She had never really liked spiders and her fear had intensified over the years. Whenever she saw a spider she panicked helplessly, couldn't move, her heart raced, her palms sweated, and she felt embarrassed at depending on other people then. She avoided walking across a lawn or going into her basement or garage lest she encountered spiders there. Having unsuccessfully tried to prevent spiders entering her home she was about to move elsewhere. Jen was told her symptoms were typical of a phobia and that she could endure them for long enough to get used to whatever was frightening her. Even the mere thought of looking at a spider evoked extreme fear and disgust so she learned to open a book with pictures of spiders at the therapist's office. She took the book home and brought herself to touch the pictures with her fingers. Next she looked at a spider in an empty glass jar for at least 30 min. without her usual attempt to remove it or turn away from it. Jen was encouraged to do exposure without her usual subtle avoidances that stopped her experiencing the fear fully and getting used to it.

Thus she looked at the spider and her own reactions in detail, and was fascinated at not being overwhelmed by fear. Her distress decreased during each exposure session and across repeated such sessions. She became more confident exposing herself to spiders at home. After 12 50-minute weekly sessions and several hours of practice at home she touched a large spider and let it crawl across her palm. Jen then cleaned out her garage, kept a spider in a jar in her kitchen and went to bed without checking for spiders. Improvement continued at follow up 8 weeks later.

# EXPRESSED EMPATHY

**Lynne ANGUS & Helen MACAULAY**, 108C Behavioural Sciences Bldg, Psychology, York University, Toronto, Canada; ph + 416 736 2100 33615

**Definition:** Actively listening to, emotionally resonating with, and understanding, another's experience followed by accurately communicating this understanding to the other.

**Elements:** Expressed empathy starts with the therapist sensing his/her own inner experience of a client's disclosure during therapy e.g. *"as she told me of her husband's tirade at the restaurant, I felt deep sadness, almost despair, about her marriage"*. The therapist then tries to highlight and put into words the most poignant and implicit aspects of a client's experience on a moment-to-moment basis, for further exploration and new meaning construction. A highly-attuned therapist focuses clients' attention on experience just outside their awareness and thus offers meaning that disentangles, clarifies, and allows clients to explore further: *"so as you sat in the restaurant, inundated by this torrent of criticism and complaint, it seemed as if you were drowning in despair, that this would simply never ever be different?"*. The therapist phrases empathic communications tentatively, leaving the door open for clients to co-construct new meanings and say if the therapist's empathic response fits their own experience of an event. Empathic explorations can be reflections, or open-ended or direct questions, to help the client expand on and differentiate their current experience. A therapist's attentive, concerned facial expression, forward lean, direct eye contact, and sensitive enquiring and tentative tone can all help convey empathic understanding to the client. Finally, clients show perception of the therapist's empathic response *"yeah, that's it, I wasn't angry, I felt sad and hopeless, that our marriage is really over"*.

**Related procedures:** *Countertransference, use of; empathy dots, use of; meaning making; metaphor, use of; validation of feelings.*

**Application:** Widely used in individual- and group-therapy across theoretical orientations to promote a working alliance and help clients understand their assumptions and process and regulate emotion.

**1st use?** Rogers CR (1957).

**References:**
1. Barrett-Lennard GT (1986). The Relationship Inventory now: Issues and advances in theory, method, and use. In LS Greenberg & WM Pinsof (Eds.),

*The psychotherapeutic process: A research handbook* (pp 439-475). New York: Guilford Press.
2. Bohart AC, Greenberg LS (1997). Empathy and psychotherapy: An introductory overview. In AC Bohart & LS Greenberg (Eds.), *Empathy reconsidered: New directions in psychotherapy* (pp 3-32). Washington, DC: American Psychological Association.
3. Macaulay HL, Toukmanian SG, Gordon KM (2007). Attunement as the core of therapist expressed empathy. *Canadian J.of Counselling*, 41, 244-254.
4. Rogers CR (1957). The necessary and sufficient conditions of therapeutic personality change. *J.of Consulting Psychology*, 21, 95-103.

**Case illustration:** (Angus & Macaulay, unpublished)
Margaret sought therapy in her mid-thirties for profound loneliness and depression after the unexpected break-up of a romantic relationship a year earlier. In session 3 Margaret reflected: 'I can (get along alone) for a while but then think "why am I doing this"? I have no problem being with myself when I know there's somebody out there, but when I'm by myself and really feel that there's nobody out there that after a while it starts to get to me.' Therapist: *'Let me see if I understand - I'm not sure if I misheard. You don't have a problem being alone if you know someone's out there'*. Margaret's answer *'Yeah, if you know'* signalled that her therapist had grasped an important aspect of her experience of loneliness which he elaborated by saying: *"So then it's alright to be alone.'*

Margaret's and the therapist's sharing of a clear understanding of her loneliness set the stage for her discovery of what was *most* painful about being on her own now. Margaret: 'Yeah, because you always know you've got someone there to talk to or want to visit or' *(T: 'Yeah')* 'it's when you feel there's nobody out there and you're alone then there's a difference between being alone and feeling lonely' *(T:* `Sure'*)* 'you know that's when you start feeling lonely - you think, oh geez.' Resonating to the core of Margaret's disclosure, her therapist responded empathically: ` *So is it that your deepest fear is of being really all totally alone'* (M:` Hm-mm'*) 'meaning "there's not even someone I can think of"* (M: `Right') *"out there whom I could contact" and then it's this terrible loneliness?*` This empathic response helped Margaret to acknowledge `Yeah, that's exactly how it felt without anyone and how I felt last year, like I'd been totally abandoned' (T: `Yes') `and that my life was going down the gutter and no one was reaching out to help and I was amazed' that set the stage for a sustained and productive focus on her relational needs in ensuing therapy sessions.

# EXPRESSIVE WRITING THERAPY

**James W PENNEBAKER,** Department of Psychology, University of Texas at Austin, Austin, TX 78712 USA; ph + 1 512 2322781

**Definition:** A method whereby people write about emotional upheavals.

**Elements:** People are encouraged to write repeatedly about emotional experiences, typically for 20 minutes per day on 4 consecutive days, though length and number of writing sessions is flexible. The writing exercises aim to help the writers explore their thoughts and feelings about one or more upheavals in order to identify, label, understand, and come to terms with their experiences. The writers receive no feedback from others - the goal is to stand back and to reassess upsetting experiences in writing for themselves alone.

**Application:** Done individually on its own or together with other psychotherapy procedures.

**Related procedures:** *Disclosure methods* in client-centered and other therapy, *religious confession, narrative exposure, prolonged exposure, goal setting.*

**1st Use?** Pennebaker & Beall (1986).

**References:**
1. Pennebaker JW, Beall SK (1986). Confronting a traumatic event: Toward an understanding of inhibition and disease. *Journal of Abnormal Psychology*, 95, 274-281.
2. Lepore SJ, Smyth, J.M. (Eds.) (2002). *The writing cure: How expressive writing promotes health and emotional well-being.* Washington, DC: American Psychological Association.
3. Pennebaker JW (1997). *Opening up: The healing power of expressing emotions.* New York: Guilford Press.
4. Frattaroli J (2006). Experimental disclosure and its moderators: A meta-analysis. *Psychological Bulletin*, 132, 823-865.

**Case illustration:** (Pennebaker 1997)
  Hal, an engineer aged 52, participated in a writing project involving over 40 laid-off workers after his company ended his 24 years of employment there. He was hostile, and had insomnia and difficulty talking with others about his experience. In the 4 months since being laid off Hal had had 4 job interviews without success. At an outplacement company contracted by

the former employer to help laid-off employees find new jobs, Hal was asked to write about his experience daily for 5 consecutive days, 30 minutes each day. All 40 laid-off employees wrote by themselves in office cubicles. Daily writings were turned in anonymously to project workers and no one ever received feedback about them. By 1-month follow-up, Hal said the writing had markedly improved how he thought about the job loss, including fewer ruminative thoughts and less anger and helplessness about it. He was now talking with his wife about the layoff and sleeping better. After his writing sessions Hal had successful job interviews and was about to start a new job at a pay level above that in his previous job.

# FAMILY FOCUSED GRIEF THERAPY

David William KISSANE, Weill Medical College of Cornell University and Memorial Sloan-Kettering Cancer Center, 1275 York Ave, New York, NY 10021, USA; ph +1 646 888 0019

**Definition:** Facilitation of a family's expression of thoughts and feelings about loss and coping with a relative's illness and death to promote shared grief and optimal family functioning, often commenced during palliative care (with the ill relative attending) and continued into bereavement after the patient's death.

**Elements:** High-risk families may be screened with the Family Relationships Index regarding communication, cohesion and conflict resolution. To prevent maladaptive outcomes, a family therapist leads family sessions through i) assessment and agreement about the focus of work, ii) active therapy, and iii) consolidation and termination. Treatment takes 6-12 sessions, each lasting 90 minutes, and extending over 6-18 months, with later consolidation sessions spaced more widely. Length of treatment depends on degree of family dysfunction.

The therapist uses circular questioning [*'Let me ask each of you to describe who gets on best with whom?'*] and confirmatory summaries to: discern patterns of communication, teamwork and conflict, role delineation, traditions, and transgenerational styles of relating; affirm strengths of family life; encourage constructive ways of relating that support mutual care and respect. The dying family-member's wishes can be harnessed to overcome prior misunderstandings and heal old grievances. The therapist attends to the family-as-a-whole, avoids alliances with individuals, and helps the family to focus on its communication, cohesion and conflict resolution. End-of-session summaries help relatives to integrate their understanding of the themes and processes discussed [*"Today, we've learned that your parents and grandparents avoided discussing feelings, as you've done too thus far. You've talked about the benefits of striving to share your feelings."*].

The therapist sensitively encourages [*"How serious is this illness? What threat to life does it bring"*] family members to safely discuss in the session the hitherto-avoided subject of death and dying. Bigger disruptions of communication and teamwork are addressed by highlighting entrenched patterns of relating often transmitted from prior generations, but once recognized, capable of being worked on differently. For example, relational styles involving much criticism may be tempered by introducing frequent affirmation [*"You've been tough on each other, yet I notice tremendous teamwork pointing to genuine care you give each other."*]. Spacing therapy over 12-18 months of bereavement [up to 12 sessions] consolidates change and family focus on improving relationships. High-conflict families need containment [e.g. therapist stops in-session arguments, showing members how these escalate and damage] and support to interrupt disruptions, respect alliances that serve members best, and recognition of the benefit of distance between relatives who differ temperamentally and don't get on. For very dysfunctional families, modest goals for change may be set.

**Related procedures**: *Anger management, anxiety management, cognitive restructuring and meaning making, communication analysis and training, genogram analysis of transgenerational patterns of relating and coping with loss, guided mourning, life review (reminiscence) therapy, prolonged-grief therapy, problem solving, relational enhancement, ritual endorsement, social skills training, use of narrative.*

**Application:** Preventive and active treatment, done in the home, hospice/hospital, or outpatient clinic, for: high-risk families whose relative of any age is having palliative care for advanced progressive illness e.g. cancer; renal/pulmonary/cardiac failure; motor neurone disease/other neurodegeneration; families carrying hereditary cancer.

**1st use?** Kissane et al (1998).

**References:**
1. Kissane DW, Bloch S, McKenzie M, McDowall C, Nitzan R (1998). Family grief therapy: a preliminary account of a new model to promote healthy family functioning during palliative care and bereavement. *Psycho-Oncology*, 7, 14-25.
2. Kissane DW, Bloch S (2002). *Family Focused Grief Therapy: A Model of Family- Centred Care during Palliative Care and Bereavement.* Open University Press, Buckingham and Philadelphia. [Translated into Japanese (2003) and Danish (2004)].
3. Kissane DW, McKenzie M, Bloch S, Moskowitz C, McKenzie DP, O'Neill I (2006). Family focused grief therapy: a randomized controlled trial in palliative care and bereavement. *American J.Psychiatry*, 163, 1208 - 1218.

**Case illustrations:**
1. *Blended family carrying unfinished business* (Kissane & Bloch 2002)
　　　　Divorce had ended a 20-year marriage of a couple with 3 daughters. The mother's terminal illness 18 years later allowed resolution of unfinished business from the divorce, her bitterness having prevented consolation of her eldest daughter's distress as a teenager. Mother knew intuitively that something remained amiss, and screening for family functioning led her to invite sorting of this out before she died. Both her current and husbands joined the 4 women in 8 family meetings, each of 90 minutes, held in her home.

Each member's perspective of the marital breakup was shared as the family retold their story. Enhanced understanding developed with greater acceptance and forgiveness. The mother's role was affirmed with gratitude. Reminiscence helped celebrate her life, while the family prepared for her loss.

2. *Family burdened by double cancer* (Kissane & Bloch 2002)

A family grieved intensely when both mother and a daughter developed cancer. The mother's family was close, while father had migrated and lost all contact. When the 2 daughters grew up the elder moved interstate for several years and was perceived as the black sheep, while the younger achieved academically and bonded to mother but developed breast cancer followed by mother getting lung cancer. These illnesses drew the family closer. In therapy for ten 90-minute sessions in the home over several months, a greater sense of reconciliation developed with the older daughter. About half-way through, the therapist invited the sons-in-law to join, thus strengthening the experience of support from family meetings. Ways were explored of creating memories for the grandchildren. Eventually, a creative outcome became evident despite the challenge of loss.

# FAMILY WORK FOR SCHIZOPHRENIA

Julian **LEFF**, Institute of Psychiatry, Kings College London, de Crespigny Park, London SE5 8AF; ph +44 207 794 9724

**Definition:** Family work tries to avert relapse in schizophrenia by helping relatives reduce high levels of negative emotion expressed to the patient such as critical comments, hostility, and over-involvement with overemotional behaviour, overprotection e.g. a mother would not let her 20 year old daughter cross the road alone when she developed schizophrenia, and lack of boundary-setting e.g. a mother allowed her son to establish a home gymnasium in her living room thus excluding her from using it.

**Elements:**
　　1. Reducing expressed emotion: Criticism and hostility can stem from ignorance about schizophrenia and are tackled initially by education about it, e.g. stating that apathy and self-neglect are caused by the illness and not by the patient being lazy or dirty.
Thereafter, critical remarks are reframed as representing a caring attitude of the relative, so allowing the relative and patient to negotiate the behaviour being criticised, e.g. reframing 'He's always wearing a dirty shirt' as *'You really care about your son's appearance'*. Overinvolvement is lessened by helping the relative and patient recognise that they maintain this in a mutually reinforcing relationship e.g. asking each partner what they would feel like if the other was absent for more than a day. Relatives' guilt is alleviated by therapist statements in education sessions that relatives cannot cause schizophrenia, and direct exploration of the guilt, e.g. a mother was asked why she allowed her son to beat her - she said she'd tried to abort the pregnancy with a knitting needle and believed this had caused his illness. Joining a group of other relatives also helps. The therapist/s relieves relatives' anxiety by congratulating them on their excellent care of the patient, saying they've earned a rest, and asking them to choose and carry out enjoyable activities outside the home which involve brief trial separations, e.g. suggesting that the parents go out together for an hour to have coffee, leaving the patient at home. The therapists encourage the patient to feel competent by choosing and carrying out a small task in the relative's absence, e.g. making her bed.
　　2. Reducing contact with a high-expressed-emotion relative: The therapist addresses this if the patient is unemployed and has no daily activity outside home, leading to long contact (over 35 hours a week) with a high-expressed-emotion relative at home e.g. elderly parents who've retired or given up their job to care for the patient, or a homemaking partner. The therapist advises the patient to attend a day hospital, day centre or sheltered workshop, and the relative to spend more time away from home in social activi-

ties, voluntary work, or attending adult education classes. Schizophrenia impairs patients' ability to form and sustain social relationships, but the therapist tries to help them increase social activities by social skills training, e.g. encouraging eye contact and smiling during conversations, and by recruiting healthy siblings to help the patient make social contacts outside the home.

**Related procedures:** *Behavioral activation, community reinforcement approach, nidotherapy, reframing, social skills training.*

**Application:** One or two therapists run sessions with individual families or any family member/s, groups of up to 10 relatives excluding patients, and multi-family groups of up to 8 families including the patients. Antipsychotic medication is usually continued in parallel.

**1st Use?** Leff et al (1982).

**References:**
1. Vaughn C, Leff JP (1976). The influence of family and social factors on the course of psychiatric illness: a comparison of schizophrenic and depressed neurotic patients. *British Journal of Psychiatry*, 129, 125-137.
2. Leff J, Kuipers L, Berkowitz R, Eberlein-Fries R, Sturgeon D (1982). A controlled trial of social intervention in the families of schizophrenic patients. *British Journal of Psychiatry*, 141, 121-134.
3. Kuipers L, Leff J, Lam D (1992). *Family Work for Schizophrenia: A Practical Guide*. London: Gaskell. 2nd ed. 2002.
4. Leff J (2005). *Advanced Family Work for Schizophrenia*. London: Gaskell.

**Case Illustration 1:** (Leff, unpublished)
    John age 19 developed schizophrenia and was admitted to hospital for 9 weeks. Antipsychotic medication reduced his delusions and hallucinations. He resumed living with mother and stepfather, but stayed in bed all morning and grew his hair long. His infuriated stepfather, a retired army officer, tried pulling John out of bed by his hair. Mother, an executive in a large company, gave up her job to look after John. Stepfather accused her of being too soft with John and she complained he was too hard.
    As is usual, 2 therapists worked with the family in their home. They began with 2 sessions of education about schizophrenia, emphasizing that John's staying in bed was part of the illness, after which stepfather stopped criticizing him. Mother said that from John's birth she'd recognised his difference from his older brother, who now lives on his own. She felt John needed more care and protection; the therapists praised her sensitivity but said it was now actually counterproductive as it hindered John from developing friendships with his peers. One-hour sessions with mother, stepfather and John together were held every 2 weeks initially, later monthly, over a year.

The therapists tried to reduce conflict between the parents, enabling them to manage John's problems together. Both parents attended a relatives-only group of up to 8 relatives meeting bi-weekly for 1.5 hours. The other group members pressed mother to return to work. She finally agreed, having developed enough confidence in stepfather's change of heart to allow him to care for John by day. He relinquished his aggressive means of getting John out of bed and, after discussion with the therapists, introduced inducements, including activities he and John could do together, e.g. constructing a barbecue in the garden. Apart from the first 2 education sessions with the parents only, the 3 family members had 15 sessions over the year, and the parents attended a relative's group together or separately 13 times in all.

**Case Illustration 2**: Reducing contact with a high expressed-emotion relative (Leff, unpublished)

Brian age 35 has suffered from schizophrenia for ten years. He lives with his mother and two younger stepbrothers, Mike and Joe, whose father died a few years ago. Brian's father separated from mother when Brian was aged 8 and lost contact with the family. Brian has paranoid delusions and tends to sit on the stairs to the upper floor holding a knife. Mother overprotects him and does not establish boundaries to his behaviour, e.g. she prepares special meals for him when he won't eat with the family. He rarely goes out and his stepbrothers never ask friends home because of embarrassment about Brian. One therapist conducted 2 education sessions attended by mother, Mike and Joe. In session 1 including all 4 family members, Mike angrily announced that in the past he'd wished Brian would die. The therapist asked Mike about his relationship with Brian before he became ill. Mike gave an account of Brian teaching him to fish and how much he'd looked up to Brian. The therapist explained that protecting Brian against contact with the outside world maintained the usual stigma of schizophrenia. At family meeting 4 Mike said he'd told his friends about Brian's illness and they'd been sympathetic. They now visit the home and stay with Brian when Mike wants to go out, and Brian stopped sitting on the stairs holding a knife. Furthermore Mike now takes Brian out fishing and though Mike says little, there is a sense of companionship. By these means contact between Brian and mother has lessened considerably. The 4 family members had 6 sessions over 4 months. No relatives group was available locally.

# FIXED-ROLE THERAPY

David WINTER, School of Psychology, University of Hertfordshire, College Lane, Hatfield, Herts, AL10 9AB, UK; ph +44 1707 285070

**Definition:** Fixed-role therapy encourages the client to enact a new role (written by the therapist) for about two weeks in order to try out alternative views of the self and the world.

**Elements:** The therapist asks the client to write a short self-description, as if written by someone who knows him/her well. Based on this the therapist, before the next session, writes a fixed-role sketch of someone with a new name whom the client might enact in and between sessions. This sketches someone not ideal or the opposite of the client, but adds features which differ from the client's main existing ones and offer testable predictions, e.g. that appropriate expression of feelings will not lead to rejection. It includes an attempt to understand other people's viewpoints.

The therapist shows the client the fixed-role sketch, asks if the character portrayed is plausible and not too threatening, and may redraft the sketch until the client finds it acceptable. The therapist then asks the client to 'become' the new character for two weeks while his/her current self is 'on vacation', during which time the client sees the therapist up to 5 times a week for brief sessions to rehearse the new role in first superficial and then progressively more intimate interpersonal situations. The fixed-role exercise allows clients to experiment with new behaviour in and between sessions while protected by 'make-believe'.

**Application:** In individual, group and couple therapy.

**Related procedures:** *Experiment, personal-construct psychotherapy, psychodrama,rehearsal, repertory grid technique, role play.*

**1st Use?** Kelly (1955).

**References:**
1. Bonarius JCJ (1970). Fixed role therapy: A double paradox. *British Journal of Medical Psychology*, 43, 213-219.
2. Epting FR, Nazario A Jr (1987). Designing a fixed role therapy: issues, techniques, and modifications. In RA Neimeyer & GJ Neimeyer (eds.), *Personal Construct Therapy Casebook* (pp. 277-289). New York: Springer.
3. Kelly GA (1955, pp. 360-451) *The Psychology of Personal Constructs.* New York: Norton (republished by Routledge, 1991).
4. Winter DA (1987). Personal construct psychotherapy as a radical alterna-

tive to social skills training. In RA Neimeyer & GJ Neimeyer (eds.), *Personal Construct Therapy Casebook* (pp. 107-123). New York: Springer.

**Case Illustration:** (Winter, 1987)
Tom was referred for continuing to feel inadequate despite extensive past treatment. In the second pre-therapy assessment session, a repertory grid (see clp entry) and other personal-construct methods such as Tschudi's ABC technique, identified Tom's dilemma of wanting to be assertive yet viewing assertive extroverts as demanding and aggressive. The therapist discussed its origin in childhood experiences and used fixed-role therapy in sessions 6-7 to help Tom see himself differently. The therapist asked Tom for a written self-description, as written by someone who knew him, which in summary was:

'I've known Tom 20 years since our schooldays together. He was a swot who pestered me for help with maths. We fished together, and in later years went to concerts and drinks with friends. He envied my settling in a good job while he after 5 years at university never settled down. Tom wasn't good company with my friends, longed for a girlfriend, joined clubs to meet women, and seemed unhappy with his girl friend. After breaking up he'd return to my social scene for a week then disappear for weeks. He was usually quiet, depressed and reticent. He stopped self-employment, preferring steady work with a company yet was anxious - it wasn't what he wanted, just like his tagging onto my friends. He moved away but remained unhappy there. When we have a drink he looks miserable, worries whether he'll marry and have children, and says little.'

The therapist now sketched a fixed-role character `Roy' which ignored searching for a girl friend and reframed as strengths what Tom saw as impediments e.g. Tom's serious intensity became Roy's *'passion and conviction which earns respect. He strives to work hard and have fun as best he can'*. Tom's tennis skills anticipating other players' moves were generalised into Roy's *'ability to see the world through other people's eyes. He mixes with many kinds of people who usually reciprocate his curiosity, and develops rewarding relationships.'* Tom's worries were reframed as `*Roy naturally has disagreements and disappointments but learns from those and looks forward without brooding on misfortunes. He's committed to causes yet tolerant of other people's right to differ.'*

On seeing the therapist's fixed-role sketch of `Roy' Tom thought it fitted his own recent new social behaviour. He said he also wanted to show more interest in people without seeming 'nosey'; to help that, Tom carried the sketch in his pocket and referred to it before entering new social situations. By session 8, the final one, Tom no longer saw assertive extraversion as undesirable, and felt more comfortable socially.

# CLP 80

# FREE ASSOCIATION

Leon HOFFMAN, 167 East 67th Street New York, NY 10065, USA; ph +1212 249 1163

**Definition:** A therapist encourages the patient to say whatever comes to mind - thoughts, feelings, sensations, memories, wishes, fantasies.

**Elements:** The therapist suggests that the patient should try to express openly all that comes to mind even if the associations seem unimportant, irrelevant, embarrassing or shameful. Both observe how and when the patient hesitates, indicating resistance to reporting that association freely. When such resistance appears the therapist suggests (interprets) that there is discomfort in being open. This line of inquiry may reveal issues in that patient's current or past interactions, worries, fears, defenses, wishes and fantasies which are unique; even though "the casts in a person's life may change, the situations may differ, but the plots endure." These plots in the patient's life are repeated in feelings and fantasies about the analyst (*transference*) which can be difficult to speak about frankly. In free associations the patient may allude to interactions reminiscent of those with the analyst. The analyst may interpret the patient's reluctance to speak directly about the analyst (*analysis of the transference*).

A free-association-equivalent in young children is the expression of central wishes and worries in play and activities. The analyst can observe how *play interruptions* may resemble adults' *resistance* to talking about certain things.

**Related procedures**: *Interpretation against painful emotions, analysis of conflicts and defenses, compromise formation* (understanding that many activities are a compromise between forbidden wishes and defenses masking those), *method of levels, close process monitoring* (detecting shifts of material in sessions and querying if those reflect avoidance of certain thoughts and feelings), *reducing affect phobia*.

**Application:** In intensive dynamic psychotherapy and psychoanalysis.

**1st use?** Freud S (1893).

**References:**
1. Freud S (1893). Frau Emmy von N-Case histories from Studies on Hysteria. In: *The Complete Psychological Works of Sigmund Freud, Volume II (1893-1895): Studies on Hysteria*, Standard Edition 2, 48-105. London: Hogarth Press.

2. Busch F (1997). Understanding the patient's use of the method of free association: an ego psychological approach. *J. Amer. Psychoanal. Assn.*, 45, 407-423.
3. Kris AO (1992). Interpretation and the method of free association. *Psychoanal. Inq.*, 12, 208-224.
4. Loewenstein RM (1963). Some considerations on free association. *J. Amer. Psychoanal. Assn.*, 11, 451-473

**Case illustration:** (Busch,1997)
Al sought treatment after he'd had several unsatisfying affairs when he'd felt discontented with his wife and realized this told him about himself. He began a session early in his four-time-a-week analysis by mentioning disturbedly that it was really quiet at home since his wife and children had gone to visit her parents in another city for two weeks. Al talked extensively about having worked feverishly all evening on references for his new 500-page book. He'd felt frustrated by the enormous task he'd tried to accom-plish in one fell swoop using a new computer program but glitches had led to his making minimal progress. However, he'd felt really good about having left his work all over the living room without his wife having a fit about it. He moved onto a camping trip he planned with his brother but wasn't crazy about being alone the first few days before his brother joined him. Therapist: `You seem bothered but yet happy by your wife's being away and the house so quiet`. Al spoke again about feeling left alone, this time in future, saying this was important and probably related to his difficulty in feeling close to his wife. He recounted irritably that she'd phoned the previous evening to ensure he had the instructions straight for taking care of the dog, and went on a diatribe about her treating him like a child. Therapist: `You've become aware of difficulties in being close to your wife but since this might be frightening you spoke instead of a rift between the two of you, which you think she caused`. Al then said his wife had cried a lot at her father's funeral, as had his sister when his mother died. Therapist: `Maybe you have difficulty knowing how you feel about your wife, especially about loss because you see this as something women feel and this feels dangerous to you`. Al replied he'd forgotten to say that the night before his wife left they'd had a wonderful evening together –he'd never felt so close to a woman before.

# GUIDED MOURNING

**Colin Murray PARKES,** 21 South Road, Chorleywood, Herts, WD3 5AS, UK; ph +44 1923 282746

**Definition:** Guided Mourning is used to improve problems resulting from the avoidance, denial or forgetting of grief. It involves reducing fear and facilitating the expression of thoughts and feelings about the loss and the lost person, along with acknowledgement of the continuing relationship with memories of that person.

**Elements:** Those who have difficulty in looking back and facing their loss are most often male, and may have recurrent nightmares, avoidance of thoughts of loss, symptoms like those of the deceased person, and unexpected break-through of delayed grief. They need time, reassurance and encouragement to accept the pain that results from looking back, and assistance in expressing grief, anger and other feelings. The therapist does not discuss future-oriented activities.

The therapist first forms a trusting relationship with the bereaved person, acknowledges their bravery in controlling their feelings, and shows understanding of its cost - a hand on the shoulder or a smile of sympathy may convey support more than words might. Bereaved people often deny anxiety while complaining of physical symptoms it produces; the therapist explains this with reassurance and instruction in self-relaxation to reduce those symptoms.

Once bereaved people feel secure enough during therapy they can start acknowledging the full reality of their loss and its implications. The therapist aids this by inviting them to bring photos or other objects linked with the lost person and talking about those, writing a 'diary' reminiscing about that person, and pretending that he or she is sitting in an empty chair nearby and conversing with them. The bereaved are helped to recognise the continuing value of their relationship with the person they've lost and the extent to which s/he 'lives on' in memory.

**Related Procedures:** Anxiety management, cognitive restructuring, exposure therapy, Gestalt therapy.

**Application:** Guided mourning helps the few bereaved people who avoid looking back, and is usually done individually. Prolonged grief therapy (see clp entry) helps another minority of bereaved people who show difficulty in looking forward and have abnormally prolonged grief.

**1st Use?** Ramsay (1979).

**References:**
1. Mawson D, Marks IM, Ramm L, Stern LS (1981). Guided mourning for morbid grief: A controlled study. *British Journal of Psychiatry*, 138, 185-93.
2. Parkes CM, Prigerson HG (4th edition 2009). *Bereavement: studies of grief in adult life*. Routledge, London & NY.
3. Ramsay RW (1979). Bereavement: a behavioural treatment for pathological grief. In: Sjoden PO, Bayes S, Dorkens WS (Eds.), *Trends in Behaviour Therapy*. Academic Press, NY.

**Case Illustration:** (Parkes, unpublished)

Arthur M was an intelligent and assertive businessman who avoided close emotional involvements and was inclined to dominate others. After his wife died from an abdominal cancer he put away anything that might remind him of her and filled his life with work and other activities. For weeks he coped well but then disturbing nightmares began and he developed abdominal pains similar to those from which his wife had suffered. These had continued for two years when he agreed reluctantly to referral for psychiatric help.

The therapist reassured Arthur that seeing a psychiatrist did not mean he was weak or inferior. During the first two weekly interviews, behind his brave exterior Arthur seemed very anxious and needing emotional support. The therapist tried to give this by saying he recognised the heroism with which Arthur battled his way through life and understood that this strategy was not easy to maintain. At the end of the 2nd interview the therapist felt that sufficient trust and empathy had developed to invite Arthur to bring a possession of his dead wife to the next interview (a 'linking object'). Arthur arrived at session 3 with a large paper parcel that he placed gently on the floor before him. The therapist moved his chair close to Arthur and, placing a hand on his shoulder, invited him to unwrap the parcel. As his wife's handbag came into view Arthur burst into tears, which continued throughout the session. His tears were accompanied by a lightening of tension and Arthur went through the contents of the handbag and smiled through his grief at the nostalgic memories they evoked. This was a turning point in therapy. In 3 subsequent interviews he expressed other distressing feelings, including anger and self-reproach. As Arthur reviewed the wreckage of their plans he discovered that his wife could remain a continuing influence; he had indeed been 'burying my treasure'. He was sleeping well and the abdominal pains had ceased.

# HABIT REVERSAL

**Gregory S CHASSON & Sabine WILHELM,** Department of Psychiatry, Massachusetts General Hospital, Harvard Medical School, Simches Research Building, 185 Cambridge Street, Floor 2, Boston, MA 02114, USA; ph +1 617 643-3076

**Definition:** Therapy to reduce distressing or impairing behaviors e.g. hair pulling, skin picking, nail biting, motor and vocal tics, by clients increasing self-awareness, using alternative responses that compete with the targeted undesired behavior, and practising general relaxation.

**Elements:**
*Train awareness* of when the target behaviors are imminent or occurring and of the cues that trigger and maintain them. Work out a hierarchy of triggers and behaviors from the least to the most distressing. Patients then watch the therapist model their target undesired behaviors, lift a finger each time they see these, and, between sessions, record on a monitoring form the frequencies of those behaviors over 30-minute intervals.

*Train a competing response:* Use alternative socially-appropriate behavior to compete with the target one until the urge to carry out the latter has subsided for about 60 seconds. Example: counter a habit of pulling out eyebrow hair by keeping one's hands in one's pockets for 60 seconds throughout any urge to pull; counter a tic of twisting one's torso to the right by slightly twisting one's torso to the left whenever the urge arises. Intermediate alternative behaviors can be introduced, in steps, to reduce target behaviors that are complex or sequential e.g. to eliminate a tic of saluting at the forehead, as an intermediate step first practise brushing back one's hair whenever an urge to salute comes on.

*Train relaxation:* Practise slow deep breathing and progressive muscle relaxation in session to lower general tension which can resemble or exacerbate urges preceding the target behaviors.

*Further elements:* Educate patients about their targeted behaviors e.g. tics, and their treatment. Raise treatment motivation e.g. design self-rewards for completion of treatment exercises. Review how the habit causes distress or inconvenience. Train generalization e.g. rehearse during sessions the competing responses to be performed whenever tics occur outside sessions. Do homework practice of self-awareness and competing responses. Recruit a relative as a supportive cotherapist. Teach relapse prevention e.g. monitor for new target behaviors starting and previously-treated behaviors worsening, and design appropriate competing responses. Continue general relaxation exercises.

**Related procedures**: *Behavior rehearsal, breathing exercises, competing responses, contingency management, functional analysis, homework, monitoring, relapse prevention, relaxation, ritual prevention, shaping.*

**Application:** To improve nail biting, hair pulling, skin picking, and tics including those of Tourette's Syndrome, habit reversal can be guided individually and by suitable self- help books and interactive internet sites.

**1st use?** Azrin & Nunn (1973).

**References:**
1. Azrin NH, Nunn RG (1973). Habit reversal: A method of eliminating nervous habits and tics. *Behaviour Research and Therapy*, 11, 619-628.
2. Bloch MH, Landeros-Weisenberger A, Dombrowski P, Kelmendi B, Wegner R, Nudel J, Pittenger C, Leckman JF, Coric V (2007). Systematic review: Pharmacological and behavioral treatment for trichotillomania. *Biological Psychiatry*, 62, 839-846.
3. Wilhelm S, Deckersbach T, Coffey BJ, Bohne A, Peterson AL, Baer L (2003). Habit reversal versus supportive psychotherapy for Tourette's disorder: A randomized controlled trial. *American Journal of Psychiatry*, 160, 1175-1177.
4. Woods D, Piacentini J, Chang S, Deckersbach T, Ginsburg G, Peterson A, Scahill L, Walkup J, Wilhelm S (2008). *Managing Tourette Syndrome: A Behavioral Intervention for Children and Adults: Therapist Guide (Treatments that Work)*. New York: Oxford University Press.

**Case illustration:** (Chasson and Wilhelm)
Jane, a 25-year-old massage therapist with Tourette's syndrome, sought help for multiple tics ranging from complex neck and mouth movements to simple throat clearing. Habit reversal therapy took 11 sessions. Each lasted 60 minutes except the first two which took 90 minutes, when she was educated about Tourette's and ranked a hierarchy of seven of her tics from the most to the least distressing ones.

Jane first targeted her distressing tic of jerking her neck to the left. On a tic-monitoring form she tallied that tic's frequency in 30-minute intervals at home and found it became more severe in her husband's presence – it annoyed him greatly. Monitoring helped Jane identify, just before each tic, a premonitory tingling urge where her left collar bone meets her neck. In session, she practised a competing response of tensing her neck muscles and turning her head to the right whenever she felt that urge. Her husband was invited to attend session 2. He learned about his impact on Jane's tics and how to help by praising her when she used her competing response and by indicating her tics with a subtle finger signal instead of showing anger. This helped reduce the frequency of her neck tic.

Jane then monitored her distressing tic of humming. She found it was preceded by a humming feeling in her throat getting louder. She practised, in and between sessions as soon as she noticed the throat feeling or actual humming, a competing response of keeping her lips tightly closed and breathing through her nose for 60 seconds until the urge passed. In sessions the therapist also trained Jane in progressive muscle relaxation with slow deep breathing. Treatment required much effort, so whenever Jane felt less motivated she reminded herself of all the inconveniences her tics had caused e.g. having to hide her tics at work, and feeling embarrassed with strangers. In sessions 10 and 11 she rehearsed her new skills to prevent relapse by: 1. monitoring current tics with the tic-monitoring form; 2. with help from her husband, practising the slow deep breathing she'd learned to reduce overall tension; 3. devising and practising competing responses which could counter future tics. After treatment ended Jane had follow-up sessions monthly for 3 months to troubleshoot her difficulty in developing a competing response for a flexing tic that had developed. The therapist helped her devise a competing response of straightening her arm whenever she felt a premonitory urge to flex it.

# HARM REDUCTION

**Diane E LOGAN & G Alan MARLATT,** Addictive Behaviors Research Center, University of Washington, Box 351629, Seattle, WA 98195, USA; ph +1 206-685-1200

**Definition:** Harm reduction aims to reduce the adverse effects of addictive and other problem behaviors by accepting clients' goals, including but not limited to abstinence, and by addressing those behaviors and the situations in which they occur.

**Elements:** The therapist and client together establish and work to meet specific goals. Some clients choose abstinence, and identify high-risk situations, alternatives to the problem behavior, and/or acceptance of urges. Others choose to not stop entirely but rather to reduce problem behavior by identifying acceptable limits and how to stay within those(drink only on weekends, no more than one drink per hour, alternate alcoholic with non-alcoholic drinks). In clients who are not ready or able to immediately change their behavior, the therapist may recommend how to increase safety (clean needles for IV drug users, condoms for sexual activity, find a designated driver).

**Related procedures:** *Alternative behaviour, working out of, motivational interviewing, relapse prevention.*

**Application:** Harm reduction is used mainly in individual and group settings for addictive behaviors and high-risk sexual behaviors, but can be tailored to almost any problem behaviour. Implementation takes 1-10 sessions, depending on client goals and progress.

**1st use?** Engelsman (1989).

**References:**
1. Engelsman EM (1989). Dutch policy on the management of drug-related problems. *British Journal of Addictions*, 84, 211-218.
2. Marlatt GA [Ed] (1998). *Harm reduction: Pragmatic Strategies for Managing High- risk Behaviors.* New York, NY, US: Guilford Press.
3. Marlatt GA, Witkiewitz K (2002). Harm reduction approaches to alcohol use: Health promotion, prevention, and treatment. *Addictive Behaviors*, 27, 867-886.

**Case illustration:** (Logan, unpublished)
Claire, a student, was referred for an alcohol evaluation and feedback session after a heavy-drinking bout on her university campus when she blac-

ked out and couldn't remember that she had caused a public scene with campus police being summoned. She said she expected an abstinence lecture and wasn't really interested in following such advice. The clinician instead explored Claire's good as well as not-so-good experiences while drinking. As the only way to avoid *all* trouble from alcohol was to not drink at all and Claire was under the legal drinking age, there was no way to remove potential legal consequences. These risks were explained, and Claire acknowledged understanding these.

She said she usually drank moderately without bad results, but at times would "go nuts" and drink heavily and black out, which impaired her relationships and academic work. She thought abstinence was unreasonable for her as her typical drinking, a couple of beers, was no problem. She and her therapist instead focussed on how to reduce harm from heavy drinking, and in exploring situations when this happened, which turned out to be drinking-games at parties. They discussed harm- reducing skills such as refereeing versus participating in drinking games, spacing her drinks, setting a limit mentally or in writing before going out, and alternating alcohol drinks with non-alcoholic drinks of water or other beverages. She agreed these tools could reduce harmful consequences and she was likely to use them.

When her single 50-minute harm-reduction session ended, Claire expressed appreciation that this was not another "confrontational abstinence session" during which she had expected to say whatever the therapist wanted to hear to "get this over with", but instead found it surprisingly useful and planned to actually implement harm- reduction tools when drinking. The therapist reiterated that though only abstinence would avoid all problems from drinking, ultimately Claire herself had to decide what to do and how to minimise potential harm. At four-week follow-up Claire said she'd been drinking more safely.

## IMAGERY REHEARSAL THERAPY OF NIGHTMARES

Lucio SIBILIA, Dipartimento di Scienze Cliniche, Università Sapienza di Roma & Center for Research in Psychotherapy, Roma, Italy; ph +39 06 86320838

**Definition:** Teaching clients to change their nightmares into new non-disturbing dreams by composing such new dreams while awake and writing them down and practising them in imagination just before sleeping in order to have those new dreams while asleep.

**Elements:** a. Record or write down a description of a nightmare (this can be bypassed). b. Change that description in any way preferred, or describe a totally-new desirable dream. c. For a few minutes before going to sleep, read this description or listen to a recording of it, and imagine experiencing that intended new dream to facilitate having it while asleep.

**Related procedures:** *Alternative practice, cognitive rehearsal, covert rehearsal, dream control, guided fantasy, homework, imagery rescripting and reprocessing, rational-emotive imagery, rehearsal relief.*

**Application:** Relief of nightmares with or without PTSD.

**1st use?** Krakow et al (1993).

**References:**
1. Bradshaw SJ (1991). Successful cognitive manipulation of a stereotypic nightmare in a 40 year old male with Down's syndrome. *Behav Psychother*, 19, 281-284.
2. Krakow B, Kellner R, Neidhardt J, Pathak D, Lambert L (1993). Imagery rehearsal treatment for chronic nightmares: A thirty month follow-up. *J.Behav Ther & Exper. Psychiat*, 24, 325–330.
3. Germain A, Krakow B, Faucher B et al. (2004). Increased mastery elements associated with imagery rehearsal treatment for nightmares in sexual assault survivors with PTSD. *Dreaming*, 14: 195–206.
4. Marks IM (1978). Rehearsal relief of a nightmare. *Brit. J.Psychiat.*, 133, 461-5.

**Case illustration 1:** (Sibilia L, unpublished)
Mara, age 5, came with mother who was midst a turbulent legal separation from Mara's father. Mara, a previously confident child, had recently insisted on her light remaining on when in bed and after a while would go to mother's bed and ask to sleep there with her. In session 1 Mara said in mo-

ther's presence that she feared a recurrence of recent nightmares. Therapist to Mara: *"Would you like to try to have better dreams?".* Mara was surprised, amused, and curious how to do this. Th: "*As a game, we'll draw together something beautiful and amusing. You'll take that picture home and look at it before sleeping, then during the night you'll dream it*". Maria was enthusiastic.

In front of her the therapist drew a circle on a blank sheet of paper. Mara exclaimed: "*It's an apple!*". Th: "*Right, now it's your turn to add something!*", gave her the pencil, and Mara added some detail. Th: "*Now it's my turn*" and added a little circle inside: "*This is a hole!*". Mara (laughing): "*There's a worm in the apple!* ". Th:: "*Then you draw the worm!*". Mara inserted a little scrawl in the `hole'. The therapist added a small smiling face to the `worm', saying "*Here's a smiling worm!*". Mara was amused. Th: *"Tonight, when you're in bed about to go to sleep, look at the drawing and you'll dream exactly what we've drawn"*. At session 2 mother said Mara reported she had the planned dream that evening and from then on slept alone.

**Case illustration 2:** (Sibilia L, unpublished)

Roberta, a reflective introverted 18-year-old, sought help for depression. She argued with father who didn't allow her out at night and with her boyfriend whom she feared would leave her. She couldn't concentrate. In session 2 she attributed morning depressions and hopelessness to nightmares which often woke her - e.g. at the bottom of a black pit she saw bleeding parts of a child's body. Therapist: *"These images may represent your depression"*. Roberta accepted this. Th: *"They'd upset anyone, so let's work together to change your nightmares into pleasant dreams. Imagine and write down something you want similar to the dream you'd like to have. You could write about a beautiful period of your life"*. Roberta couldn't remember anything pleasant. Th: *"Relax and imagine you're lying in a sunny meadow"*. Roberta: "This reminds me of something". Th: *"Stay with this good memory; remember everything you felt then"*. Roberta described this. Th: *"Please sit at the desk and write down the details and pleasant feelings of that good memory"*. Roberta left this session with her written desirable dream, and was instructed: *"Just before going to sleep read and imagine what you've just written and resolve to dream it"*. At session 3, Roberta said with surprise she'd had pleasant dreams for the first time in ages, though they weren't what she'd written.

## IMAGERY RESCRIPTING THERAPY

Mervin R. SMUCKER. Department of Psychiatry, Medical College of Wisconsin, Milwaukee, Wisconsin, USA

**Definition:** Helping clients to relive and then transform recurring, distressing images (e.g. flashbacks, nightmares) into mastery and self-soothing imagery.

**Elements:** Imagery rescripting is conducted within a 60-90 minute session in 3 phases which are audio-recorded:
1. Imaginal reliving: Clients are asked to visualize and verbalize all their distressing imagery including accompanying sounds, smells, and sensations.
2. Mastery imagery: The therapist encourages clients to create their own mastery imagery e.g. Therapist: *Can you imagine yourself as an adult today entering the scene?* Client: Yes. Th: *What would you like to do or say to him now?* Client: I tell him to leave the CHILD alone. Th: *Can you see yourself saying that to him directly?* Client: I look him straight in the eye and say, "Get out of here, or I'll call the police". Th: *How does he respond?* Client: He leaves.
3. Self-calming imagery: The therapist asks clients to create their own imagery reassuring their previous traumatized self e.g. Th: *What would you like to do or say today to the CHILD?* Client: I go to my bed and say, "I'm here now to protect you." Th: *How does the CHILD respond?* Client: The CHILD wants to come with me, respects me standing up to my father and winning, and trusts me for this. Th: *Where do you take the CHILD?* Client: Out the front door to my car. We drive to my present home. Th: *How does the CHILD feel now?* Client: She has no fear anymore and seems happy to be with me.
   The therapist uses Socratic questioning to empower clients to develop their own mastery and self-soothing imagery, and asks clients to listen daily to the entire audio-recording of their imagery session for up to a week, or until the next session.

**Related Procedures:** *Cognitive rehearsal, cognitive restructuring within reliving imagery, guided imagery, imagery rehearsal of nightmares, rehearsal relief of nightmares, Socratic imagery, triumphant imagery, two-chair dialogue.*

**Application:** Relief of intrusive, recurring images (e.g., flashbacks or nightmares) with or without PTSD.

**1st Use?** Smucker & Niederee (1994).

**References:**
1. Smucker MR, Niederee J (1994). Imagery Rescripting: A multifaceted treatment for childhood sexual abuse survivors experiencing posttraumatic stress. In L VandeCreek, S Knapp, T Jackson. Eds. *Innovations in Clinical Practice: A Source Book*, Vol. 13, Sarasota, FL: Professional Resource Press.
2. Smucker MR, Dancu CV, Foa EB, Niederee J (1995). Imagery Rescripting: A new treatment for survivors of childhood sexual abuse suffering from posttraumatic stress. *Journal of Cognitive Psychotherapy: An International Quarterly*, 9(1), 3-17.
3. Smucker MR, Niederee J (1995). Treating incest-relate PTSD and pathogenic schemas through imaginal exposure and rescripting. *Cognitive and Behavioral Practice*, 2, 63-93.
4. Smucker MR, Dancu CV (1999/2005). *Cognitive-Behavioral Treatment for Adult Survivors of Childhood Trauma: Imagery Rescripting and Reprocessing*. New York: Roman & Littlefield Publishers.

**Case Illustration:** (Smucker, unpublished)
Nicole, age 24, reported that from ages 6–13 her brother Joe (4 years older) had enticed her repeatedly to have oral, anal, and vaginal sex with him in his room. At age 8, she told her mother, who discussed it with her father; they decided this was fabricated. Joe denied the abuse, saying she was crazy. The abuse stopped when Nicole started menstruating at age 13. Thereafter she became anorexic, depressed, and suicidal, with frequent flashbacks and nightmares, and two suicide attempts at age 16.

At evaluation Nicole reported recurring abuse-related flashbacks, nightmares, depression, anger, guilt, and shame; sex disgusted her. Her 60-minute imagery-rescripting session was audiotaped. The therapist asked: *"Can you visualize and describe with eyes closed, in detail in the presence tense, your most upsetting memory"*. After Nicole described anal abuse at age 8 for five minutes, the therapist said: *"Can you again imagine and describe that scene"*, but at the most upsetting moment asked: *"Can you see yourself as an ADULT today entering the room? What would you do or say now to Joe?"* Nicole described imagining herself pushing Joe to the floor, stopping him getting up, and saying angrily she knows what he did, she isn't crazy, and he'll never hurt her [the CHILD] again. She `saw' Joe fearing her [the ADULT] and avoiding her gaze (an empowering moment), laughed at him, left the room together with herself as a CHILD, and went to her present apartment. Nicole then imagined herself as an ADULT today comforting herself as a CHILD: "You're not to blame for this, you were too young to know it was wrong, nobody believed you when you told mother." The therapist asked: *"And how does the CHILD respond?".* Nicole replied: "She [the CHILD] wants to believe, but doesn't know how." After Nicole described the

ADULT giving heart-felt reassurances, apologizing for blaming her as a CHILD, not believing her, and ignoring her, the CHILD accepted the ADULT's soothing reassurance. Nicole concluded as the ADULT: "I love you. I'm sorry I didn't before. I'm sorry for everything you've felt. I now see how strong and brave you are, an incredible little girl." Therapist: *"What does the little girl reply?"* Client: "She gives me a big hug." Nicole opened her eyes, smiled broadly, and said she felt better than in a very long time.

Nicole took an audiotape of the entire imagery session home with her and listened to it daily for 3 weeks. This single imagery- rescripting session was the only therapy she had. At 9 months follow-up she was free of flashbacks, nightmares, guilt, shame and anger, and was having her first loving sexual relationship with a man.

# CLP 80

## IMAGO RELATIONSHIP THERAPY

Sam LISON, PO Box 84850, Jerusalem 90805; ph +972 2 5341545/ 544682638

**Definition:** Teaching couples structured dialogues to change their relationship from a power struggle to one of mature love with mutual commitment, awareness, safety and comfort.

**Elements:** *Dialogue:* The partners sit opposite and look at one another. One partner asks for a dialogue on a particular issue. The other listens and *mirrors* back (*reflects*) what was said e.g. `I hear you saying. ... Did I hear you? Am I with you?' When the sending partner says that's all on that issue the receiving partner summarizes, and then *validates* what was heard by expressing understanding (e.g. Oh, I get it, you... I see your point now, you...') and empathy ('I guess what you feel regarding... is sad and frustrated (each feeling one word). The receiver might now ask to switch roles and become the sender with the partner as receiver.

A couple might: convey frustration and ask the partner to change behavior in a specific positive way (e.g. `every 2nd day from Monday for 2 weeks when I come home from work I want you to (behavior-change request) hug me for 10 seconds'); role-play a parent and child; express appreciation and feeling cared for; share a vision of their dream relationship; ask to make amends.

*Guided imagery:* The therapist guides the couple with their eyes closed to: imagine themselves in a safe place which need not be shared (e.g. in nature, from a good childhood memory); remember childhood experiences with parents; be in a dream relationship. The partners are also asked to open their eyes and share with each other their best relationship dream.

*Positive flooding:* The sender circles and warmly describes the seated partner's good physical, personal and behavioral characteristics.

*Cradling:* One partner cradles the other as they lie seated on the floor and asks what it was like and how it should have been at home as a child.

*Homework* between sessions: The couple is asked to: practice dialogue (mirroring, validating, empathizing); implement unconditionally whichever behavior change has been agreed; gift pleasant surprises; repeat caring behaviors.

*Relaxation:* Any method e.g. progressive muscle relaxation; meditation with gongs marking the start and end of meditation, imagining their inner centre and neutrally noticing present feelings.

*High energy fun:* e.g.: couples animatedly express positive and negative feelings in gibberish; talk with their lips covering their teeth; impersonate rockstars, tigers and lovers - to try to have fun and laugh.

**Related procedures:** *Active listening, communication training, couple/marital therapy, social skills training; gestalt therapy, guided imagery, homework, mirroring, reflection, psychodrama, role-play, relaxation, reinforcement, reward.*

**Application:** With individual couples and in couples workshops.

**1st Use?** Hendrix, Harville (1988).

**References:**
1. Hendrix H (1988). *Getting the Love You Want - Guide for Couples.* Henry Holt, NY.
2. Brown R (1999). *Imago Relationship Therapy: an Introduction to Theory and Practice.* Wiley, NY.
3. Stuart R (1980). *Helping Couples Change: Social Learning Approach to Marital Therapy.* Guilford, NY.

**Case illustration:**
Sara and Joe were considering divorce after 30 years marriage. He angrily sensed her hostility and she was upset that he acted towards her like an automatic, silent robot. In session 1 each described the other's main complaints; she knew it disturbed him that she held grudges for years, and he said she disliked his very predictable behavior. Before starting a dialogue they jointly practiced progressive muscle relaxation and then each imagined their own safe place. When relaxed, Joe could more easily listen and mirror back what he heard Sara saying about feeling loneliness and pain when he disengaged from her even as she spoke to him. They reviewed what they did alone: Joe sat silently reading for hours and Sara spoke on the phone with friends. They agreed to do more together – go out at least once a week and acknowledge each other's presence at home by discussing a book Joe had read, and Joe being present while Sara practiced on the piano. They discussed their dream relationship e.g. going on cruises, freely expressing negative and positive feelings which they heard and related to. They detailed instances of such feelings and prepared plans to practice benignly expressing them in dialogue (*homework*).

Joe felt frustrated that Sara ignored him while preparing for Sabbath, reinforcing memories of feeling 'invisible' as a child in his parents' home. He asked that for the next two Fridays Sara would find the time to serve him at 12 noon a salad including Bulgarian cheese, black olives, and green onions. She agreed to this, understanding its value for him and for herself, realizing she might manage more than she'd originally thought she could.

After session 13 they went on their first cruise but returned disappointed, each having felt neglected and ignored by the other. Nevertheless, they could now dialogue: listen, express understanding of the other's point of view without necessarily agreeing, and empathize with one another, giving a sense of confidence and more calm and pleasure with one another. Joe initiated their going to plays and expressed interest in what Sara enjoyed. She learned to express herself freely without upsetting him. They rediscovered that they liked one another. Therapy over 9 months involved 30 1-2-hour sessions. At 3- and 6-month follow-up they were pleased at the transformation of their relationship.

# INFLATED RESPONSIBILITY, REDUCING

**Adam S RADOMSKY**, Department of Psychology, Concordia University, 7141 Sherbrooke St. W., Montreal, QC, H4B 1R6, Canada; ph +1 514 848 2424

**Definition:** A way of reducing inflated beliefs that one can provoke or prevent negative events, situations and/or outcomes.

**Elements:** The therapist encourages patients to review, reconsider and reduce the degree to which they feel responsible for protecting themselves and / or others from harm, and discusses appropriate levels of responsibility for particular threats to aim at as treatment goals.

***Related procedures:*** *Cognitive restructuring, behavioural experiment, reframing, giving perspective.*

**Application:** Usually individually, for obsessive-compulsive disorder. Can also be done in groups.

**1st Use?** Salkovskis (1985).

**References:**
1. Salkovskis PM (1985). Obsessional-compulsive problems: A cognitive-behavioural analysis. *Behaviour Research & Therapy*, 23, 571-583.
2. Lopatka C, Rachman S (1995). Perceived responsibility and compulsive checking: An experimental analysis. *Behaviour Research & Therapy*, 33, 673-684.
3. Ashbaugh AR, Gelfand LA, Radomsky AS (2006). Interpersonal aspects of responsibility and obsessive-compulsive symptoms. *Journal of Behavioural and Cognitive Psychotherapy*, 34, 151-163.
4. Ladouceur RL, Rhéaume J, Dubé D (1996). Correction of inflated responsibility in the treatment of obsessive-compulsive disorder. *Behaviour Research & Therapy*, 34, 767-774.

**Case illustration:** (Radomsky, unpublished)
Fay aged 43 checked at home for up to 4 hours a day the kitchen appliances, doors, windows and sell-by (best-before) dates on foods for her 2 children and husband. This led her to leave her part-time job and to her husband and children complaining that she spent too little time with them. She said she checked so much as she felt responsible for protecting her family from harm from burglaries, unpredictable accidents and food poisoning, that if something bad happened to them she'd feel highly responsible and "incre-

dibly guilty", and that checking made her feel "responsible in a good way" and temporarily reduced her anxiety about accidents at home.

Over 8 sessions the therapist helped Fay reduce her inflated responsibility in several ways; the two ways described here comprised 2 sessions. First, the therapist asked her to draw a pie graph showing how responsible she'd feel if her children were poisoned by rotten eggs, and drew this at 100%. In discussion she agreed responsibility for the threat of poisoning might also stem from other sources (supermarket, farmer, ministry of agriculture, etc.). Fay drew further pie graphs to show the proportion of responsibility from each of these sources on the understanding that she could accept the remaining portion. The final pie graph revealed that she would be, at most, 17% responsible for such poisoning.

Second, the therapist helped Fay draw up 2 responsibility contracts. 1. `I agree to accept all (100%) responsibility for burglary at my home between 8pm and 9pm this Saturday. I understand that during this time, nobody else will be responsible if a burglary occurs'. 2. `I agree to share responsibility for burglary at my home between 8pm and 9pm this Monday equally among the members of my family who will be home at the time. This results in my agreeing to accept no more than 25% responsibility for this particular outcome during this time'. The therapist encouraged Fay to record her anxiety, perception of threat and amount of harm felt after each of the critical hours. Her record showed that when Fay shared (lower) responsibility with other family members she felt less anxious and threatened, but felt identical amounts of harm (i.e. none), compared to when she had sole (inflated) responsibility. She said the pie charts and the contracts method helped her take a more realistic amount of responsibility for harm and markedly reduced her anxiety, guilt and checking. The procedure may have led to some exposure and ritual prevention but this was minimal with emphasis being on explicitly reducing how much responsibility she felt rather than alteration of her behaviour.

# INTERNALIZED-OTHER INTERVIEWING

Karl TOMM, Department of Psychiatry, University of Calgary, Calgary, AB, T2S 3C2 Canada; ph +1 403 8021680

**Definition:** A method to explore, enhance, and/or modify a client's inner experience of another person's inner experience, and potentially alter the virtual and lived relationships between the client and the other person.

**Elements:** When a therapist anticipates that an experiential shift within a client, of another person's experience and/or their relationship with that person, might move therapy forward, the therapist may invite the client to try an "experiment" of internalized other interviewing. *"When we get to know someone well, we create an image of that other person within ourselves and the 'other' becomes part of us. By questioning that 'other' within you, and inviting you to respond from as deeply as you can enter into that person's inner experience, rather than role playing that person's outer visible behavior, some interesting understandings might emerge. Are you willing to try that?"* If the client accepts, the therapist addresses the client in the other person's name (to ground him/her in the experience of the other) and asks reflexive questions whose content varies enormously according to what is salient in the clinical situation. For instance, if a man has abused his wife, the therapist could ask his internalized wife about her experience of that abuse and what concrete changes she'd value in her husband; this could help him enter into his wife's fear and pain and appreciate more fully the consequences of his actions. If a woman is depressed with self-deprecating thoughts, the therapist might interview several of her significant others in turn, asking each one what they appreciate, admire, value and respect in her so that she can appreciate herself through those other people's eyes. The therapist ends internalized- other interviewing by thanking each internalized other of the client and then, using the client's own name, asks about his/her experience in being interviewed as the other. If the internalized-other person has actually been present during the interview, the therapist asks that real other person *"Which of (the client's) answers as you 'fit' for you and which reflected significant misunderstandings?"*, in order to facilitate further congruence between the other person's real experience and the clients' understanding of that person's experience. An internalized-other interview might last 5-20 minutes as part of a session and may be used again in subsequent sessions.

**Application:** *May be carried out in individual therapy, couple therapy, family therapy, grief therapy, training, coaching, supervision, etc.*

**Related Procedures:** becoming, empathy, family constellation, gestalt therapy, meeting one's 'distributed self', experience-of-experience questioning, psychodrama, two-chair dialogue.

**1st Use?** Epston (1988).

**References:**
1. Epston D (1993). Internalized other questioning with couples: The New Zealand version. Chapter in *Therapeutic Conversations* edited by Stephen Gilligan and Reese Price, New York: Norton Press.
2. Nylund D, Corsiglia V (1993). Internalized other questioning with men who are violent. *Dulwich Centre Newsletter*, 2, 29-34.
3. Burnham J (2000). Internalized other interviewing: evaluating and enhancing empathy. *Clincial Psychology Forum*, 140, 16-20.
4. Tomm K, Hoyt M, Madigan S (1998). Honoring our internalized others and the ethics of caring: A conversation with Karl Tomm. *The Handbook of Constructive Therapies*, Edited by Michael Hoyt, pp 198-218.

**Case Illustration:** (Tomm, unpublished)
A middle-aged divorced man, Bob, had extensive drug and alcohol abuse and recovered substantially during several years of involvement in AA and therapy. After having been 'clean' for a few months, he became acutely suicidal on suddenly realizing that he'd been taking cough syrup for a cold not just as an expectorant but for its 'codeine kick.' He was seen the next morning in a consultation interview. No one had criticized him for his misuse of the medication, yet he felt it reflected a profound failure on his part after so many years of treatment for his addictions, and that he "might as well get it over with."

The therapist asked Bob: *"Of everyone who knows you, who would have been most upset if they'd known you abused the codeine?"* Bob: "My mother, Agnes." Though Bob had not seen or spoken with his mother for years (because they'd had so much conflict), he was invited to speak from the 'I position' of her inner experience. Th: *"Let me speak to you as if you were Agnes for a while. Agnes, is it true that Bob got into a lot of trouble because of his drug abuse?"* B: "Yes, he certainly did!" Th: *"Is it also true, Agnes, that you criticized him a lot for abusing drugs?"* B: "Yes, I guess I did." Th: *"Is it reasonable to say that you came to rely on criticism as a way to raise him?"* B: "I suppose so." Th: *"If you were aware that your criticism may have been internalized over the years, so that he became so critical of himself for using, that he was now contemplating suicide for having taken the codeine, would you have some regrets for having resorted to so much criticism in your efforts to raise him, Agnes?"* (After a long pause) B: "I think I would." Th: *"If you were to express those regrets, and perhaps even apologize for criticizing him so much in the past, would he be able to accept your apology?"* B: "I think he could." Th: *"And if you actually did apologize, do you imagine that Bob might be able to forgive you?"* At this point Bob began to weep heavily. The questions seemed to have triggered a shift within him from a pattern of his internalized mother blaming/shaming him, to her apologizing and him forgiving her. Had Agnes really been present to witness his answers, she'd have been invited to comment so as to further potentiate the effect of this healing process. This internalized- other interview lasted about 10 minutes during a single consultation.

## INTERNET-BASED THERAPY

Georg W ALPERS, University of Wuerzburg, Biological Psychology, Clinical Psychology & Psychotherapy, Marcusstrasse 9-11, D-97070 Wuerzburg, Germany; ph +49 931-312840/2; **Andrew J WINZELBERG** & **C Barr TAYLOR**, Behavioral Medicine Laboratory, Stanford University School of Medicine, Stanford USA

**Definition:** Any psychosocial intervention delivered over the Internet (web) designed and/or delivered by health-care professionals.

**Elements:** Internet use to complete and submit behavioral assignments and get peer support and therapist education, feedback and support, by e-mail, web pages, chat-rooms. Can be synchronous (all participants on-line at the same time) in a chat-room or asynchronous in a news-group (messages posted and read at any time). Content can be more or less structured. Groups can be open to any Internet-user or closed with a defined membership.

**Related procedures:** *Internet-delivered therapy, computer-mediated therapy, on-line psychotherapy, cyber-psychotherapy, cybercounseling, online counseling, e-therapy, web-based CBT, e-mail therapy.*

**1st Use?** Gustafson et al. (1993).

**References:**
1. Gustafson D, Wise M, McTavish F et al (1993). Development and pilot evaluation of a computer-based support system for women with breast cancer.*J.Psychosoc Oncolog*, 11, 69-93.
2. Lange A, Schrieken B, van de Ven JP et al. (2000). "Interapy": Effects of a short protocolled treatment of posttraumatic stress and pathological grief through the Internet. *Behavioural and Cognitive Psychotherapy*, 28, 175-192.
3. Taylor CB, Bryson S, Luce KH et al (2006). Prevention of eating disorders in at-risk college-age women. *Archives of General Psychiatry*, in press.
4. Winzelberg AJ, Classen C, Alpers GW et al (2003). Evaluation of an Internet Support Group for Women with Primary Breast Cancer. *Cancer*, 97, 1164-1173.

**Case illustration:** (Winzelberg et al 2003)
At age 46 Emily was diagnosed with breast cancer and a congenital condition made surgery impossible. She was married and distressed that she might not see her child grow up. Participation in a face-to-face group stopped due to scheduling difficulties. 7 months post-diagnosis, media ads alerted her to a closed 12-week Bosom Buddies group (12 members, news-

group format, professionally moderated). Answering the moderator's question what group members wanted from it, Emily said she hoped to express her inner feelings without making someone else feel bad, and that giving back to others might help her make her cancer experience more positive. She logged onto the web-site regularly, read it, and posted 56 messages over 12 weeks. In week 2, on feeling new pains and worry about recurrence, she posted "I need a hug!". The group and moderator sent her 15 messages encouraging her to make appointments for her dreaded medical examinations, acknowledged her anxieties, and gave support including "cyber hugs". In several messages Emily reflected on other's expression of emotions. She said she was sometimes sad and cried but also grateful. Group discussion on how to interact with one's medical team prompted her to discuss and resolve her concerns with her doctor. The moderator asked group members how they felt about their bodies. She said she had gradually learned to accept her loss of sexual desire (later confiding this was easier to disclose as she did not wait for facial feedback while writing). Other group members appreciated her openness. Near the end of the group Emily stated she did not think cancer was either bad or good, just something that happened and that she had to make the best of it. Her depression and traumatic stress scores fell markedly. She found it very comforting to know she could log on at any time and talk or listen.

# INTERPERSONAL PSYCHOTHERAPY (IPT)

**Bridget BAILEY,** Ohio State University, College of Social Work, 1947 College Road, Columbus, Ohio 43210, USA; ph +1 412 613 8580

**Definition:** A way of treating depression by improving interpersonal relationships associated with the onset or perpetuation of depression.

**Elements:** Interpersonal therapy (IPT) helps the patient evaluate how the depression might have been triggered and sustained by events in relationships, and develop skills to manage those. IPT uses an *interpersonal inventory* to review the patient's current social and family life. Focus is on the present, through time-limited treatment with an active therapist, without discussing transference. Treatment focuses on one of 4 problem areas associated with the current depressive episode.
1. *Grief* if the depression began with the death, or association with that, of a close loved person. Focus is on mourning and evaluating good and bad aspects of the lost relationship, rebuilding a supportive social network, and "moving on" with life.
2. *Role dispute* when the depression concerns an ongoing disagreement with someone important e.g. a young adult argues with parents about career choice, a couple quarrel about parenting roles. The therapist tries to help the patient problem-solve the dispute, process emotion around it, change expectations, and improve communication skills by role play and by eliciting and analysing a detailed account of a patient's conversation to understand its meaning and methods of communication, and analysing decisions by considering alternative actions and their consequences.
3. *Role transition* if the depression relates to a major life change e.g. relocation, divorce, or job change. The therapist and patient discuss good and bad aspects of the former and new roles, help the patient to process emotion about the lost role, and develop social skills to help master the new role.
4. *Interpersonal deficits* if the patient has long-standing difficulties in forming and keeping close relationships. The therapist helps the patient examine the good and bad aspects of past relationships, improve social skills, increase interpersonal contacts, and decrease interpersonal discomfort.

**Related procedures:** *Communication analysis and training, grief therapy, problem-solving, role play, social skills training.*

**Application:** For primary or comorbid depression, in 12-16 one-hour individual sessions, in adolescents, adults and the elderly. Has also been used for anxiety, eating disorders, and borderline personality disorder, and been adapted to a group format.

**1st Use?** Klerman et al (1984).

**References:**
1. Klerman GL, Weissman MM, Rounsaville B, Chevron E (1984). *Interpersonal psychotherapy of depression.* New York: Basic books.
2. Weissman MM, Markowitz JC, Klerman GL (2000). *Comprehensive guide to interpersonal psychotherapy.* New York: basic Books.
3. Mufson L, Weissman MM, Moreau D, Garfinkel R (1999). Efficacy of interpersonal psychotherapy for depressed adolescents. *Archives of General Psychiatry,* 56, 573-579.
4. Frank E, Spanier C (1995). Interpersonal psychotherapy for depression: Overview, clinical efficacy, and future directions. *Clinical Psychology: Science and Practice,* 2, 349-369.

**Case illustration:** (Holly Swartz, unpublished)
Ann had children aged 3 and 1 and recently became depressed when her husband's work made him travel away often. She felt sad, lonely and angry during his absences. He thought she should appreciate his earning more for the family. Therapist: *"Your mood dropped a month after Jeff began his work travels. After optimism about his promotion the realities of his new responsibilities began to take their toll on you. It was hard to be alone with your children during the week, with no help when they got cranky in the evenings or woke up at night. Even harder was Jeff's not seeming to hear your concerns and anger with you for not appreciating his efforts to provide for the family. Your dispute with him seems a main issue to focus on. Your low energy, low mood, poor concentration, insomnia and anxiety made it still harder to care for the children on your own. Spending our 12 sessions focusing on this role dispute could resolve issues with Jeff, improve your depression, and make it easier to cope with challenges at home. Also, if you can help Jeff understand your difficulties at home you may both find ways to ease those. This may sound improbable to you now because depression makes you feel hopeless but we can help you feel better within weeks. How does that sound to you?"*
Sessions focused on improving Ann's communication with Jeff. The therapist encouraged her to identify her needs regarding Jeff. Her first goal was to tell him how she felt. A communications analysis of what exactly each party said with its tone, setting and body language - revealed that when Jeff returned from a trip she badgered him with a litany of complaints, so he felt attacked and shut down. The therapist role- played with Ann how to ask Jeff to set up regular phone calls during his travels so they could both review the day's events and he could support her emotionally, and to plan "date nights" when his schedule permitted so they had pre-set times to talk when they weren't exhausted. As Ann learned to make requests more constructively, Jeff

responded favourably. He became more attentive, her mood improved, and she became able to handle the demands of caring for her children by herself. The therapist indicated the link between her mood and her relationship with Jeff.

As therapy neared its end, the therapist helped Ann anticipate potential stressors (*"What happens if Jeff is promoted again?"*), encouraging her to express her needs directly to Jeff in an acceptable way. They reviewed signs of any imminent relapse and how to seek treatment again if needed.

# INTERPRETING DEFENSES AGAINST UNPLEASANT FEELINGS

Leon HOFFMAN, 167 East 67th Street New York, NY 10065, USA; ph +1 212 249 1163

**Definition:** Helping a patient realize that what s/he says or does in a session or in real life may be an attempt to avoid unpleasant feelings.

**Elements:** Therapists have to be sensitive to a patient's feelings which may be too painful to talk about right away, and work out how to gently help the patient to gradually become aware of and discuss those feelings willingly. A therapist senses patients' defenses against unpleasant feelings when patients spontaneously change the topic under discussion, or children change their play activity, and resist the therapist's attempts to explore the original topic. The patients may deny feeling discomfort or may express opposite feelings. The therapist listens empathically and respectfully, may seek clarification, and points out that not continuing with the original subject may reflect avoidance of an unpleasant feeling e.g. *"it feels better to fight than to feel scared"; "it's easier to feel tired and fall asleep than to think about uncomfortable stuff."*

Over time, the patient becomes more comfortable discussing (or the child playing out) discomfiting topics. They may discuss the distress involved more openly, and reveal other awkward events in their life, and tricky transference feelings. This allows them to discuss (or play out) conflicts more adaptively, e.g. by using humor or play- acting aggression rather than being really aggressive towards the therapist/analyst.

**Related procedures:** *Analysis of conflicts and defenses, compromise formation* (understanding patients' forbidden wishes and defenses to mask those), *method of levels, close process monitoring* (detecting shifts of material in sessions and querying if those reflect avoidance of certain thoughts and feelings), *reducing affect phobia*.

**Application:** In almost any treatment from its start onward.

**1st use?** Bornstein B (1945).

**References:**
1. Bornstein B (1945). Clinical notes on child analysis. *Psychoanalytic Study of the Child*, 1, 151-166.
2. Hoffman L (2007). Do children get better when we interpret their defenses against painful feelings? *Psychoanalytic Study of the Child*, 62, 291-313.

3. Hoffman L (1989). The psychoanalytic process and the development of insight in child analysis: A case study. *Psychoanalytic Quarterly*, 58, 63-80.
4. Hoffman RS (2002). Practical psychotherapy: working with a patient's defenses in supportive psychotherapy. *Psychiatric Services*, 53, 141-142.

**Case illustration:** (Hoffman 1989 & 2007)

Leo aged 9, was in four-times-a-week analysis for enuresis, tantrums, and nightmares. Within a few months he became aggressive in sessions, trying to cut the analyst's beard off and intruding into his closet making noises to scare him. Leo alluded to his parents' fierce arguments in their bedroom and said he wet less when he built a fort around his bed. In sessions he built a model fort with blocks and other toys, saying he wanted to play "hit the donkey on the butt." Leo presented his clothed butt to the analyst, asking him to throw a soft ball at it. Before the analyst could respond, Leo said he was tired, "Never mind, I don't want to play." The analyst said "*maybe you feel tired because you feel uncomfortable.*" Leo ignored this, but said his older half brother could beat anyone because *he* was not afraid, and came close to the analyst's face with a menacing expression. The analyst suggested *"Leo, you're acting tough so you don't have to worry about getting hurt"* and thought to himself that Leo seemed to be provoking him to hurt Leo. Leo's truculence subsided.

A few weeks later Leo missed a couple of sessions because of illness. On returning, he threw lighted matches toward the analyst, and, in an off-hand barely-audible whisper said, "I'm going to the orthodontist right after the session." Leo calmed down when the analyst said, "*It's easier to attack me with matches than to worry about getting hurt by the orthodontist.*" Leo replied he worried *he* (Leo) would get hurt if he didn't attack, and jokingly asked if the analyst thought words could hurt him. Leo took a dictionary and playfully threw it at the analyst, who said *"You get angry and attack when you worry about being hurt."* Leo became friendlier and demonstrated karate moves saying the analyst could learn how to defend himself if he were mugged. The analyst said *"You're teaching me how to protect myself when you attack me!"* Leo laughed: "I get you angry, don't I?" The analyst replied *"You know how to do that well."*

In the earlier session above the analyst had pointed out to Leo that he (1) warded off uncomfortable feelings by becoming tired and (2) acted tough to avoid scary feelings. In the later session, the analyst interpreted Leo's defence of turning passive into active in order to avoid painful feelings about the dentist, after which Leo behaved more adaptively.

## LIFE-REVIEW (REMINISCENCE) THERAPY

Ernst BOHLMEIJER, Trimbos-institute, PO Box725, 3500 AS Utrecht, Netherlands; ph +31 30 2971100, fax +31 30 2971111

**Definition:** A structured way to reminisce therapeutically about one's past.

**Elements:** Patients review their positive and negative memories, over the whole life-span, in order to build integrated, meaningful, mastery-enhancing life-stories that might reduce or prevent anxiety and depression. Integrative reminiscence focuses on resolving, or lending meaning and coherence to, past and current conflicts or other experiences. Instrumental reminiscence reviews successful past coping experiences to try to solve current problems. Creative reminiscence focuses on building a meaningful life-story by stimulating the imagination and artistic expression of past experiences.

**Application:** Done individually or in groups, in older adults and other age groups, on its own or in combination with other therapies (e.g. cognitive therapy, narrative therapy, creative therapy).

**Related procedures:** *Activation of memories, story-telling, narrative therapy, mastery training, expressive writing, psychoanalytic free association, using metaphor, solution-focussed therapy, giving perspective.*

**1st Use?** Butler (1963).

**References:**
1. Bohlmeijer E, Smit F & Cuijpers P (2003). Effects of reminiscence and life review on late-life depression: a meta-analysis. *International Journal of Geriatric Psychiatry*, 18, 1088-1094.
2. Bohlmeijer E (2007). Reminiscence and depression in later life. PhD Dissertation. Amsterdam: Free University.
3. Butler RN (1963). The life-review: an interpretation of reminiscence in the aged. *Psychiatry,* 26, 65-76.
4. Watt LM & Cappeliez P (2000). Integrative and instrumental reminiscence therapies for depression in older adults: intervention strategies and treatment effectiveness. *Aging and mental health*, 4, 166-177.

**Case illustration:** (Bohlmeijer 2007)
Robert aged 66 had been depressed since being made redundant 5 years earlier and then starting a consultancy business despite having enough money. To answer why he felt miserable and why work, achievement and money were so important to him he joined a life-review group (4 people aged

at least 55, seven 2-hour sessions).

Two memories stood out in Robert's stories. First, as a small boy he'd played outdoors a lot, giving an intense feeling of freedom that ended abruptly when he started school. In group discussion the topic of 'lost freedom' placed his problematic transition from work to more free time in a more positive light. After this he felt he could again enjoy the freedom he'd abandoned in his youth.

The second distinctive memory concerned Robert's drive to achieve. Throughout his schooling he'd always been the youngest in his class and felt he had to push himself, especially as he found schoolwork less easy than his rival older brother did and because good grades earned his father's attention. Later Robert wanted to achieve a good social position to obtain security through a good income. During the life-review meetings Robert came to see that his drive for success stopped him enjoying freedom like that he'd had in early childhood but gave him other things he wanted: social status, interesting work, and financial security.

In sessions 6 and 7 Robert began to realise he wanted to enjoy freedom in the years ahead and discussed what this might involve and how to achieve it. He became keen to contact and spend ample time with friends he'd neglected because of his work ambitions. Asked for a *metaphor* for his life, Robert replied 'I am a traveler in the desert; this is my yearning for freedom more than a need to find the right way'. After the life-review group Robert felt much less depressed and more optimistic about his future.

# LINKING CURRENT, PAST AND TRANSFERENCE RELATIONSHIPS (TRIANGLE OF PERSON)

**Jeremy Holmes** Department of Clinical Psychology, Washington Singer Building, University of Exeter EX4 4QG

**Definition:** Pointing out of common links among ways in which the patient relates to his/her significant others, parental figures in the past, and the therapist.

**Elements:** The therapist seeks common factors across the 'triangle of person' across: a) current relationship difficulties, b) earlier relationships, especially with parents, and c) how s/he relates to the therapist (transference). The therapist then interprets such links, often along one or other 'side' of the 'triangle' (e.g. link of significant others to therapist: *'Your descriptions of tentative connections with your boyfriends remind me of the cautious way in which you approach me'*).

**Related procedures:** *Transference interpretation; describing overgeneralisation* (part of *cognitive restructuring*), using the *'triangle of defense'*.

**Application:** Individual and sometimes group psychoanalytic psychotherapy.

**1st Use?** Malan (1976).

**References:**
1. Malan D (1976). *The Frontier of Brief Psychotherapy*. New York: Plenum.
2. Malan D & Della Selva P (2006). *Lives Transformed: a Revolutionary Method of Dynamic psychotherapy*. London: Karnac.
3. Abbass A (2002). Short-term dynamic therapies in the treatment of major depression. *Canadian Journal of Psychiatry,* 47, 193-2004.

**Case illustration:** (Holmes, unpublished)
Naomi sought help for depression triggered by the failure of her 3rd marriage. In session 4 the therapist pointed out that she seemed to accept almost unthinkingly the contractual arrangements – times, session frequency, use of the couch - without considering whether this form of therapy and this therapist were right for *her*. She replied – "oh, but I've Googled you and you tick all the boxes". It emerged that she had also chosen her husbands by their CVs – tall, handsome, successful – rather than asking herself whether she really liked or trusted them. As a child Naomi had gained her mother's attention by bending to her every wish and becoming the clever, well-

groomed, socially adept girl that her mother insisted one had to be in order to succeed in life. Feelings were irrelevant, approval and appearances were what mattered. The therapist then suggested there was a common theme linking her 3 failed marriages (current problem), her childhood relationships, and her relationship with her therapist (transference). He suggested that, to her ultimate detriment, she gauged people by their external features (their curriculum vitae) rather than by her own spontaneous reactions to them. He linked her unquestioning acceptance of her therapist and each husband to her mother's over-valuation of appearances and ignoring of feelings. Her task in therapy was to learn to identify and trust her feelings and use them as a guide to action. In session 7 she began speaking of how she had found a house which she really liked, and despite some difficulty in raising the money, she had decided to follow her instincts and go ahead with it, especially as it was very suitable for her beloved cats.

## MENTALIZING, PROMOTION OF

Jon GALLEN, Menninger Clinic, PO Box 809045, 2801 Gessner Drive, Houston, TX 77280, Menninger Department of Psychiatry & Behavioral Sciences at Baylor College of Medicine, Houston, Texas, **Anthony W BATEMAN**, Halliwick Unit, St Ann's Hospital, Barnet, Enfield & Haringey Mental Health Trust, London, UK, **Peter FONAGY,** University College London & Anna Freud Centre, London, UK

**Definition:** Attending to intentional mental states in oneself and others and interpreting behavior accordingly.

**Elements:** Mentalizing interventions promote an enquiring, open-minded understanding by the patient and therapist of one's own and others' mental states. These include past, present and anticipated mental states ranging from ordinary thoughts and feelings to abnormal hallucinations and dissociations, and from intuited emotional resonances to explicitly spoken material. Mentalizing procedures can concern just one current feeling or a broad autobiographical narrative.

**Related procedures:** *Transference interpretation, countertransference, use of; Socratic questioning; mindfulness meditation; cognitive restructuring; metacognitive monitoring; promoting reflection, psychological mindedness, observing ego, empathy.*

**Application:** In individual, group, and family therapy based on any theoretical orientation.

**1st Use?** Fonagy (1991).

**References:**
1. Allen JG, Fonagy P, Bateman AW (2008). *Mentalizing in Clinical Practice.* Washington, DC: American Psychiatric Publishing.
2. Bateman AW, Fonagy P (2006). *Mentalization-Based Treatment for Borderline Personality Disorder: A Practical Guide.* New York: Oxford University Press.
3. Fonagy P (1991). Thinking about thinking: Some clinical and theoretical considerations in the treatment of a borderline patient. *Internat J.Psychoanalysis*, 76, 39-44.
4. Fonagy P, Gergely G, Jurist E, Target M (2002). *Affect Regulation, Mentalization, and the Development of the Self.* New York: Other Press.

**Case Illustration 1:**
Karen recounted an incident hours before her psychotherapy session. Her husband had left a phone message that he'd decided to stay away on his trip for a few more days, without any explanation. She reacted with "instant fury", slamming her fist onto marble tiles on the kitchen wall, with results visible on her swollen hand. The therapist asked *"Looking back, what do you make of that now?"* Karen answered "What else was I going to do?", as if unthinkingly injuring herself were an utterly natural response to feeling angry or frustrated. The therapist remained puzzled and asked Karen if she could help him understand the link: *"What is the connection between feeling furious and smashing your fist?"* Karen again answered "It's what you do!" The therapist persisted: *"It's what you do, but to me it's a bit of a puzzle".* The therapist asked if she ever refrained from hurting herself when she was furious; astoundingly, she replied she couldn't remember a time when she'd refrained. The therapist asked how much time elapsed between her feeling of fury and smashing herself. Karen reflected for a moment and replied, "A second or two." The therapist exclaimed *"Good! That gives you some time to think — to push the pause button".* He pointed out it might be useful for her to cultivate some experience of refraining from action when she felt furious. Further exploration suggested that Karen felt an immediate and intolerable loss of the excitement of looking forward to seeing her husband. Smashing her fist cleared her mind. Subsequent discussion addressed self-injury as an expression of her anger that exacerbated her marital conflict, creating a vicious circle of feeling rejected and angry, injuring herself, and evoking more rejection.

**Case Illustration 2:**
Jake reported a "weird" dream in which he was holding a gun to his head in a therapy session and, in the dream, felt a tremendous sense of power as he saw the look of panic on the therapist's face. The therapist asked what made the dream seem "weird." Jake replied that the last thing he would want to do is frighten his therapist and, besides, "It doesn't seem to faze you when I talk about wanting to kill myself". The therapist challenged him: *"How do you know it doesn't faze me?"* In a non-sequitur, Jake responded, "My parents never seemed to care about all the crazy self-destructive stuff I was doing." The therapist reiterated: *"What makes you think I'm not fazed — how do you know?"* Jake replied he assumed that the therapist really didn't "give a damn" about him once he'd left the office. Persisting, the therapist responded emphatically, *"How do you know?"* Finally, Jake reflected for a moment and said, "I don't, for sure." The therapist then replied that he didn't think Jake's dream was "weird" at all; rather it wasn't that far from the truth. The therapist explained that although not feeling panicky he'd worried more than usual that Jake was becoming more suicidal and may have noticed the therapist's anxiety, and it was good that Jake had talked about the dream. Jake

said the therapist had seemed a bit tense in the previous session when Jake was talking about dropping out of school as everything was so pointless and futile. The therapist confirmed that hearing the words "pointless and futile" had troubled him. Jake responded, "But I didn't want to worry you." The therapist replied *"Why not? Might there be something to gain in having me worry?"* This led to productive discussion of Jake's belief "out of sight out of mind" and that keeping the therapist on edge might be the best way to ensure that he wouldn't take Jake for granted and would remain invested in helping him.

# METACOGNITIVE THERAPY (MCT)

Michael SIMONS, Beate HERPERTZ-DAHLMANN, RWTH Aachen University, Germany; & Sylvie SCHNEIDER, University of Basel, Switzerland

**Definition:** A way to improve emotional disorders by challenging negative and positive beliefs about cognitive processes like ruminating and worrying e.g. positive: "Ruminating/worrying helps me cope"; negative: "I can't control my ruminating/worrying". Whereas cognitive restructuring or danger-ideation-reduction therapy challenge thought content e.g. reasons for & against believing one is contaminated, MCT helps patients to manage thinking about thinking ("Having this thought means...", "Washing helps me feel better"), thought suppression (mental avoidance), and selective attention to threatening cues.

**Elements:** The therapist uncovers metacognitive beliefs like fusion of thoughts with: 1. actions e.g. `Thinking I could harm someone makes it more likely that I'll really harm somebody'; 2. events e.g. `Because I think my dad could be killed in an accident, he is in real danger'; 3. intentions e.g. `Thinking I could have sex with grandpa means I want to have sex with him'. The patient is persuaded to modify such beliefs by experiments e.g. for thought-action fusion: *"Try to lift a stone just by thinking about it";* for thought- event fusion: *"Try to change the weather just by mental power"*; for thought-intention fusion by Socratic dialogue e.g. *"You believe thinking something means you want it to happen. So, if you're thinking about bad marks at school, does that mean you want bad marks?"* .

The therapist asks patients about attempts at thought suppression (*"What do you do when this thought pops into your mind?"*) and fusion beliefs (*"What does having this thought mean to you?"*). Patients are encouraged to try thought-suppression experiments (e.g. *"Try not to think of X!"*) in order to find out how hard it is to suppress thoughts and that trying to do so can worsen them.

Selective attention is challenged by Socratic dialogue (e.g.*"How does it help to always attend to possible dangers like dirt?"*), and detached mindfulness exercises are advised (e.g. *"Observe your thoughts as they come and go as if they were scrolling on the CNN news ticker, without trying to change them"*). Other metacognitive beliefs are challenged by brief (5-10 minutes) exposure and ritual prevention exercises (exposure exercises to produce habituation usually last 30 minutes or longer).

**Related procedures:** *Experiment, detached mindfulness, cognitive restructuring, reframing, giving perspective, exposure.*

**Application:** For depression, anxiety, PTSD and OCD in individual sessions, if need be together with relatives in children and adolescents.

**1st Use?** Wells (1999).

**References:**
1. Simons M, Schneider S, Herpertz-Dahlmann B (2006). Metacognitive therapy versus exposure and response prevention for pediatric OCD: case series with randomized allocation. *Psychotherapy & Psychosomatics*, 75, 257-264.
2. Wells A (1999). A metacognitive model and therapy for generalized anxiety disorder. *Clinical Psychology and Psychotherapy*, 6, 86-95.
3. Wells A (2000). *Emotional disorders and metacognition. Innovative cognitive therapy.* Chichester: Wiley.

**Case illustration:** (Simons, unpublished)
Kevin aged 14 suffered for 6 months from contamination ideas and washing rituals, and obsessive thoughts about Hitler and Nazi ideas and fears that he himself might be a Nazi. The therapist's asking him *'What does it mean to have such thoughts?'* uncovered Kevin's fear that 'thinking about Hitler and Nazis means I want to be a Nazi' (thought-intention fusion). Asking him *'How do you react when you have these thoughts?'* disclosed his excessive monitoring and suppressing of politically incorrect thoughts and checking whether he may have said anything against foreigners. The therapist asked Kevin to test these ideas by doing *experiments* such as 1. *'Think about something you don't want such as a bad mark in school'* - Kevin found that thinking about a bad mark did not mean that he wanted one, and 2. *'Try for a minute not to think of a crocodile sitting on my head'* - Kevin found that trying to suppress the thought actually made it more intrusive. His problem was thus not his thoughts but rather his fruitless efforts to stop them. He learned "detached mindfulness" to the intrusions (*'Just observe your thoughts coming and going like waves and say to yourself: "This is just a thought"'*). After 3 weeks of daily self-training *("Whenever these thoughts pop into your mind, just recognize them; watch them coming and going")*, without recording thoughts, such thoughts ceased to disturb him without any prolonged exposure exercises to them. Washing rituals decreased mainly by exposure with ritual prevention targeted at gradual shortening of shower time by 10 minutes a week, from 1 hour to 15 minutes a day. After ten weekly 50-minute sessions of MCT for the repugnant thoughts and exposure and ritual prevention for the washing rituals, these problems ceased. Therapy gains were maintained at 1 year follow-up.

# CLP 80

## METAPHOR, USE OF

**Jeremy HOLMES**, Department of Clinical Psychology, Washington Singer Building, University of Exeter EX4 4QG, UK

**Definition:** Metaphors (literally 'carrying over', like 'transference') link one thing with another and are commonly used to make otherwise-inaccessible feelings visible to others (e.g. 'when my husband left me it was like a red hot poker had been driven through my heart').

**Elements:** The therapist helps patients use metaphors to depict what troubles them e.g. by asking *"What was it like to ... be an only child with elderly parents?"* ('like being a helper in an old people's home'); *"... find yourself at that party knowing not a soul?"* ('like being in a foreign country unable to speak a word'); *"... come home from school and find that your father had died?"* ('like falling out of an airplane without a parachute'). The therapist may offer a metaphor (see below) to try to describe how the patient might be feeling, which can then be examined, dismissed, played with, or modified.

**Related procedures:** *Narrative therapy, story telling, psychodrama imagery, giving perspective, cognitive restructuring.*

**Application:** Psychodynamic psychotherapy - individual and group.

**1st Use?** Winnicott DW (1971).

**References:**
1. Bateman A, Brown D, Pedder J (2000). *Introduction to Psychotherapy: An Outline of Psychodynamic Principles and Practice.* London: Routledge.
2. Berlin R. et al (1991). Metaphor and psychotherapy. *American Journal of Psychotherapy*, 45, 359-367.
3. Holmes J (1992). *Between Art and Science.* London Routledge.
4. Winnicott DW (1971). *Playing and Reality.* London: Penguin.

**Case Illustrations** (Holmes J, unpublished)
1.*Patient-generated playful metaphor to enhance a sense of creativity and interactive competency*
 Anna sought therapy for depression and chronic low self-esteem. In session 3 she said her boss at work was demanding, never satisfied, and able to sack her at any moment. The therapist asked *"What's it like when you're summoned to his office?"*. Anna replied "As though I'm alone in a field with a raging bull". The therapist suggested that she needed to develop matador skills, and to remember that, though less powerful than her boss she

could, with grace and skill, and knowledge of his lumbering mentality, outwit and ultimately defeat him. This metaphor struck a chord, and in the ensuing 2 years of therapy both patient and therapist often referred to it.

2. *Therapist-generated metaphor*

John, an only child aged 22 sought help through a student health service for feeling desperately upset when his apparently happily married parents split up. He made great efforts to stay on good terms with both of them. It emerged that he had been very close to his parents throughout his childhood, with little or no conflict in his teenage years. He usually confided any difficulties to his parents rather than to friends. When they became preoccupied with their own problems and separated he felt doubly bereft.

In session 6 the therapist suggested that the divorce of John's parents was like a tsunami engulfing the whole family including John, and that, like villagers living on the side of an island facing the huge wave, he was at much more risk of drowning than people on the other side. Thus his intimacy with his parents was both a blessing and a curse. The tsunami image seemed to help John gain some distance from his difficulties. Over the next 6 months he became more financially and emotionally independent, getting a job, forming a close relationship with a girl, and becoming able to tell his parents how angry he had felt about their failure to stay together.

## METHOD OF LEVELS (MOL)

Tim **CAREY**, Centre for Applied Psychology, University of Canberra, Canberra, ACT, Australia 2601; ph +61 (0) 2 6201 2950 & **Warren MANSELL**, School of Psychological Sciences, University of Manchester, Manchester, UK, M13 9PL; ph +44 161 275 8589

**Definition**: A Method-of-Levels (MOL) therapist helps people to explore their immediate experience of distress and shift their awareness to their (level of) beliefs and values assumed to produce the distress.

**Elements:** 1. Converse with clients about an area of current concern and focus on their experience of that concern as they describe it to the therapist. As the conversation proceeds, clients usually pause at times and may look away, shake their head, or smile.
2. On noticing these disruptions to their word flow the therapist asks clients what they've fleetingly become aware of. By asking *"What popped into your mind just then when you looked away?"*, *"What occurred to you that made you pause?"*, *"What made you smile just now?"* etc, the therapist helps to focus the client's attention on a different level of their experience. The conversation then continues until the therapist detects another disruption. A MOL therapist thus iteratively helps clients to explore current areas of dissatisfaction and other aspects of themselves that might underlie their distress. Through this kind of conversation, clients might find out, for example, that their anxiety in team meetings occurs because they want to remain friends with the team members while disagreeing with some of their views. In order to alert clients to each shift in awareness at the time it occurs, therapy conversations can appear disjointed. The therapist will often gently interrupt clients to immediately ask about what the therapist just noticed rather than let clients finish what they were saying and only then try to recapture the moment. This draws attention to disruptions right away, enabling the patient to shift awareness back to a potential source of conflict. As the conversation continues in this way clients often seem to suddenly realise something, or become quietly reflective or confused on questioning what they were once sure of. Sometimes they feel as though they've stepped back and are looking at their problem rather than being in it. When this happens the therapist asks *"Is this a place we should leave it for today?"* and leaves it to the client to schedule the next session.

**Related Procedures:** *Attention control, downward arrow technique, free association, metacognitive therapy, mindfulness, polarities experiential exercise, Socratic questioning, thought catching, values exploration and construction.*

# CLP 80

**Application:** Individually for distressed adults, children and adolescents.

**1st Use?** Carey (2001).

**References:**
1. Carey TA (2001). Investigating the role of redirecting awareness in the change process: A case study using the method of levels. *International Journal of Reality Therapy*, 20(2), 26-30.
2. Carey TA (2008a). *Hold that thought! Two steps to effective counseling and psychotherapy with the Method of Levels.* Chapel Hill, NC: Newview Publications.
3. Carey TA (2008b). Perceptual Control Theory and the Method of Levels: Further contributions to a transdiagnostic perspective. *International Journal of Cognitive Therapy*, 1(3), 237-255.
(http://www.atypon-link.com/GPI/toc/ijct/1/3)
4. Mansell W (2008). Perceptual Control Theory as an integrative framework and Method of Levels as a cognitive therapy: what are the pros and cons? *The Cognitive Behaviour Therapist.* Doi: 10.1017/S1754470X08000093

**Case illustration:** (Carey 2001; cited in Carey 2008b)
Mia, a young woman, sought help for severe depression and anxiety she'd felt for several months. In session 1 she reported distress about how she should live her life, wanting to please her family yet also decide her own future. Her family disapproved of Mia's decisions on how to live her life but she was dissatisfied when living as they wished e.g. she liked her current job but her parents were unhappy with her choice and found a job vacancy elsewhere which they thought she should apply for but she did not want that. The therapist helped Mia explore her conflict by asking her to describe both sides of the conflict: *"How do you feel when you make your own decisions?", "What's important to you about making your own decisions?",* and *"Have you always enjoyed your parents' approval?", "How do you know when your parents approve of you?"* As Mia answered the therapist asked about distractions to shift her attention to another level: *"What's going through your mind as you discuss approval just now?", "What were you thinking when you looked away just then?", "You seem to be slowing down your talking - what's going through your mind as that's happening?"* At the end of session 1 Mia said she thought she should accept herself as she is before expecting others to accept her, that she'd never thought of this before, and that if she could accept herself she would solve her own problem. In session 2 Mia dwelt on her current distress despite her therapist's questions trying to shift her awareness to a level above the distress. However, in session 3 she shifted to focus on what independence meant to her, relaxed and laughed, and said she thought she should start taking her own advice by making independent decisions and being satisfied with those. In session 4 Mia said she'd reduc-

ed her contact with her parents, had joined a local social club, was exercising daily, and was thinking clearly without depression or anxiety, so therapy ended. At 10-week follow-up Mia remained improved.

## MINDFULNESS TRAINING

Alistair SMITH, Psychology Services, LCT, 18 Euxton Lane, Chorley, Lancs. PR7 1PS, UK; ph +44 1257 245537

**Definition:** Raising present-moment awareness and non-judgmental acceptance of one's own sensations, emotions and thoughts through meditation practice.

**Elements:** Classes train mindfulness meditation with non-judgmental attention focussing (e.g. persistently attending to ordinary breathing, then body sensations, then sounds, then thoughts) and learning to return repeatedly from mind-wandering to awareness of the present, accepting unpleasant along with other thoughts as they arise while meditating. After practice periods the therapist inquires into participants' experiences, and helps them learn to disengage from the self-criticism which usually arises. Similar daily intensive practice at home, with audiotaped and printed guidance, is combined with mindfulness during everyday activities (e.g. when washing dishes, do so with attention to the process of washing, rather than to 'get the dishes done and on to the next thing'; eat attentively instead of daydreaming at the same time). Training includes practice of mindful movement (e.g. walking, stretching), body-awareness during 40 minutes of body scanning, and sitting silently while focusing on, among others: breath, hearing, thoughts and feelings arising and passing. Many people value the frequent practice of 3-minute breathing spaces to pause and disengage from anxiety or depression and to see these as passing events. Mindfulness-Based Stress Reduction (MBSR) teaches the effects of mindless constant activity ('automatic pilot') on our body, emotions, thoughts, what we eat, and how we react to events. Mindfulness-based Cognitive Therapy (MBCT) for recurring depression teaches people to observe negative thoughts without changing their content, thus relating towards them in a new way. People are helped to reflect on aspects of their lives and thoughts which nourish or drain them emotionally. Each person writes an outline of their 'relapse signature' and what they will do on detecting this. They are encouraged to develop options for what to do after mindfully considering what will be most helpful e.g. sitting silently meditating on what is being experienced, go for a mindful walk, or do something that is pleasurable or will give a sense of mastery.

**Related Procedures**: *Attention training, acceptance and commitment therapy* (but without behavioural experiments or metaphor and paradox to contact avoided thoughts, feelings, memories, and sensations), *compassionate mind training* (but without creating compassionate instead of critical images and thoughts), *Buddhist mindfulness meditation, hatha yoga* emphasising physical control and postures in training consciousness towards insight and equanimity.

**Application**: 8 weekly 2½-hour group sessions (20 or more people for MBSR, about 12 for MBCT), plus one all-day session for MBSR. 1-3-monthly maintenance classes are usual for a year or more. Individual sessions are less efficient. Used for stress e.g. with chronic pain, cancer/multiple sclerosis/fibromyalgia/ psoriasis, general anxiety, panic, being in prison, intensive studying. MBCT is used for recurring depression and eating disorders.

**1st Use**? Kabat-Zinn (1982)

**References:**
1. Follette VM, Linehan MM, Hayes SC (2004). *Mindfulness and Acceptance*. New York: Guilford Press.
2. Kabat-Zinn J (1982). An outpatient program in behavioral medicine for chronic pain patients based on the practice of mindfulness meditation: theoretical considerations and preliminary results. *General Hospital Psychiatry*, 4, 33-47.
3. Kabat-Zinn J (1990). *Full Catastrophe Living: How to cope with stress, pain and illness using mindfulness meditation.* London: Piatkus.
4. Segal Z, Williams JMG, Teasdale J (2002). *Mindfulness-Based Cognitive Therapy for Depression: A New Approach to Preventing Relapse.* New York: Guilford Press.

**Case illustration:**
Derek, aged 66, had recurring depression for 8 years after an accident caused spinal damage and chronic pain, so he stopped working, driving and sports. He was `... fine one moment and break down the next. I can't handle things going wrong...'. Derek practised mindfulness enthusiastically. During session 1's body scan he focused attention so much that `My big toe felt like the whole world'. In session 2's guided- sitting meditation, while attending to breath, sounds, thoughts etc his thoughts changed constantly; mindfully attending to his precise pain sensations instead of worrying about them often stopped his pain. Mindful movement too shifted attention from unhelpful thinking. He found body scanning refreshing and sitting meditation enjoyable. At session 2 Derek said he suddenly realised he had suffered unduly for years as he had not fully accepted his accident's reality, and denial had kept him resenting pain and focussing on (an impossible) cure for his injuries. Liberated by this insight, he stopped antidepressants, drastically cut his analgesics, and spent 3 hours daily in formal mindfulness practice until the therapist asked him to emphasise informal practice more e.g. when out for a walk, washing dishes, doing other regular activities. He disliked very slow walking as formal meditation practice, but enjoyed a mindful 4-mile

walk most days, and 3-minute breathing spaces helped him detach from gloomy thoughts. At session 8, Derek wrote 'I am living with the pain ... meditation has helped me so much I find it hard to believe how much I actually enjoy it' and later said he felt 90% better: 'before, the minute the pain started I would run and take painkillers. Now I can handle it. I meditate'. His wife and friends said he was much less irritable. Mindfulness practice was refreshing and 'part of my life'. Instead of 'getting in a mess turning [worries] over in my mind all the time' now 'yesterday has gone and tomorrow you don't know what will happen'. Mindfulness's most useful aspect was 'learning to accept the things you can't change...'. 13 months later he said: 'I'm fine. I still go to bed and cry with pain, but I'm back doing all sorts of things. I have learned to live and handle the pain, so I don't have the anxiety'. He still spent an hour daily in mindfulness practice, came to one reunion, then decided to practise mindfulness alone. He wrote 'The pain is slowly getting worse, but I cope so much better.' His depression had gone by the end of his course and remained absent over the next year.

## CLP 80

## MORITA THERAPY

**Kei NAKAMURA**, Psychiatry Department, Jikei University, Daisan Hospital, 4-11-1, Izumi-honcho, Komae, Tokyo 201-8601; ph +81 334801151

**Definition**: Morita therapy leads patients from preoccupation with and attempts to eliminate neurotic symptoms towards accepting anxiety as natural (arugamama) while engaging in constructive behaviors.

**Elements**: Morita therapy tries to give corrective experience, over 4 phases if an inpatient:
1. Bed-rest in isolation for 7 days (time out), during which patients stay in their room all day with activity restricted to meals, a morning wash, and going to the toilet, and no access to reading, radio, TB, CD, computer or games.
2. Light work for 4-7 days. During this the patient: a) initiates, under therapist guidance, graded activity and work needed in daily living at the hospital; b) writes in a diary what s/he did by day and every day submits this to the therapist who reads it, writes in comments, and returns it to the patient (diary guidance); c) has interviews 2-3 times a week with the therapist who does not regard symptoms as foremost and focuses on daily activities (strategic inattention to symptoms, contingency management).
3. Work for 1-2 months with gradual engagement in activities such as gardening, caring for animals and cooking and eventually doing these together with other patients.
4. Preparation for normal daily living over 1-4 weeks which may include commuting to work or school from the ward.
Today Morita therapy is commonly done with outpatients weekly or two-weekly. The therapist asks about their daily life and symptoms, encourages them to start constructive activities to return to normal living while remaining anxious, and often also gives diary guidance.

**Related procedures**: *Arugamama, behavioural activation, community reinforcement approach, contingency management, diary-keeping, exposure and ritual prevention, goal-setting, problem-solving, activation of desire for life, time out, work therapy.*

**Application**: In- or outpatient guidance (individual and group) in clinical, work and school settings and self-help groups such as Seikatsu-no Hakken Kai (Circle for Group Learning of Morita Therapy).

**1st Use**? Shoma Morita (1919).

**References:**
Morita S (1919). *Shinkeishitsu no hontai oyobi ryoho*. (1998). In English: *Morita Therapy and the True Nature of Anxiety-Based Disorders (Shinkeishitsu)*. State University of New York Press, Albany, NY.

**Case Illustration 1:** INpatient Morita Therapy
A woman aged 25 had social anxiety disorder for 2.5 years. In front of others she trembled and avoided writing, which disrupted her work. She asked for inpatient Morita therapy. During her bed-rest phase, her hands often trembled when observed and later she felt bored. The therapist wrote in her diary about stepping out of her room to join life on the ward: *"Take it a step at a time, while holding anxiety."* (Diary guidance to practise arugamama including exposure but aimed more at helping her do daily activities on the ward than at decreasing her fear). The patient ardently desired activity and began wood-carving but became tense and her hands often shook when attending the large group at patients' daily meetings. The therapist did not regard her tension and tremor as major issues (contingency management). She was encouraged to be active despite feeling tense, and the therapist commented in interviews and diary entries on her progress towards each goal e.g calling her conscientious setting of meals on a table despite her hands shaking a success as her goal was not to abolish tremor but to give patients meals. In her month-long work phase she had more chances to work with other patients and became less anxious and less preoccupied with her tremor. Thereafter she started commuting to work from the ward. On her first day back at work her hands shook as she held a microphone to address a meeting of colleagues, but she was happy that she could greet them. She wrote in her diary that she had 'many things to be anxious about that I want to do' (accepting self as arugamama). As she continued commuting she lost almost all fear of writing in the presence of others and communicated better with colleagues. She had no medication during treatment.

**Case Illustration 2:** OUTpatient Morita Therapy
A woman aged 33 had feared contamination since age 14 and developed compulsive washing. When first seen she was over 2 months pregnant and had stopped housework for fear of mercury contaminating her child, herself and her family. She knew her fear was irrational. She had outpatient sessions every 2 weeks to a total of 6 hour-long sessions. The therapist said her fear of illness and misfortune for herself and her family was natural and asked what she wanted. She expressed a strong desire for health and security for herself, her family and especially her child. The therapist said her fear arose from deep care for her family; it could not be eliminated but did not need to be. He noted the vicious circle of compulsive washing and sense that this was inadequate causing yet more washing. He

proposed that she wait for her fears to fade away naturally without trying to deny them (arugamama, exposure and ritual prevention) and to promote her family's health and security in a more constructive way (behavioural activation). As she wanted to be able to cook for children he negotiated with her a goal of cooking at least one dish by the next session. She returned saying she had cooked several times with her husband's help, which the therapist called major progress. She wanted to do more housework but panicked at the thought of being the main person doing it. The therapist pointed out her mindset that "everything must be in a certain fixed way" (noting all-or-nothing or black-and-white thinking errors). He suggested that she think about doing housework together with her family, do what she felt like doing without postponing it, and to broaden her goals beyond housework (problem-solving, activation of desire for life). Though her fear of mercury recurred at times, after cooking with her husband's help for some time she began to cook by herself. She decided to do shopping as her next goal, which she accomplished. She gradually resumed normal living and delivered her baby several months later.

# MOTIVATIONAL ENHANCEMENT THERAPY (MET)

**David C HODGINS**, Department of Psychology, University of Calgary, Calgary, Alberta, Canada; ph +1 403 220 3371 & **Katherine M DISKIN**, Mental Health Services, CFB Esquimalt, Victoria, BC, Canada: ph +1 250 363 4411

**Definition**: Giving the client personalized feedback on assessment results and formulating a change plan in addition to standard motivational-interviewing elements (see separate clp entry#) of expressing empathy through reflection, developing discrepancies between clients' present behaviours and their values and goals, avoiding client resistance, and supporting client self-efficacy.

**Elements:** MET adds to motivational interviewing by helping clients understand how their problem's status compares with that of the average person. Clients complete a structured assessment of problem behaviours (e.g. for an alcohol problem this might include measures of alcohol dependence, frequency and intensity of drinking, and of other alcohol-related problems such as liver function). The therapist then asks if clients wish to learn the results, gives those in relation to available norms and interpretation guidelines, and discusses the clients' reactions to the results, which often jars with their values and goals.

**Related Procedures:** *Decisional balance exercise, motivational interviewing.*

**Application:** MET is used mainly for alcohol and drug dependence and gambling, to enhance motivation before therapy or as a standalone procedure. It is often offered individually in 1-4 sessions but can also be used in groups.

**1st Use?** Miller et al (1992).

**References:**
1. Miller WR, Zweben A, DiClemente CC, Rychtarik RG (1992). *Motivational enhancement therapy manual: a clinical research guide for therapists treating individuals with alcohol abuse and dependence.* Rockville, MD: National Institute on Alcohol Abuse and Alcoholism.
2. Miller WR, Rollnick S (2003). *Motivational interviewing: Preparing people to change. Second edition.* New York: Guilford.
3. Project Match Research Group (1997). Matching alcoholism treatments to client heterogeneity: Project MATCH post-treatment drinking outcomes. *Journal of Studies on Alcohol*, 58, 7-29.

**Case illustration:** (Hodgins, unpublished)
Tom's fiancée enquired about individual therapy for Tom's serious online sports betting. She accompanied Tom to his first appointment but remained in the waiting room while he saw the therapist. In motivational-interview style the therapist explored the specifics of Tom's gambling and his readiness to change, his fiancée's and his own concerns, and what Tom liked about sports betting in order to help him recognise ambivalence about giving it up. Discussion and reflection of Tom's experiences clarified that his betting impeded his goals of financial stability, buying a home, and starting a family (*"What I hear you saying is that though you really love the challenge of picking winners, you're thinking that this costs way too much money - it will be very difficult to save enough money to purchase a house if it keeps on. Buying a house is important if you and your wife start a family. Is that right?"*). At times Tom expressed frustration at his fiancée's insistence that he deal with this issue. The therapist reflected back Tom's feelings about this without taking sides or exploring it in more detail (*"It's hard for you that your fiancée is taking this so seriously"*), and reflected his strengths including his reduction of alcohol consumption over recent years. To explore how much Tom should be concerned the therapist invited Tom to estimate his expenditures on gambling, time spent gambling, and problem severity, and presented his scores in relation to Canadian norms from a prevalence survey. Tom was not surprised that he gambled much more than the average Canadian man but was a bit taken aback that he was spending 25% of his income on gambling and that his problem severity was moderately-high. The therapist encouraged Tom to reflect upon these results using a motivational-interviewing style (*"This is surprising to you. You don't see yourself as someone who spends that much on a leisure activity. In other areas of your life you're quite responsible"*), and toward the end of the session asked him what he was thinking about his goals. Tom now said he strongly wanted to address his online sports betting.
He did this in cognitive behaviour therapy over six subsequent sessions.

## MOTIVATIONAL INTERVIEWING (MI)

Hal ARKOWITZ, Department of Psychology, Arizona University, Tucson, Arizona 85721 USA; ph +15203254837

**Definition:** A way of enhancing motivation to change by exploring and resolving ambivalence about it without the therapist advocating, or directly influencing, the client to change.

**Elements:** MI is a way of relating to clients to increase their motivation by:
1) *Expressing empathy through reflection* (e.g.: Client: "I feel nervous about seeing my father again after all these years"; Therapist: "You're afraid you'll be disappointed by the reunion");
2) *Developing discrepancies between clients' present maladaptive behaviors and their values and goals* (e.g.: Therapist: "While it seems important to you to be a good mother to your son, your depression often makes you unavailable to him when he needs you");
3) *Rolling with clients' resistance, seeing it as information about perceived pros and cons of change to be respected and worked with, not an obstacle to overcome* (e.g. Therapist: "It seems you'd like to stop drinking because it causes problems in your marriage, but you're afraid stopping would leave you without friends and a way of handling stress");
4) *Supporting client's beliefs that they can help themselves* (e.g. asking about past successful change attempts in other areas).

**Related procedures:** *Analysing secondary gain, motivational enhancement therapy, client-centered therapy.*

**Application:** MI has mostly been used to treat addictions and included giving clients feedback about their substance use and how it relates to norms of such use, though such feedback is not a defining feature of MI nor usually used with MI for other disorders.

**1st Use?** Miller WR (1983).

**References:**
1. Arkowitz H, Westra H (2004). Integrating motivational interviewing and CBT in the treatment of depression and anxiety, *J.Cognitive Psychotherapy*, 18, 337-350.
2. Burke B, Arkowitz H, Menchola H (2003). The efficacy of motivational interviewing: A meta-analysis of controlled clinical trials. *J.Consulting & Clinical Psychology*, 71, 843-861.
3. Miller WR (1983). Motivational interviewing with problem drinkers. *Behav*

*Psychother*, 11, 147-172.
4. Miller WR, Rollnick S (2003). *Motivational interviewing: Preparing people to change*, 2nd edition. New York: Guilford.

**Case illustration:** (Arkowitz, unpublished)
Brad sought help for depression and anxiety. Initial sessions explored his ambivalence about change in a supportive non-judgmental manner by discussing pros *(analysing secondary gain)* and cons of his depression. He said disadvantages of being depressed were his suffering and inability to do enjoyable things and its adverse effects on family and friends. He described secondary gains that depression and anxiety postponed having to make difficult decisions on his college major and career as he felt he couldn't decide those while depressed, and that he felt less pressure from his parents about these issues while he was depressed. He thought concerns about school and his future may have partly precipitated his depression.

When asked what activities might improve his mood *(behavioural activation, homework)*, Brad proposed doing more outside home such as playing his guitar, seeing friends, and attending a meeting he usually enjoyed. By the next session he hadn't done any of these and felt less hopeful that anything would help. The therapist helped him explore pros and cons of doing these things. He concluded he expected too much of himself even in these activities. Discussion led to his reducing their extent and he agreed to try doing one (unspecified) thing outside the house which he otherwise wouldn't do. The next week he said he'd gone out to lunch with a friend and felt good about that. Over the next few weeks his activities increased and included some of the others above. Doing more and becoming less demanding of himself about school coincided with marked improvement in his depression.

# NARRATIVE EXPOSURE

Frank NEUNER, Maggie SCHAUER, Thomas ELBERT, Psychology Department, University of Konstanz, Fach D25, D-78476, Germany

**Definition:** A form of exposure for clients with PTSD which encourages them to tell their detailed life history chronologically to someone who writes it down, reads it back to them, helps them integrate fragmented traumatic memories into a coherent narrative, and gives that to them at the end as written testimony. Describing personal experiences in detail facilitates *imaginal exposure* to traumatic memories. Developed for refugees from diverse backgrounds who live in unsafe conditions, narrative exposure serves not only therapeutic but also social and political purposes by recording human rights violations.

**Elements:** Narrative exposure targets fragments of traumatic memories (sensory, physiological, cognitive, emotional) and aids their integration. It includes:
- *Education* about PTSD symptoms and need to face the traumas (*exposure*);
- Helping the client narrate and relive the traumas in detail with accompanying sensations and feelings *(imaginal exposure);*
- *Reframing* the victim's role into a survivor's role by contributing to the fight against human rights violations with their own testimony.

**Related procedures:** *Prolonged exposure, life reminiscence therapy, testimony therapy, guided fantasy, behaviour rehearsal.*

**Application:** Individual sessions with a client and a helper in psychology/medical clinics or huts/tents in refugee settlements. Helpers may be psychologists, psychiatrists, or briefly trained local therapists (e.g. refugees) without psychological or medical education.

**1st Use?** Called testimony therapy by Kornfeld L, Weinstein E (1983).

**References:**
1. Kornfeld L, Weinstein E in Cienfuegos J, Monelli C (1983). The testimony of political repression as a therapeutic instrument. *American Journal of Orthopsychiatry,* 53, 43-51.
2. Neuner F, Schauer M, Elbert T, Roth WT (2002). Narrative exposure treatment in a Macedonian refugee camp: case report. *J.Behav & Cognitive Psychotherapy,* 30, 205- 209.
3. Neuner F, Schauer M, Karunakara U, Klaschik C, Elbert T (2004). A com-

parison of narrative exposure therapy, supportive counseling and psychoeducation for treating PTSD in an African refugee settlement. *J.Consult Clin Psychol*, 72, 579-587.

**Case illustration:**
During the Rwandan civil war Eric fled from his village to Uganda and stayed in a refugee settlement for ten years. He had recurring intrusive images and nightmares of past events. At age 24, in the camp he met a Rwandan therapist via an aid organization. The therapist encouraged Eric to overcome avoidance and talk at length about his traumatic past. During six 90-minute sessions the therapist wrote down Eric's description in Kinyarwanda. It included Eric's life from birth and childhood in the peaceful period prior to the war to the current situation. His telling of the death of his family was hard to follow as it was often fragmented by intrusive memories of hiding in the grass, his mother crying, seeing her and four siblings being shot by armed rebels, noises of bullets, deformed bloody bodies. The therapist helped Eric to face these feelings (*imaginal exposure*) and sensations (heart beating fast, feeling his legs running), put them into words, and integrate them into the narrative. After giving detailed descriptions Eric felt some relief. The therapist reread the written narrative to Eric, asking him to listen carefully and to add to and correct it as needed. Thereafter the therapist helped him explore later traumas in the same way and continue thus until he reached the present. In session 6 the therapist reread Eric's full narrative to him and presented him with a handwritten copy of the testimony. Eric still felt strong grief and loss around his family's death, but with significant relief as he could talk about and share these events for the first time in his life. At 6-month follow-up his symptoms were so reduced that PTSD criteria were no longer met. Though Eric could not read, he kept his written testimony in his hut as he wished to show it to his children once they were grown.

# NIDOTHERAPY

Peter TYRER, Imperial College, London UK

**Definition:** Collaborative assessment and change of the environment (not the patient) to reduce the impact of mental disorder on the patient and society. More a form of environmental therapy (nidus = Latin for nest) than of psychotherapy.

**Elements:** Targets relevant relatives, neighbours, health and social authorities, police and others as needed to promote tolerance of the patients' eccentricities and a life style to fit the patients' needs. Includes *problem-solving* and *target/goal setting* by the therapist/team more than by the patient.

**Related procedures:** *Case management, community therapy.*

**Application:** Cases of persistent mental or personality disorder who resist change.

**1st Use?** Tyrer P (2002). Nidotherapy: A new approach to the treatment of personality disorder. *Acta Psychiatr Scand*, 105, 469-471.

**References:**
Tyrer P, Sensky T, Mitchard S (2003). Principles of nidotherapy in the treatment of persistent mental and personality disorders *Psychotherapy & Psychosomatics*, 72, 350-357.

**Case illustration:**
John persistently complained about his neighbours and the local authority housing department, believing in a conspiracy to place him in substandard housing to make him ill. He frequently lost his temper when his complaints were not taken seriously, and was often moved elsewhere, where the problems would resurface. He felt harassed, not ill. After 15 home visits over many months, he agreed to the community team acting for him in dealings with neighbours or housing authorities. Thereafter he concentrated on making his apartment into a permanent home for the first time, and the team gave him suitable plants for his garden to screen him from prying eyes.

# CLP 80

## PROBLEM-SOLVING THERAPY (PST)

**Arthur M NEZU** & **Christine M NEZU**, Psychology Department, Drexel University, Philadelphia PA 19102, USA; & **Thomas J D'ZURILLA**, SUNY at Stony Brook NY

**Definition:** A multi-component procedure to help people view and manage stressful life problems effectively.

**Elements:** PST teaches general skills to manage current and future problems. Patients learn to view and react to problems effectively by practising: changing attitudinal and emotional barriers to solving problems; accurately defining problems and setting realistic goals; breaking down problems into manageable sub-problem areas; brainstorming many options to attain their goals; working out probable tradeoffs of each option to decide which seem likely to work best for everyone affected; trying out the apparently-best options to see which help in fact. These skills are to help clients reduce ineffective ways of reacting to problems such as avoidance, impulsivity, careless or excessive behavior, emotional intolerance, procrastination, passivity, and overdependence on others. Clients learn problem solving as a way of coping via explanations (e.g. how lack of problem-solving ability contributes to current distress), skills training (e.g. how to visualize success and use negative feelings as a clue to defining problems), role-play exercises, and homework tasks.

**Related Procedures:** *Cognitive restructuring, problem and goal setting, role play/rehearsal, reframing, emotional validation, acceptance.*

**Application:** Individually or in groups, face to face or by phone.

**1st Use?** D'Zurilla TJ, Goldfried MR (1971).

**References:**
1. D'Zurilla TJ, Goldfried MR (1971). Problem solving and behavior modification. *Journal of Abnormal Psychology*, 78, 107-126.
2. Mynors-Wallis LM, Gath DH (1995). Randomised controlled trial comparing problem solving treatment with amitriptyline and placebo for major depression in primary care. *Brit Med J*, 310, 441-445.
3. Nezu AM, Nezu CM, Lombardo E (2003). Problem-solving therapy. Pp 301-307 in O'Donohue W, Fisher JE, Hayes SC (Eds.), *Cognitive behavior therapy: Applying empirically supported techniques in your practice*, Hoboken, NJ; John Wiley & Son.

**Case Illustration:**
Jennifer aged 40 felt depressed, worthless and hopeless and unable to deal with her husband's and teenage daughter's behavior. They refused to join in treatment so she had individual CBT. Initially she saw her problems as signs she had failed as a spouse and parent. Often she dealt impulsively with problems or avoided thinking about them e.g. she quickly gave into her husband's unreasonable spending and fantasized about leaving. She blocked out her anger and fears by drinking wine or calling a friend who always needed her rather than attending to her own problems. Worry about confronting problems led her to ignore her daughter's poor grades and breaking evening curfews.

Jennifer was asked to see herself as a problem solver who knew how to work toward change despite barriers. She was guided to view problems as challenges rather than catastrophes and to reframe negative feelings as signs of a problem to manage rather than to dread (e.g. see her daughter's difficulties as behaviors needing change, not evidence she was a bad mother). She learned to reduce negative self-talk by separating facts from assumptions e.g. she was asked to describe photos her therapist chose from magazines and then make statements distinguishing known facts such as "this photo shows two women and a man seated at a table" from assumptions such as "the man looks angry" which needed more information for verification. In reverse role-playing dialogues her therapist played Jennifer voicing Jennifer's beliefs e.g. "my marriage is hopeless as it has problems" and asked her to argue against them. She learned to use discomfort to cue problem solving e.g. anxiety when her husband raised his voice prompted her to STOP and THINK, define the problem, brainstorm, and evaluate options. She discovered that at the point her anxiety rose she was trying to control her husband's emotions, and brainstormed ways to accept others' feelings and to constructively change future problems. This helped her to improve rather than avoid marital difficulties and worry he did not love her.

She became less self-critical and less depressed as she applied problem-solving skills to her husband's spending under stress by finding ways to support him and help him cope better e.g. taking long walks together. She set her daughter simple contingencies to manage her behavior e.g. adhering to curfews and completing chores and homework consistently earned a monetary allowance while non-adherence led to loss of cellphone and internet access. After 25 sessions Jennifer felt more confident of being able to solve future problems and to recognize and accept those that she could/should not change e.g. when her aunt developed cancer Jennifer worked out how to give practical help while accepting the diagnosis.

## PROLONGED EXPOSURE COUNTERCONDITIONING

Nenad PAUNOVIC, Department of Psychology, Stockholm University, Stockholm, Sweden; ph +46-(0)8-749 25 75

**Definition:** Prolonged imagining of past/current most-pleasant/mastery experiences before and after shorter imagining of main traumatic ones.

**Elements:**
- Identification of past/current most-pleasant/mastery and trauma experiences in detail;
- With much therapist prompting, prolonged imaginal reliving of pleasant/mastery experiences just before and after briefer imagining of main trauma scenes (*exposure*);
- Daily *homework* listening to an audiotaped cassette of each session.

**Related procedures:** *Covert reinforcement, counterconditioning, systematic desensitization* (with prolonged pleasant/mastery personal experiences rather than brief relaxation, and more intense and longer *imaginal exposure/implosion*), *behaviour/cognitive rehearsal, behavioral /cognitive experiment* confirming self-esteem/positive world-view, *guided fantasy, well-being therapy.*

**Application:** Individual therapy.

**1st Use?** Paunovic N (2002).

**References:**
1. Paunovic N (2002). Prolonged exposure counterconditioning (PEC) as a treatment for chronic post-traumatic stress disorder and major depression in an adult survivor of repeated child sexual and physical abuse. *Clinical Case Studies*, 1, 148-169.
2. Paunovic N (2003). Prolonged exposure counterconditioning as a treatment for chronic posttraumatic stress disorder. *Journal of Anxiety Disorders*, 17, 479-499.

A woman aged 29 developed PTSD after three sexual assaults by her uncle when she was 14 and another by a stranger at age 19, and felt severe depression and guilt. Her therapist asked her to identify her 3 most enjoyable events ever concerning: her achievements, best friends, most valued activities, praise/affection from others, other life events; say which events had made her feel most happy/glad/well; describe each in detail - what happened, what she saw, heard, felt, did, and what other people did then. The therapist wrote down the details.

In sessions she imagined with eyes shut the pleasant/mastery experiences: driving a helicopter on her birthday, barbecuing with friends, picking mushrooms with her boyfriend in a forest, lighting a fire with her family at their country home, and giving a present to her mother-in-law. The therapist repeated aloud continuously each pleasurable event while she imagined it with her eyes shut eg: "You: ... build a fireplace with your friends (naming them); pick branches to sit on; arrange stones; collect wood; play with your dog, see your friends (naming each); hear the fire crackle; hear your dog whining; grill pork fillet and marshmallows; feel the taste; see your dog and your friends sitting beside you; feel your dog's head on your back pushing you down; feel satisfied and happy".

In sessions 1-4 (85-100 mins.) she was asked to imagine the main details of her traumatic experiences for 5 mins. by listening to short descriptions from the therapist and then describing them aloud herself. In sessions 5-6 (90 mins.) she saw video scenes of sexual/physical violence for 1-2 minutes and was then asked with her eyes shut to describe for 5 mins. her main traumas, what she saw, heard, did, and what the perpetrator did when she felt most afraid, and heard the therapist say: "You hear him say, 'you want to', but your whole body says 'no'; you hear him blame you, he says 'you want to'". At the peak of her distress the therapist asked her to switch to imagine her most pleasurable events; she imagined these before and after the trauma exposure for: in sessions 1-2, 45 mins. before 1 trauma exposure, after, 40 mins.; in sessions 3-4, 30 mins. before the first trauma exposure and 25 mins. after two trauma exposures; during sessions 5-6, 20 mins. before the first trauma exposure and 15 mins. after three trauma exposures. All sessions were audiotaped and the patient was asked to listen to them once daily. From pre- to posttreatment her PTSD, depression and guilt fell to a non-clinical level.

# PROLONGED-GRIEF THERAPY

Colin Murray PARKES, 21 South Road, Chorleywood, Herts, WD3 5AS, UK; ph +44 1923 282746

**Definition:** This gives sufferers from abnormally prolonged grief, who have difficulty in looking forward, time, reassurance and other help to put their grief aside and revise their assumptions about the world and their own future.

**Elements:** In prolonged-grief therapy the therapist establishes a trusting relationship, which allows the bereaved person to start exploring the future. This is accomplished by listening respectfully to the person's account of their loss and its effects on their lives, and giving verbal and non-verbal support in a matter-of-fact way that does not reward emotional expression. The therapist explains that when people lose their main source of support it is normal for them to feel anxious, that everyday assumptions are disrupted, and to have bodily symptoms of anxiety and feelings of chaos, and that all these will gradually diminish. S/he then works with the bereaved person to re-integrate the past with the future, saying the aim is not to forget the lost person but to discover how much they learned from the lost person that helps them to move forward and find new meaning in life. At the end of each session targets are agreed for forward-looking activities e.g. *"What could you do that would make your wife/husband proud of you?"* These targets are reviewed at the start of the next session and small successes are rewarded by congratulations and non-verbal expression of delight. Failures are analysed matter-of-factly to find lessons that can be learned from them e.g. *"Shall we keep this one on the list for next time or consider a less ambitious aim?"*. In this way bereaved people discover bit by bit their capacity for autonomy. Cognitive restructuring (see clp entry) may be used to identify and modify negative thinking. Prolonged-grief therapy avoids pity and, unlike guided mourning (see clp entry) does not aid the expression of grief and other negative affects. The therapist thus helps bereaved people to recognise the continuing value of their relationship with the lost person, and to let go of that person 'out there' while discovering that that person 'in here' is never lost.

**Related Procedures:** *Anxiety management, behavioural activation, cognitive restructuring, constructivist psychotherapy, family-focussed grief therapy, traumatic stress management, management of shattered assumptions, family-focussed grief therapy.*

**Application:** The normal course of uncomplicated, grief involves oscillation between looking back and looking forward; block in either process can impede recovery. For unduly-prolonged grief, with difficulty in looking forward, prolonged-grief therapy is given. In contrast, delayed or avoided grief associated with difficulty in looking back is treated by guided mourning (see clp entry).

**1st Use?** Parkes (1998). Developed further by Shear et al. (2005).

**References:**
1. Boelen PA (2008). Cognitive behaviour therapy for complicated grief. *Bereavement Care*, 27, 27-30.
2. Parkes CM, (3rd editon 1998 and, with Prigerson HG, 4th edition 2009). *Bereavement: studies of grief in adult life*. Routledge, London & NY.
3. Prigerson HG, Vanderwerker LC, Maciejewski PK (2008). A Case for Inclusion of Prolonged Grief Disorder in DSM-V. Chap.8, pp 165-186 in *Handbook of Bereavement Research and Practice: Advances in theory and intervention*. Eds. MS Stroebe, RO Hansson, H Schut and W Stroebe. Americam Psychological Association, Washington, DC.
4. Shear K, Frank E, Houck PR, Reynolds CF (2005). Treatment of Complicated Grief: A Randomized Controlled Trial. *J. Amer. Med. Ass.*, 293, 2601-2608.

**Case Illustration:** (Parkes, unpublished)

Molly, the youngest of a large family, was always treated as the 'baby' of the family. Although a pretty, bright child, she was seen as frail and was over-protected by her mother. She did well at school and went on to university but then found separation from her mother and home very hard. She fell in love with her professor, an older man who reciprocated her love and with whom she had a happy marriage in which she was dependent on her 'wonderful' husband and intolerant of any separation from him. He died when Molly was 55, leaving her shattered and afraid. She missed him terribly and, when referred for therapy two years later, still behaved as if he had died yesterday. She felt she could not survive without him and had shut herself up at home and withdrawn from social relationships. Molly was in a state of perpetual grieving and did not avoid grief, so Guided Mourning was inappropriate.

The therapist decided that Molly had had a powerful and dependent attachment to her husband following anxious clinging to her family since her early childhood; now that she was on her own and unprotected, she had an opportunity to discover that she could survive without depending on her mother, her husband or her therapist. (to enable Molly to discover her true worth and potential for autonomy, it was important for the therapist to avoid any suggestion of pity for her predicament, and engage with her in a programme that respected her obvious strengths. ("My respect for your true worth and potential is of more use to you than any pity I may feel for your current weakness") He worked with her to identify aims and encourage her to reach targets that would be rewarding and meaningful e.g. to renew an earlier interest in painting. Next she joined a painting group that would get her out of the house and into contact with others. She remarked that the group 'don't think of me as being a widow', and escaped from a pitiable, stigmatised identity. Another step forward was to accompany the group to paint pictures of mountains in Switzerland.

After that success, on returning from the mountains Molly sacked the man who'd been managing her husband's business and took over the management herself. She felt that she was moving forward while remaining faithful to the memory of her husband. She still missed him, but knew she could survive without him and took comfort from continuing the business he'd enjoyed.

# PROMOTING RESILIENCE (SOCIAL/EMOTIONAL COMPETENCE) IN YOUNG CHILDREN

**Paula BARRETT & Kristine PAHL,** PO Box 5699, West End, Brisbane, Queensland, Australia, 4101; ph +61 7 3846 4443

**Definition:** Promotion of cooperative behaviour, initiation and maintaining of peer and adult relationships, managing of conflict, sense of mastery and self-worth, and emotional control.

**Elements:**
- Teach children in role-play games to detect and react to other people's feelings and to feel self-esteem and competent. Example: Seat the children in a circle, pass a soft ball around and ask each child to introduce him/herself and say what colour their own hair is, how many brothers and sisters they have, what they like doing, etc. ;
- Teach interaction with other children and adults: Make eye contact, smile, speak confidently, share.
- Encourage helpful green thoughts rather than unhelpful red ones: Ask each child to hold a hand puppet which has a red sad face on one side and a green happy face on the other, read out to the children green thoughts (e.g. "I can do it!") and red thoughts (e.g. "I'm not good enough"), and ask them to show if each thought in turn is green or red by displaying their hand puppet's green happy face or red sad face.
- Promote support networks of people with whom to share love and emulate their good qualities e.g. a brave and helpful older brother or sister. Example: as a group, make a collage of drawings of support people. Have each child draw themselves together on the same poster-sized paper. To show the children how to do it, the facilitator also draws him/herself onto the same collage.
- Adjust to new situations and detect and manage their own feelings and sense what other people feel. Example: Feelings role plays (children take turns spinning a wheel with 4 feelings on it: sad, angry, happy, scared. The feeling it lands on is acted out through facial expressions and body language), say what people in magazine pictures are feeling.
- Relax: Sense and react to body clues (breathing rate, muscle tension), and self-soothe by slow deep breathing, progressive muscle relaxation, guided imagery. Example: after relaxation have children imagine their favorite place (e.g. beach, park). Ask them to imagine what they see, hear, smell, taste, and touch.
- Help the children work with parents to set realistic goals and plan small manageable steps to attain those goals, in graded exposure hierarchies to conquer fears (e.g. of the dark), and to face challenges (e.g. learn how to ride a

bike).
**Related Procedures:** *Cognitive restructuring, problem solving, relaxation, role play, social skills training.*

**Application:** Teach skill elements in playful experiential learning such as the Fun FRIENDS Program for children aged 4 to 7, in groups of 6-10 children or individually, in a clinic or school. One or more parents attend to help their child maintain and generalize skills across many settings. Children in groups are also offered 3 supplementary individual sessions.

**1st Use**? Barrett PM (2007).

**References**:
1. Barrett PM (2007). *Fun Friends: teaching and training manual for group leaders.* Brisbane, Australia: Fun Friends Publishing.
2. Barrett PM (2007). *Fun Friends: Family learning adventure: Resilience building activities for 4, 5, & 6 year old children.* Brisbane, Australia: Fun Friends Publishing.
3. Pahl KM, Barrett PM (2007). Development of social-emotional competence in preschool-aged children: Introduction of the Fun FRIENDS program. *Australian Journal of Guidance and Counselling*, 17 (1), 81-90.
4. Heckman JJ (2000). *Invest in the very young.* Chicago, IL: Ounce of Prevention Fund.
www.ounceofprevention.org/downloads/publications/Heckman.pdf

**Case Illustration:** (Barrett & Pahl, unpublished)
Sally aged 5 showed separation anxiety since starting preschool 6 weeks earlier. Sally clung to mother (Liz) causing much distress each morning when going to school and when with peers, and was distant from her teacher despite efforts to engage Sally through activities and rewards. Liz usually remained in the class for its first 15-30 minutes until Sally calmed down. Liz enrolled Sally in a Fun FRIENDS group program run at a clinic by a psychologist in ten 1.5 hour weekly sessions. The group contained 6 children including Sally. Parents were invited to attend the last part of each session: at every session each child had at least one parent present and 6-10 parents attended. Over the 10 weeks Sally also had 3 individual sessions to enhance particular skills.

At group sessions 1-3 Sally cried and was clingy when Liz left her. The psychologist who did individual work with Sally contacted her teacher to offer new rewards to promote independent behavior (e.g. reward chart using stickers, sitting in the special helper chair as a reward for positive behavior). In the Fun FRIENDS group Liz helped Sally create a 'step plan' (exposure hierarchy) to reduce separation fears, which ceased by session 8.

Sally was distant from her peers in group sessions 1 and 2 but thereafter slowly interacted more with other children. Skill training that helped her do this included: encouragement of mixing with other children using a brave voice and looking them in the eye, recognizing and expressing her feelings (e.g. doing a role-play acting out her feelings with facial expressions and body language), discussing how to be good friends (sharing, helping, listening, smiling), relaxation, and having helpful green thoughts rather than unhelpful red ones. By session 5 she engaged as much as her peers did. By session 8, Liz and the teacher noticed Sally sharing with other children and holding hands and helping and smiling at them. By the end of 10 group and 3 individual sessions, Sally showed no separation fear and related confidently and well to other children.

# CLP 80

## PUPPET PLAY PREPARING CHILDREN FOR SURGERY

Eftychia ATHANASSIADOU, Stelios CHRISTOGIORGOS, Gerasimos KOLAITIS & John TSIANTIS, 6 Gatopoulou St 152, 37 Filothei (Athens), Greece; ph +30 210 6815767 / +30 694 4787904.

**Definition:** Puppet play to prepare children for hospital and surgery by expressing feelings and learning what's involved.

**Elements:** The therapist first, in a semi-structured interview with mother (preferably alone) asks open-ended questions about: 1.`What do you feel about (child)'s operation, and what hospital and surgery experiences have you and relatives had?`; 2.`What emotional support do you and (child) get from father and other relatives?`; 3.`What have you and others told (child) about the operation, why it's being done, and how it will be done?`; 4.`What else troubles you and (child)?`. The therapist listens, contrasts mother's imagined dangers with real risks of the operation, and encourages her to talk to others about her fears and to share responsibility for the child's care in hospital and at home. Mother role-plays examples the therapist shows her of how to win trust by telling her child correctly about the hospital stay, surgery, and post-surgery pain. Semi-structured puppet play of a hospital scenario then follows with mother observing if the child asks for this. The therapist role-plays a child patient while holding a puppet child-patient, and the child holds and role-plays a puppet doctor. The puppet child-patient (therapist) talks about the hospital stay, medical procedures, surgery, and anaesthesia induction and recovery, and encourages the real child to express feelings and ask about the hospital stay and surgery. The puppet-play session concerns 1. learning to do puppet play e.g. `Let's start with the puppet making a funny comment or sound (cough). Would you like to try it?`; 2. visiting the doctor, e.g. the therapist gives the child toy medical instruments and suggests that he use these as a puppet doctor to examine the puppet patient's throat, ears and chest.; 3. being in hospital e.g.*"The puppet patient must go into hospital where he'll stay in a room with other children and perhaps his parents but he won't be able to go to school or see friends for a few days. This (puppet) patient says he misses his friends and he doesn't like doctors' examinations or injections. What can we tell him, doctor?"*; and exploring of: 4. guilt e.g. *"Am I in hospital away from my home and friends because I did something wrong?'*, 5. separation anxiety e.g. *"Will they take me away from my mother?"*, 6. fantasies about the operation and recovery e.g. *"Will it hurt? Will I see them cutting my tonsils? Will they take out only my tonsils? Will I wake up again?"*

**Related Procedures:** *Play therapy, reverse role play, role play.*

**Application:** Children hospitalized for surgery.

**1st use:** Cassell S, Paul M (1967).

**References:**
1. Cassell S, Paul M (1967). The role of puppet therapy on the emotional responses of children hospitalized for cardiac catheterization. *Pediatrics*, 71, 233-9.
2. Linn S, Beardslee W, Patenaude A F (1986). Puppet therapy with pediatric bone marrow transplant patients. *J.Pediatr Psychol*, 11, 1.
3. Abbott K (1990). Therapeutic use of play in the psychological preparation of preschool children undergoing cardiac surgery. *Issues Compreh Pediatr Nurs*, 13, 265- 277.
4. Athanassiadou E, Tsiantis J, Christogiorgos S, Kolaitis G (2009). Evaluation of the effectiveness of psychological preparation of children for minor surgery by puppet play and brief mother counseling. *Psychother & Psychosom*, 78, 62-63.

**Case Illustration:** (Athanassiadou, unpublished)
Nick aged 5 became hyperactive and anxious before admission for a tonsillectomy (his first time in a hospital). When Nick was admitted the day before operation a therapist asked if he'd like to play with puppets about his hospital stay and operation while mother looked on but did not participate. Nick held, and role-played being, a puppet doctor. The therapist held, and role-played being, a puppet child-patient: *"I'm here to have my tonsils out but don't know what will happen to me. I'm frightened and want to ask lots of questions. Will I have an injection?"* Nick took a play syringe from a doctor's play kit and began `injecting' the puppet-child-patient held by the therapist while saying to himself repeatedly `I'm afraid of injections - I don't want another one. Therapist (holding and speaking as the puppet-patient): *"Yes, I too am afraid of injections. They hurt a bit, but while having them I use tricks like counting to 10 and imagining I'm doing something else I really like such as swimming on a lovely beach. Doctor, why am I going to have an operation? What's wrong with me? Am I being punished for something?"* The therapist outside role play encouraged Nick to role-play the puppet doctor's replies: `*Tell him why he's having the operation - he seems worried*". Nick seemed distracted and hyperactive, walking back and forth holding the play-syringe, and said `I must have done something wrong. My mother often says if I'm not a good boy I'll go into hospital. I don't know what tonsils are and why mine must come out'. The therapist asked outside puppet play if Nick understood how tonsils are removed. Nick said his friend told him they would cut open his head and then close it. Resuming role play as puppet doctor, Nick became aggressive, hitting the puppet patient with the syringe as he thought doctors would do to him. The therapist reassured Nick outside puppet play

that nothing like that would happen – the operation aimed to make him better and stop future pain. Therapist as puppet-patient: `Are you sure they won't cut anything else off my body?', `Will it hurt a lot, doctor?' Outside role play the therapist prompted Nick to answer as the puppet doctor that nothing else would be cut off. - therapist as puppet patient: "You can tell our little patient that he won't feel anything because he'll have medicine to sleep during the operation". Nick: "Will he wake up afterwards?" Therapist: `Yes, of course. After the operation is over he'll wake up as he wakes from sleep every morning.
Some days after surgery Nick appeared to be happier and calmer.

# RECIPROCAL ROLE PROCEDURES, DESCRIBING & CHANGING

Anthony RYLE, Westerlands Lodge, Lavington Common, Petworth, West Sussex, GU 28 OQL, UK

**Definition:** Helping patients describe, recognise and change dysfunctional Reciprocal Role Procedures (RRPs). RRPs are patterns evident in the patients' relationships and self-management e.g. care-dependency, control-submission, abuse-victimisation.

**Elements:** Based on the patient's history, interaction with the therapist, and diary keeping, the therapist and patient identify, discuss and record dysfunctional states - the feelings and behaviours that accompany the patient's enacting a given role with reciprocating others. As dysfunctional RRPs are identified their antecedents and consequences (including switches to other RRPs) are summarised in writing and in sequential diagrams. These extend the patient's self reflection and help the therapist avoid reciprocating and reinforcing dysfunctional RRPs. For example: A patient may show the RRP anxious striving in relation to critical conditional acceptance through perfectionism and excessive striving to please others, including the therapist. He might come to feel exhausted and abused, at which point striving to please might be replaced by resentful striving, expressed as passive resistance. The sequential diagram (see below) demonstrates how both striving and resentment maintain the existing RRP. The therapist may be seen as offering critical and conditional acceptance and can challenge that perception and help the patient see the impact of these RRPs and explore alternatives. In Borderline Personality Disorder, more or less dissociated RRPs such as bully in relation to victim, ideal care seeking in relation to perfect carer and soldiering on, or affectless zombie in relation to perceived demand are common and switches are frequent between them and may seem unprovoked. This may confuse patients and evoke counter-hostility or unrealistic offers of care from staff. In such cases use of the diagrams in daily life and in sessions to recognise, control and replace dysfunctional RRPs by more adaptive ones is particularly valuable.

Sequential Diagram

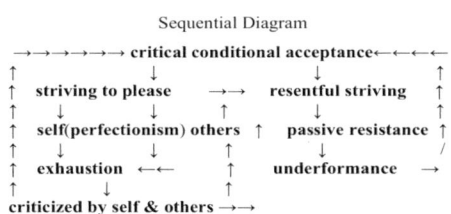

## CLP 80

**Application**: Supporting constructive, collaborative non-collusive work in therapy and management in individual and group settings. In teaching and supervision, can enlarge clinicians' awareness of intra- and interpersonal reactions.

**Related procedures**: *Transference interpretation, use of countertransference, diary keeping, writing therapy, reframing, personal construct techniques.*

**1st Use?** Ryle A (1975). *Frames and Cages.* Pp 36. London: Chatto & Windus for Sussex University Press.

**References:**
1. Ryle A (1975). *Frames and Cages.* Pp 36. London: Chatto & Windus for Sussex University Press.
2. Ryle A, Kerr IB (2002). *Introducing Cognitive Analytic Therapy.* Chichester, Wiley.

**Case Illustration:** *(*Ryle, unpublished)
M had had numerous contacts with mental health services since her father's death and the birth of a congenitally handicapped child six years ago. She had broken off contact from therapy and counselling several times. Care workers called her 'overpoweringly loud'. She had had a brief admission to a psychiatric ward 2 years previously. She described low mood, suicidal ideas, panics and anger, and had Borderline Personality Disorder. She received 24 sessions of cognitive analytic therapy). The patient said she had been raised by her grandmother apart from her siblings, who never accepted her (rejecting to rejected RRP). Grandmother could be overprotective and at other times harsh; M was the same with her children (either overprotective or harsh in relation to depending RRP). Over sessions 1-4 M and the therapist identified three recurrent dysfunctional states and associated RRPs, and drew a sequential diagram linking these:
1. VICTIMISED state: RRP victim in relation to controlling neglect.
2. RAGE state: RRP anger in relation to perceived threat or rejection.
3. POWERFUL CARETAKER state: RRP controlling care in relation to submissive dependence.

The therapist and patient traced the sequences between the states. When M sees others as being or likely to be neglecting or controlling she feels she is or will become a victim. When anticipating or responding to this she gets angry (RAGE state), shouting and ignoring others and provoking rejection. She is most secure in the POWERFUL CARETAKER state where she feels in control but where others are submissive and dependent and don't meet her needs. She risks dependency only with her husband.

As M and the therapist came to recognise these states and RRPs as they appeared in sessions the therapist suggested that they were developing a new listening in relation to listened to RRP. Gradually M became more able to reflect and care for herself and lessen control of her children. In session 19, however, she arrived in a bad mood, dismissed the therapy as useless and refused to take off her coat, saying she was leaving. The therapist suggested she was angry because of perceived rejection implied by the impending end of therapy. They used the summary of state sequences to understand this. For sessions 20-23 M conversed calmly and acknowledged how her loud voice had been a way to hide her insecurity. They exchanged 'goodbye letters' in session 24; in hers, M expressed gratitude for the changes achieved. Scores on a measure of identity diffusion fell from a borderline to a normal level.

# REPAIRING RUPTURE

**Jeremy D SAFRAN,** Department of Psychology, 65 Fifth Ave. New School for Social Research, New York, NY 10003; ph +1 212 229-5727 / fax 3259

**Definition:** The therapist repairs a rupture in the therapeutic alliance with the patient by using one or more different procedures. In *confrontation ruptures* the patient shows problems in the alliance by expressing hostility or criticism toward the therapist. In *withdrawal ruptures* the patient manifests alliance problems by withdrawing from the therapeutic process or by deferring or expressing negative feelings indirectly.

**Elements:** a) The therapist senses a rupture in the therapeutic alliance, b) draws it to the patient's attention (e.g. *'I sense a feeling of tension in our relationship right now. Do you feel the same?'*), c) explores the patient's experience of the rupture (*'Do you have any sense of what you're experiencing right now?'*), and d) tries to resolve the rupture in different ways such as 1) clarifying any misunderstanding, 2) reiterating the therapeutic rationale (*'Exploring that's going on between you and me may help us understand what's going on in your relationship with other people'*) in order to strengthen the alliance, 3) empathizing with the patient's experience, 4) accepting responsibility for his/her own contribution to the rupture, 5) responding non-defensively to the patient's concern, 6) collaborating with the patient to try to establish a shared perspective on what is taking place in the relationship (*'We're both feeling criticized and trying to blame the other person for what's taking place between us'*).

**Related procedures:** *Transference interpretation, addressing empathic failures.*

**Application:** This therapeutic principle is relevant to a range of different therapeutic modalities.

**1st Use?** Safran JD et al (1990)

**References:**
1. Horvath AO, Bedi RP (2002). The Alliance. In JC Norcross (Ed.) *Psychotherapy relationships that work.* New York: Oxford.
2. Safran JD, Muran JC (2000). *Negotiating the therapeutic alliance: A relational treatment guide.* New York: Guilford Publications.
3. Safran JD, Crocker P, McMain S, Murray P (1990). Therapeutic alliance rupture as a therapy event for empirical investigation *Psychotherapy*, 27, 154-165.
4. Strauss JL, Hayes AM, Johnson SL, Newman CF, Brown GK, Barber JP, Laurenceau J-P, Beck AT (2006). Early alliance, alliance ruptures, and

symptom change in a nonrandomized trial of cognitive therapy for avoidant and obsessive-compulsive personality disorders. *J.Consult Clinical Psychology*, 74, 337-345.

**Case Illustrations** (Safran & Muran 2000)

*1. Repair of confrontation rupture*

Susan was depressed, in her early 20s, and on an antidepressant. She'd improved once three years earlier with an antidepressant, but relapsed one month ago for no clear reason. She was extremely ambivalent about psychotherapy, feeling this implied she was to blame for her problems. More than once she asked her therapist if he felt she should be on antidepressants; he sensed she was testing him to see if he could accept that her depression was biological and therefore beyond her control. The therapist tried to explore the meaning of her question and to convey that he'd support whatever she decided, but she seemed to regard any exploration of her experience as intrusive and any reassurance as hollow. During such exchanges the therapist felt cautious, unspontaneous, and concerned about saying the wrong thing. On one occasion he said: *"It feels to me as if we're two chess players, carefully sizing one another up and trying to decide their next move. Do you know what I mean?"* Susan said the image fitted her too, so he asked her what it felt like to be playing chess with him. This led to exploration of her need to act with extreme caution in order to protect herself from him, which in turn helped her to start exploring her deep mistrust and feelings of vulnerability.

*2. Repair of withdrawal rupture*

Sam was a middle-aged writer who sought treatment for a writer's block and associated depression. From the start his therapist was struck with his thoughtfulness, intelligence and psychological maturity. Sam had clearly struggled deeply with important issues in his life and worked out a well-articulated philosophy. In their first few sessions the therapist found herself greatly admiring Sam and doubting her own ability to help him. To try to explore what might be going on in their relationship she said to Sam *"You know, I find myself really admiring you. You've obviously thought about things deeply, and I find myself respecting your wisdom. At the same time, I find myself wondering if anything I could say or do would be of value to you. You seem to be generating your own answers as you raise the questions, and you seem very self-sufficient to me."* This opened the door to a core relational theme for Sam that was interfering with the establishment of an alliance. Over time he was able to talk about his sense that others could not be counted on and that he would ultimately have to look after himself. A related link was between his self-esteem and experiencing himself as wise, and his difficulty in seeking help from another since this would threaten his self-esteem.

# REPERTORY GRID TECHNIQUE

**David WINTER**, School of Psychology, University of Hertfordshire, College Lane, Hatfield, Herts., AL10 9AB, UK; ph +44 1707 285070

**Definition:** The therapist uses repertory grid (RG) technique to assess a client's system of personal constructs - bipolar dimensions (e.g. conservative-radical, deep-superficial) used to interpret and anticipate events.

**Elements:** The therapist first elicits (e.g. by asking for names fitting role titles such as 'someone I like', 'someone I dislike', 'my partner') *elements* of the client's world (the term has a different meaning from this section's heading). RG *elements* usually concern significant others and/or aspects of the self (e.g. `myself now'; `how I would like to be'; `myself as others see me'), but may relate to life events, relationships, or therapy sessions. Next, the therapist elicits *constructs* from the client, usually by taking triads of *elements* elicited (e.g. `myself now'; mother'; `father'), and, for each triad, asking for some important way in which two of the triad's *elements* are similar and thereby different from the third. Finally, all the RG *elements* are sorted on all of the constructs, usually by the patient rating them on a 1-7 scale where 1 and 7 denote the contrasting poles of the construct, or by ranking them. After the session the therapist can use software to analyse the resulting grid of ratings statistically, or simply 'eyeball' the grid without any computer analysis. Statistical analysis, if used, reveals similarities and differences in how the client construes *elements*; relationships between his/her *constructs*; conflicts and dilemmas; and aspects of the structure of the construct system, such as the strength of relationships between constructs. The therapist may also scrutinise the content of the client's constructs. The grid may indicate aspects of the client's view of the world of which s/he was previously unaware and on which therapy might usefully focus (e.g. positive implications of the client's symptoms revealed by correlations between constructs describing the symptoms and other constructs in the grid), and a pictorial representation of these may be shown to the client. It also yields individualised measures to monitor therapy outcome e.g. dissimilarity in construing of self and ideal self; correlations between constructs indicating dilemmas.

**Related Procedures**: *Laddering.*

**Application:** Usually with individuals, but also with couples, families, and groups, particularly in personal construct psychotherapy, which focuses on the client's reconstruction of his/her world, involving revision of existing constructs and experimentation with new ones.

**1st Use**? Kelly (1955).

**References:**
1. Kelly GA (1955). *The Psychology of Personal Constructs.* New York: Norton (republished by Routledge, 1991).
2. Fransella F, Bell R, Bannister D (2004). *A Manual for Repertory Grid Technique.* Chichester: Wiley.
3. Winter DA (1992). *Personal Construct Psychology in Clinical Practice: Theory, Research and Applications.* London: Routledge.
4. Winter DA (1988). Reconstructing an erection and elaborating ejaculation: personal construct theory perspectives on sex therapy. *International Journal of Personal Construct Psychology*, 1, 81-99.

**Case Illustration:** (Winter 1988)
Sam, aged 25, came for psychotherapy for help with difficulties in obtaining an erection of five years duration. The therapist elicited the following *elements:* 14 people fitting the role titles mother, father, other close relatives, a man and a woman I like, a man and a woman I dislike, someone in authority, women with whom I've had a sexual relationship, together with 'myself', 'my ideal self', and 'myself without a sexual problem'. The therapist then elicited 12 *constructs* by asking Sam to compare and contrast the people in 12 triads of these *elements*, plus the construct 'has sexual difficulties – does not', and 2 constructs that Sam had used in discussing his problems - 'sexually attractive – unattractive' and 'lovable – unlovable'. The grid was completed by asking Sam to rate his *elements* on a 1-7 scale on each *construct*. After the session, the therapist entered the grid into a computer, and statistical analysis showed, surprisingly, that Sam rated 'myself without a sexual problem' as further from 'my ideal self' and less honest and lovable than 'myself now', and also that Sam's ratings of people as 'sexually attractive' and as 'often like to dominate' were correlated. The grid gave a clue to the origin of such constructs by showing that his ratings of 'myself without a sexual problem' resembled his ratings of 'my father'. Feedback of such grid results to Sam led him to recall occasions from his childhood when he had seen his father flirting with other women, and being 'ridiculous' in front of his mother. Sam imagined that if he could obtain an erection he might behave as sexually inappropriately as his father had, even to the extent of becoming a rapist. Discussion of insights from Sam's repertory grid allowed him to accept that his negative view of sexuality based on his childhood perception of his father were now obsolete, freeing him to explore alternative views of his adult relationships. After 6 1- hour sessions, a repeat grid assessment showed that he now rated 'myself without sexual problems' more like he rated 'my ideal self' and as honest and lovable, and that he no longer rated sexually attractive people as dominating. He had begun sexual relationships again, and on most such occasions obtained an erection.

## RITUAL (RESPONSE) PREVENTION

**Brian PILECKI** & **Dean McKAY**, Department of Psychology, Fordham University, Bronx, NY, USA; ph +1-718-817-4498

**Definition:** A method to help patients learn to stop carrying out obsessive-compulsive rituals which switch off the anxiety triggered by obsessive thoughts. Ritual prevention is typically preceded by exposure to feared/avoided stimuli that trigger the rituals, hence the term exposure with ritual prevention (ERP).

**Elements:** The therapist encourages patients to confront feared/avoided situations while refraining from carrying out rituals (compulsions) that they've been using to reduce distress. The patient eventually discovers that distress dies down anyway without the use of rituals and that not carrying out rituals incurs no harmful consequences. Ritual prevention may be guided by a therapist, family members, or by patients themselves. It involves real and/or imagined stimuli. Ritual prevention is accomplished by simple abstinence, encouraging replacement behavior incompatible with the ritual (e.g. playing the piano instead of washing hands repeatedly, or watching an enjoyable television show instead of doing ordering rituals like re-arranging items on a shelf), self-reward of successfully-prevented rituals by good food, money or other incentives, or other ways of breaking the cycle of obsessions and rituals. With repeated exposure to the initially anxiety-evoking stimuli plus prevention of the formerly-ensuing rituals the patient learns that not ritualizing is unlikely to bring on feared outcomes. The goal is to completely master urges to engage in rituals.

**Related procedures:** *Exposure, flooding, modification of expectations, modeling, behavioral experiments.*

**Application:** ERP can be guided individually or in a group, as an in- or outpatient and/or at home, with involvement of partners and/or other relatives, and with cognitive restructuring or medication.

**1st Use?** Meyer V (1966).

**References:**
1. Meyer V (1966). Modification of expectations in cases with obsessional rituals. *Behaviour Research and Therapy*, 4, 273-280.
2. Abramowitz JS (1996). Variants of exposure and response prevention in the treatment of obsessive-compulsive disorder: a meta-analysis. *Behavior Therapy*, 27, 583-600.

3. Meyer V, Levy R (1973). Modification of behavior in obsessive-compulsive disorders. In Adams HE & Unikel IP (Eds) *Issues and trends in behavior therapy* (pp 77- 137). Springfield, IL: Thomas.
4. McKay D (1997). A maintenance program for obsessive-compulsive disorder using exposure with response prevention: 2 year follow-up. *Behaviour Research and Therapy*, 35, 267-269.

**Case Illustration:** (McKay 1997)

Karen was referred for psychotherapy after asking her dermatologist for a prescription hand lotion for severely chapped hands and wrists. He saw she had no chapping on any other body area, and on inquiry found she had washed her hands and wrists excessively over the past 15 years. Her washing had worsened just prior to initiating treatment, recently for up to 100 times per day. On seeing a psychologist she was surprised to hear that she had obsessive-compulsive disorder, and reported further symptoms such as ordering objects at home, maintaining symmetry of items on her bedroom dresser, and checking doors and locks for as long as she could remember. She was extremely hesitant about starting therapy by exposure with ritual prevention (ERP). It began with her therapist modeling ERP for her - washing his hands in her presence, then touching a clean napkin to the floor, and asking her to rub her hands with that napkin. She did this and felt mild anxiety that diminished within 5 minutes. By the end of her first 90-minute ERP session she was touching the floor with her hand directly, and was asked to continue practicing ERP between sessions. Her between-session work included keeping a homework diary to track her improvement. After six 90-minute sessions she could touch feared contaminants, such as public garbage pails and doors to enter public places, without washing afterwards. Further, she only washed after using the bathroom, which was about 3-5 times a day. The therapist visited her home to develop ERP tasks in which she deliberately disordered things around her home and re- arranged items on her dresser asymmetrically. Her marked anxiety evoked by disordering tasks dissipated after about 30 minutes. In order to promote greater habituation, the therapist reminded her of the disorderly nature of her environment every 3-5 minutes. For her checking rituals, she had home sessions where she deliberately left her front door unlocked and walked around her block. She was asked to do this daily between sessions. After 23 90-minute sessions - 5 at home, the rest as an outpatient - her rituals decreased markedly, her hands stopped being chapped, and she spent little time in ordering/arranging items. Checking rituals persisted but were fewer than at the start of treatment. She then had a year-long maintenance program consisting only of twice-monthly phone calls to the therapist for guidance of daily self-directed ERP.

By 2-year follow-up her checking and other rituals had improved further.

# SCHEMA FOCUSSED EMOTIVE BEHAVIOR THERAPY (SET)

**Peter ZORN,** University Psychiatric Services, University Hospital of Psychiatry, Department of Psychotherapy, Bolligenstrasse 111, CH-3000 Bern 60, Switzerland; ph +41 31 930 99 15 / fax 88

**Definition:** In SET a therapist and a group of patients discuss structured case histories of people with various personality disorders. This is to activate, clarify and modify each patient's maladaptive schemas and associated feelings that drive distorted ways of relating to others, and so help them feel less injured and accept themselves more.

**Elements:** The group discusses each case portrayed in 4 parts – that person's:
1. Formative relationships generating negative core schemas e.g. repeatedly feeling rejected, ordinary, dependent, a devalued outcast.
2. Maladaptive ways of interacting with others (e.g. trying to be superior in order to avoid feeling inferior).
3. Ensuing bias of perceptions, interactions with others, and emotional responsiveness (e.g. self-centredness in relationships, compensatory achievement at work, inability to enjoy leisure time).
4. Activation of crises (e.g. failure to meet ones own standards, so confirming a sense of inferiority; loss of work preventing compensatory achievement).
Each patient's beliefs and feelings are modified primarily by schema-therapy methods (e.g. reframing childhood experiences as negligent or abusive), modifying negative core schemas, role-playing becoming satisfied with hitherto frustrated needs, improving self- acceptance of one's own needs. Relating to the therapist and patients in the group leads to new and corrective experiences.

**Related Procedures:** *Cognitive restructuring, interpersonal reconstructive therapy, problem solving, role play, schema-focussed therapy, transference interpretation.*

**Application:** In closed 90-minute twice-weekly groups of 6-9 out- or in-patients who have any personality disorder, to a total of 30-40 sessions.

**1st Use?** Zorn et al (2003).

**References:**
1. Zorn P, Roder V, Tschacher W, Thommen M, von Osterhausen K, Lächler

M (2003). Evaluation eines neuen kognitiv behaviouralen Gruppenprogramms (BIT) für Patienten mit Persönlichkeitsstörungen – erste Ergebnisse. (Evaluation of a New Cognitive Behavioural Group Therapy Programme (BIT) for Patients with Personality Disorders – First Results). *Nervenarzt*, 74 (Suppl. 2), S311.
2. Zorn P, Roder V, Müller DR, Tschacher W, Thommen M (2007). Schemazentrierte emotive-behaviorale Therapie (SET): Eine randomisierte Evaluationsstudie an Patienten mit Persönlichkeitsstörungen aus den Clustern B und C (Schema Focussed Emotive Behavioral Therapy (SET): Randomised controlled trial of patients with Cluster B and C personality disorders). *Verhaltenstherapie*, 17, 233-241.
3. Zorn P, Roder V, Soravia L, Tschacher W (2008). Evaluation der "Schemazentrierten emotiv-behavioralen Therapie" (SET) für Patienten mit Persönlichkeitsstörungen: Ergebnisse einer randomisierten Untersuchung (Schema-focussed emotive behaviour therapy (SET) for patients with personality disorders: Randomised controlled trial). *Psychotherapie, Psychosomatik, Medizinische Psychologie*, 58, 371-378.
4. Zorn P, Roder V, Tschacher W (2009). Schemazentrierte emotive-behaviorale Therapie (SET) – Theorie, gruppentherapeutisches Konzept und empirische Befunde zur Behandlung einer Patientin mit narzisstischer Persönlichkeitsstörung (Schema- focussed emotive behaviour therapy (SET) – Theory, concept of group therapy, and empirical results in a patient with narcissistic personality disorder). *Persönlichkeitsstörungen*, 13 (2), 104-115.

**Case illustration:** (Zorn et al, 2009)
In her thirties Ann entered a SET group of 9 patients for her `lonely depression ... at all times'. 6 years earlier she had her first of several admissions for major depression. Years before she had become anxious and begun to beat herself, mostly by hitting her face. Her group SET sessions began with the therapist describing `Mr. Great' (narcissistic personality disorder) who alternately felt excessive admiration for his "grandiose" abilities and cold scorn when he failed to live up to those, so his quest for unconditional love remained unfulfilled. This prompted Ann to recall unpleasant memories of childhood and adolescence, saying she'd struggled for love from her mother, who mostly faced Ann with contempt and approved of Ann only when she achieved something her mother hadn't attained. Ann's father had been emotionally distant but spoiled her materially. Ann became her parents' `little princess' when she got top marks. If Ann failed, her parents didn't speak to her for weeks, making her feel inferior and deserving of punishment. Ann now understood that, like Mr Great, she'd always tried to excel to please her parents, and saw similar patterns in her seeking approval from others. She chose cold unapproachable partners and tried to gain their love by excelling, e.g. by trying to be a `perfect` housewife while also excelling in her job. If she failed, she made demands on herself and punished herself as her pa-

rents had with her. Group discussions clarified such feelings and behaviours to help her become aware of and modify those. A key therapy scene was Mr Great's dream of being lost in space without contact to Earth. Hearing this led Ann to feel her chronic unbearable loneliness and frantic ineffectual attempts 'to be included'. She remembered a childhood dream of being an angel soaring through space desperately seeking, but not finding, her home planet. This activated grieving over her isolated cold childhood. For the first time Ann began to give herself the affection she had lacked by treating herself more tolerantly, regarding herself lovingly, harming herself much less, and gradually spending more time on recreation and well-being. Near the end of her SET groups her self-esteem improved and she fell in love with a more-available man who related well to others. She decided to end her current relationship and in group sessions role-played ending it without feeling guilty. By the end of session 31 she also felt less depressed and less anxious.

# SELF AS CONTEXT

**John T BLACKLEDGE**, Morehead State University, Kentucky 40351, USA; ph +1 606-783-2982; & Association for Contextual Behavioral Science Board of Directors

**Definition:** Helping people see that they have thoughts which can change, and because they can notice that change, they themselves are more stable than the shifting thoughts they notice.

**Elements:** The therapist helps a client contrast the ever-changing content of one's thoughts and feelings with the constant perspective of one's self which perceives those. For example, a client may be asked while noticing something to notice who is noticing that thing. A client thus learns that her view of her shifting thoughts and feelings etc is always from the same continuous perspective; in other words, that thoughts, feelings, and sensations are always viewed *there* and *then* from a perspective of *I*, right *here*, and right *now*.

**Related procedures:** *Cognitive defusion, mindfulness, meditation, metacognitive awareness, distancing, giving perspective, some mystical practices.*

**Application:** In individual or group ACT (acceptance and commitment therapy).

**1st Use?** Hayes et al (1999) in ACT, long preceded by related procedures in other therapies and religious observances e.g. psychosynthesis (Assagioli 1971) and mystical practices (Deikman 1982).

**References:**
1. Assagioli R (1971). *The act of will*. New York: Viking.
2. Deikman AJ (1982). *The observing self: Mysticism and psychotherapy*. Boston: Beacon Press.
3. Hayes SC (1984). Making sense of spirituality. *Behaviorism*, 12, 99-110.
4. Hayes SC, Strosahl KD, Wilson KG (1999). *Acceptance and commitment therapy: An experiential approach to behavior change*. New York: Guilford.

**Case illustration:** (Blackledge, unpublished)
   Jim was distressed by the thought that he was a "bad father" for having been unsupportive of his children, especially as he felt they mattered very much to him. The idea consumed Jim so much that he was reluctant to interact more with his children for fear that his "ineptitude" as a father might further harm them. To help Jim get distance from the thought "I'm a bad fa-

ther", the therapist said *"I'd like you to look at a few items around this room. Just look around, and when something catches your eye, tell me what it is."* Jim: "The lamp". Therapist: *"As you look at that lamp, is that lamp you or something that you are noticing?"* Jim: "It's something I'm noticing" *"Now look at that table. Is that table you, or something you are noticing?"* Jim: "It's certainly not me - it's something I'm noticing". The therapist repeated the exercise with a chair, the humming of an air conditioner, and tension in Jim's shoulders *("Is that tension you, or something you are noticing?")*. In all cases Jim said the object (or sensation) was indeed not him, but something he noticed. Therapist: *"Write the thought `I am a bad father' on an index card and place it on the table in front of you"*, and once Jim did this, asked *"Is that thought you, or something you notice?"* Jim: "It's just something I'm noticing, but it sure does describe me really well." Therapist: *"Write that thought down -`It sure does describe me really well'. As you look at that, is that thought you, or something you are noticing?"* Jim: "It's not me - I'm just noticing it". Therapist: *"So, you're still the same Jim who walked into my office 30 minutes ago? You're still 'you', right? Look at all the different things, sounds, sensations and thoughts you've noticed over the past few minutes. As you do so, notice that you are the one noticing them. So many different things to notice, and you've told me repeatedly that none of these things are you? What if you are the one who's doing the noticing, if this thought `I'm a bad father' isn't you any more than that lamp, or that tension in your back? What if you could notice that thought and carry it with you while you interact with your kids, just like you could carry that lamp or muscle tension with you while you interact with your kids?".*

# SELF-CONTROL SKILLS TRAINING

Michael ROSENBAUM & Tammie RONEN, Department of Psychology & Bob Shapell School of Social Work, Tel-Aviv University, 69978, Israel; ph +972 3 0546615215

**Definition:** Training in goal-directed skills to accept and change one's immediate experiences - feelings, thoughts, and behaviors.

**Elements:** Self-control skills training involves learning to:
1. Monitor and *accept* one's immediate experiences openly and non-judgmentally through concentration and relaxation exercises.
2. *Change* one's immediate experiences through four modules: a. cognitive restructuring (reframing thoughts e.g. *"You're not a bad mother; you came here to learn how to stop hitting your child, which means you're a good person who wants to learn to act differently"*); b. problem analysis (planning e.g. *"Let's draw a road map showing what you plan to do this week"*; evaluating alternatives e.g. *"Let's look at each of your options to see which is best for you to take"*; anticipating consequences e.g. *"Imagine 10 years have passed and you reflect on changes in your life - what were they?"*); c. increasing awareness of internal stimuli and behavior e.g. *"Close your eyes and imagine touring inside your own body and meeting your sensations during your emotions and actions: see what you meet inside when you start feeling depressed"*; and d. practising self-control exercises such as delaying gratification e.g. *"If I stood in front of you holding the remote-controlled toy car you're dying to buy and I promised to give it to you once you stopped hitting your friends, could you resist your temptation to hit?"*

**Related procedures:** *Affect regulation, delay of gratification, cognitive restructuring, problem solving, redefinition, reframing, meditation, relaxation, self-evaluation, self-observation, self-reward, self-talk, skills acquisition.*

**Application:** Help to cope with emotional and behavioral problems and stressful situations, and to enhance academic and interpersonal skills and well-being.

**1st Use?** Meichenbaum D (1985).

**References:**
1. Meichenbaum D (1985). *Stress Inoculation Training.* New York: Pergamon Press.
2. Ronen T, Rosenbaum M (2001). Helping children to help themselves: A case study of enuresis and nail biting. *Research in Social Work Practice*, 11,

338-356.
3. Rosenbaum M (1990). The role of learned resourcefulness in self-control of health behavior. In Rosenbaum M (Ed) *Learned resourcefulness: On Coping Skills, Self- Control and Adaptive Behavior* (pp 3-30), New York: Springer.
4. Rosenbaum M (1998). Opening versus closing strategies in controlling one's responses to experience. In Kofta M, Weary G, Sedek G (Eds) *Personal Control in Action: Cognitive and Motivational Mechanisms* (pp 61- 84), New York: Plenum Press.

**Case illustration:** (Ronen & Rosenbaum, 2001)
Daniel, aged 10, was referred for nightly bedwetting. His parents attended Daniel's self-control skills training sessions mainly to praise his progress. Daniel did charting, practising, and reporting. The therapist began with cognitive restructuring, saying Daniel could start to control his bedwetting by identifying and reframing maladaptive thoughts e.g. from *"I can't stop wetting, I feel nothing at night"* to *"I'll try now to control things in my sleep"*; from *"It's a sickness"* to *"I can learn how to stop wetting my bed"*.

In stage 2, problem analysis, Daniel observed links between thoughts, feelings, and behaviors (*"It's not under my control" "I don't notice when my bladder is full at night"* →*"pressure in my bladder makes me wee in bed"*), and was asked *"Every day this week write down an automatic thought you had and what you then felt and did."* Daniel wrote *"I wanted an ice-cream, took one out of the refrigerator,then thought I can practise delaying temptation, and put it back"* ).

In stage 3, Daniel was trained to raise awareness of relevant internal stimuli and behavior e.g. *"Try not to urinate immediately your urge comes - instead hold it in for a while and notice what you feel, where you feel it, how much longer you can hold it in"*, aided by relaxation and self-monitoring e.g. *"Close your eyes, focus on yourself, check if you feel any pressure in your body"*.

In stage 4, Daniel was trained to do daily self-control exercises e.g. *"Every day rate how well you resisted temptations"*), to practise: changing helpless to confident thoughts (*"Write down every time you find yourself saying* 'I won't be able to' *and immediately tell yourself* "Why I think I can do it"); delaying gratification (*"When you want to empty your bladder, try to delay weeing for 5 more minutes"*); using self-talk (*"Praise yourself immediately after you've delayed urinating"*); problem solving (*"I fear I'll wet the bed on my school trip, so I drink nothing before going to sleep"*); and having positive imagery (*"Imagine how your life will improve once you stop wetting the bed"*).

By the end of 11 weekly sessions (including intake & assessment) Daniel had stopped bedwetting. In week 12, he was asked to generalize his new skills to manage another problem with only minimal therapist guidance.

He chose nailbiting and overcame this by applying techniques resembling those he'd used with bedwetting. He asked for help only on how to measure biting and used a 1-10 scale to rate his effort to refrain from biting. Within 6 weeks he'd stopped biting his nails. At 1-month follow-up he'd wet the bed only twice. At 5-month follow-up he was completely dry and had not bitten his nails.

# SELF-PRAISE TRAINING

**Douglas H RUBEN**, Best Impressions International, 4211Okemos Road, Suite 22, Okemos, Michigan 48864, USA; ph +1 517-347-0944

**Definition:** A way of teaching passive people to say appropriately positive things about themselves without boasting, or fear of bragging, or crumbling if listeners are critical, and to sound like other healthy people sharing information.

**Elements:** In role rehearsal, the therapist first teaches the client to 'convert' other people's comments into relevant self-praise e.g. if someone says 'Hey, Garrett, my day today was great', the client replies with a remark that is relevant and converts the topic to something nice about him/herself e.g. 'I'm so pleased to hear that. I also had a great day today and really enjoyed the weather." Next, clients are taught to 'shift' conversation more markedly to something positive about themselves after acknowledging what has been said e.g. on hearing 'I really got annoyed today at my boss' the client acknowledges with a transitional "Gee, sorry to hear that. How awful. I hope things get better at work" and then invites a new topic, which is positive about themselves, e.g. "May I tell you what happened today? My kids bought me 2 concert tickets for my birthday next week.' The client practises converting and shifting daily for a month in varied company (men, women, older, younger, etc.). Finally the client rehearses and then directly solicits somebody else's opinion e.g. "Do you like my scarf/new car etc?" If the reply is critical, self-praisers are told to just say "thank you".

**Related Procedures:** *Covert desensitization, assertiveness training, social skills training, social disinhibition, role rehearsal, exposure.*

**Application:** Passive (unassertive, introvert) adults and adolescents, adult children of alcoholic families and family abuse, in homes, residential facilities, colleges, schools, and hospitals.

**1st Use?** Ruben DH (1992).

**References:**
1. Ruben DH (1992). Interbehavioral analysis of adult children of alcoholics: etiological predictors. *Alcoholism Treatment Quarterly*, 9, 1-21.
2. Ruben DH (1993). *No More Guilt: Ten Steps to a Shame-free Life*. Bedford, MA: Mills & Sanderson.
3. Ruben DH (2000). *Treating adult children of alcoholics: A behavioral approach*. NY: Academic Press.

**Case illustration:**
Maggie aged 35 feared talking in crowds or in front of coworkers, kept quiet during conversations, and always agreed with what people said. She felt her opinions were stupid, that she had no good qualities, and put herself down even if praised by others e.g. when told her dress looked lovely she instantly said 'Not really, It's a hand- me-down from my older sister and looks old and ugly on me.' This relieved her fear of being scrutinised and seeming to brag. In her first week of self-praise training a therapist role-rehearsed with her how to 'convert' people's comments into something relevant and good in her life e.g. if a friend said 'I have to plant my garden today' Maggie might reply 'Yes, I love planting. I also really like cutting the grass' Maggie practised such 'conversions' for a week between sessions. The therapist then role-rehearsed with her 'shifting' conversation more markedly to saying something positive about herself e.g. if a friend said 'I went to a new hamburger restaurant yesterday and it was good', Maggie might reply 'That's nice, I hope the food was good there. I'll have to check it out." She immediately goes on to say 'Incidentally, I must tell you about the guy I'm dating; he's so neat!'. Maggie rehearsed such shifting in real life for a week. Finally she role-rehearsed a task she found very hard - soliciting others for compliments, e.g. 'Do you like the color of my sweater?'. If people said they liked it, she thanked them without her former self-put-downs. She rehearsed soliciting compliments for a week. After nearly a month of practising self-compliments, Maggie found it easier to start conversations, not be put off by unflattering remarks, and acknowledge nice things people said of her. Her former severe anxiety dropped, and she became a regular contributor to impromptu conversations.

# CLP 80

## SIBLING FIGHTING-REDUCTION TRAINING

Douglas H RUBEN, Best Impressions International, 4211Okemos Road, Suite 22, Okemos, Michigan 48864, USA; ph +1 517-347-0944

**Definition:** A method for a parent to stop siblings fighting by having them correct the problem together as a shared task, and once they are calm and polite, allowing them to resume their pre-fight activity.

**Elements:** Resisting being a referee or listening to complaints, the parent asks each fighting child to apologize to the other e.g. both must "say sorry" to each other before they can resume their pre-fight play. If only one child says 'sorry' and the other refuses, the parent does not correct the unremorseful child but instead asks both to give each other a hug, or to shake hands if they are adolescents. If both comply, they can resume their pre-fight play. If instead, one child's attempted hug or handshake is rejected by the other, the parent ignores this and asks both children to immediately share completion of a boring simple task with a clear end-point. Afterward, they may resume their pre-fight play e.g. "Garrett and Andrew, I want you both to pick up the lint on the carpet. Garrett, you pick up the lint on the left side of the room, and Andrew you pick up the lint on the right side of the room. When you are both done you can go back to playing as before". If they complete their shared task without fuss, they resume their previous play. If one child completes the task but the other does not, the obedient child can resume the pre- fight play, whereas the dissenting child/ren are not allowed to resume this play for 10 minutes. If neither child does the shared task, the parent ignores refusals or protests and forbids both from resuming play for 10 mins. Finally, the parent is taught to praise the siblings whenever they are nice to each other. The method is repeated each time fights break out, even 10-30 times a day, until conflicts gradually subside.

**Related Procedures:** *Restitution and overcorrection (positive practice), shame aversion, contingency management, time-out response interruption.*

**Application:** Children ages 3 to 18 in households (for parents); classrooms (classmates, instead of siblings); institutional settings, camps.

**1st Use?** Adams CD, Kelley ML (1992).

**References:**
1. Adams CD, Kelley ML (1992). Managing sibling aggression: *Behavior Ther*, 23, 707- 717.
2. Olson RJ, Roberts MW (1987). Alternative treatments for sibling aggres-

sion. *Behavior Therapy*, 18, 243-250.
3. Ruben DH (2002). *Bratbusters: Say Good-bye to Tantrums and Disobedience.* New Orleans, LA: Wellness Institute, Inc. (updated, 2nd printing).
4. Macciomei NR, Ruben DH (1999). *Behavioral Management in the Public Schools: An Urban Approach.* NY: Praeger Press.

**Case illustration:**
Casey's twins aged 7 (Sherwood and Toby) were fighting and swearing in the family room, wrestling and hitting one another on the floor after having disagreed on which video cartoons to watch. Casey entered the room and told them to come to her even though they were running to her. Ignoring their tattling and "I hate you's" to each other, she asked them to each apologize to the other by saying, respectively,"I'm sorry Sherwood," and "I'm sorry Toby". After each apologized, she asked them to hug each other. Sherwood began a hug but Toby flinched from it saying 'I hate you', which Casey ignored. She asked both children to count the number of tiles on the ceiling, Toby to count the tiles on the left and Sherwood the tiles on the right side of the ceiling. "Count quietly together and work like a team, and you can return to watching cartoons." Toby counted the tiles but Sherwood didn't, blaming Toby for the fights, which Casey ignored while allowing only Toby to watch cartoons. Casey told Sherwood he could watch them in 10 minutes time. Casey resisted her temptation to scold Sherwood for his disobedience. Rather, she patiently followed the procedure 10 times more that day whenever the children argued. She continued this procedure over the next two days. By day 3 the fights had almost stopped. Casey watched for when Sherwood and Toby were happy together and praised them for getting along nicely. Two weeks later 1-2 fights reappeared and Casey immediately re-applied the same method, which stopped fights for several more days. She continued to use the method effectively when the twins got out of hand occasionally.

# SKILLS-DIRECTED THERAPY (SDT)

Tammie RONEN & Michael ROSENBAUM, Bob Shapell School of Social Work, Tel-Aviv University, 69978, Israel; ph +972 3 0546615215

**Definition:** Skills-directed therapy (SDT) trains children to develop skills that help them feel good and accord with long-term goals.

**Elements:** The therapist assesses the child to see which skills s/he: 1. performs competently; 2. lacks and how that affects behavior; 3. requires to resolve existing problems and adapt better. Parents, teachers, and peers are involved as needed. The child learns new skills in verbal (conversation, role play, behavior rehearsal) and nonverbal (drawing, sculpting, imagery) exercises in order to understand and to change thoughts, feelings, and behaviors.

**Related procedures:** *Behavior rehearsal, cognitive restructuring, contingency management, linking thoughts, feelings, and behaviors, learned resourcefulness, promoting resilience, role play, self-control, self-monitoring, self-reward, well-being therapy.*

**Application:** To reduce children's aggression and other problems and increase self- control, social, and coping skills. Given individually or in groups, with significant others involved as required.

**1st use?** Ronen T (2004).

**References:**
1. Ronen T (2004). Imparting self-control skills to decrease aggressive behaviour in a 12-year old boy. *Journal of Social Work*, 4, 269-288.
2. Ronen T, Rosenbaum M (2001). Helping children to help themselves: A case study of enuresis and nail biting. *Research in Social Work Practice*, 11, 338-356.
3. Ronen T (2006). Cognitive behaviour therapy with children: Skills-directed therapy (SDT). *The Hellenic Journal of Psychology* [Greece], 3: 1-22.
4. Ronen T, Rosenbaum M (2009 in press). Developing learned resourcefulness in adolescents to help them reduce their aggressive behavior: Preliminary findings. *Research in Social Work Practice*.

**Case illustration:** (Ronen 2004)
David age 12 lived alone with his mother. He was referred for aggressive, undisciplined behaviour over the last year at home and school, and worsening school grades over 4 months. He mistreated and fought other children and was rude to adults. David truanted or came late to school, whe-

re he was disruptive, often moved around class, wandered in hallways, ignored teachers, and did no homework. Friends stopped playing with him or inviting him home and complained about him. At home he sat still playing on his computer or watching television.

The therapist assessed David together with his mother and alone, and then saw his mother and teacher (each alone), to pinpoint skills he needed to improve e.g. resist temptation in order to sit still in class, converse with children. SDT for David included counselling of:

A. *Main teacher*, in two 40-minute meetings at school plus 20-minute phone calls twice weekly over 5 weeks, to reward positive behavior, ignore undesirable behavior, and encourage David in positive assignments e.g. lecture the class on basketball.

B. *Mother*, in four 45-minute weekly clinic sessions, to reward David's good actions, ignore unwanted behavior, and talk differently about him e.g. replace "He's hard to handle" with *"He uses my inconsistencies to get what he wants"*; replace "I'm a weak mother" with *"I need to learn skills to have him obey me"*.

C. *David*, in twelve 40-minute sessions, first weekly then 2-weekly, to develop self-control skills. In a *'research course as a scientist'* he was asked to hypothesise about his behavior and seek support for his hypotheses e.g. *"When subjects are interesting it's easier to sit still and attend"*, and to rate his own and friends' behaviors over the next week for interest levels and disruptions in each class. David learned to use: (a) *cognitive restructuring* e.g. redefine "I'm strong because I can disturb others" as *"Disturbing others is weak because I can't delay temptation; I'll prove I'm strong by sitting still and not hitting others"*; (b) *problem analysis* to link his behaviour with others' reactions to him e.g. *"I think my teacher hates me (which angers me) after I've been loud and disruptive"*; (c) *focus* on feelings affecting his behaviour e.g. "what I feel when shouting compared to what I feel when my teacher praises me"; and (d) *exercises and practice* to relax when angry, restrain urges to hurt others, imagine rewards for success e.g. *"I see and hear my mother saying she'll give me the amazing robot she's holding if I complete my homework this week"*, and when successful to praise himself e.g. *"I was wonderful today"*. By termination at week 24, David had behaved mainly positively over 6 consecutive weeks.

# SOCRATIC QUESTIONING

**Keith S DOBSON,** Department of Psychology, University of Calgary, 2500 University Drive, NW Calgary, Alberta, Canada T2N 1N4; ph +1 403 220 5096

**Definition:** Socratic questioning involves asking strategic questions to understand clients' perspectives and help them work out solutions to their problems.

**Elements:** In Socratic questioning the therapist tries to open therapeutic opportunities e.g. *"When you're depressed you seem to believe your negative thoughts rather uncritically. Are your negative thoughts always correct? Might some be unrealistically negative? Could positive thoughts be even more accurate? Perhaps we could explore how accurate your thinking is?"*. This Socratic style differs from direct instruction such as "Depressed people see things too blackly; your thinking needs to become more accurate".

Further examples of Socratic questioning aiding assessment of clients' problems and ways of dealing with those, and leading clients to develop successful strategies are: *"When a stressful situation occurs, do you always get depressed? Could one see that situation in other ways in order to feel better?"*; *"When you get angry with your partner, what does that say about your overall relationship?"*; *"Does getting anxious mean you never cope with problems?"*.

At times a direct non-Socratic style is also called for e.g.: when gathering information during initial assessment ("What signs of depression do you notice?"); in a suicidal crisis demanding quick action; telling clients about social services or how therapy might unfold; teaching assertiveness skills by role play in sessions; answering clients' requests for expert knowledge or advice about dilemmas.

**Related procedures:** *Therapeutic alliance, validation of feelings.*

**Application:** Can be used with individual clients and in group settings.

**1st use?** Beck et al (1979).

**References:**
1. Beck AT, Rush AJ, Shaw BF, Emery G (1979). *Cognitive therapy for depression.* New York, NY: Guilford Press.
2. Carey TA, Mullan RJ (2004). What is Socratic questioning? *Psychotherapy: Theory, Research, Practice, Training,* 41, 217-226.
3. Castonguay LF, Beutler LE (2006). *Principles of therapeutic changes that*

*work.* New York, NY: Oxford University Press.
4. Dobson DJA, Dobson KS (2009). *Evidence-based practice of cognitive-behavioral therapy.* New York, NY: Guilford Press.

**Case Illustration:** (Dobson unpublished)
Mia (has procrastinated asking her parents to repay money she loaned them): It would be good if I just did it. *Therapist: What would be good about it?* Mia: We'd not have this awkward issue between us. *Th: Further advantages?* Mia: I might get the money back, and use it. *Th: To buy?* Mia: A new refrigerator - ours hasn't worked well recently. *Th: Any 'pluses' for your parents?* Mia: Maybe they find it embarrassing to owe me money, and would be relieved to get this over with. *Th: Quite a few advantages. What about risks, downsides?* Mia: My parents have money - it wasn't much, and they inherited money recently. Mostly, I fear it'll be awkward. *Th: For you? them? both?* Mia: Both. But mostly I'm embarrassed to ask. *Th: Your embarrassment is in the way? Perhaps you fear what might happen?* Mia: They might be embarrassed or resent me. *Th: What's the worst that might happen?* Mia: My mom might cry. My dad might say something hurtful, that I'm cheap or forcing them to pay too soon. *Th: Pretty powerful fears! What's the best possible outcome?* Mia: They pay me and we all forget about this. *Th: This is the best? Might you see something even more positive: that you helped your parents when needed and now they can repay you? Could such support strengthen your relationship?* Mia: I never thought of it that way. I didn't think my parents would. *Th: So what's the mostly likely outcome?* Mia: Mostly likely, they'll pay me. I'll feel awkward but relieved to get it and buy a new refrigerator. *Th: Or maybe they won't have the money, or have it but want to keep it for other purposes. But at least you can talk about that openly. On balance, do you think it's worth the risk?* Mia: Yes, I think so, but I'll be nervous. *Th: That's part of your prediction. Would it help to plan your making this request, and when?* Mia: I think I'm ready. [Mia and the therapist role play her requesting the money and a date and time to meet. She's also asked to predict what will happen, how she'll feel, and her parents' reaction, for comparison with the actual outcomes at the next session. Finally, Mia is encouraged to recognize her goal is to make the effort, and the outcome is uncertain.].

# SOLUTION-FOCUSED QUESTIONING / BRIEF THERAPY

**Kirstine POSTMA,** Easington Mental Health Services, Merrick House, Easington SR8 3DY, Tees, Esk & Wear Valleys NHS Trust, UK; ph +44 0191 5275050; & **Nasa Sanjay Kumar RAO,** Logos Centre for CBT and mental health promotion, North Road, Durham DH1 4TS, UK

**Definition:** A questioning style to explore clients' possible preferred futures and their realisation based on existing resources and behaviours.

**Elements:** *Problem-free talk*: Conversation on any topic - family, work, personal interests - apart from the problem presented - in order to encourage thinking beyond that problem and reveal resources, competencies and strengths; e.g. *'Considering all that how did you manage to get up and come here this morning?', -'What does it say about you that you still managed to get your children to school on time?'*
- *Miracle question/preferred future*: Pointing out small, observable signs that are realistic and significant to the client and measurable (see below) e.g. `Imagine that tonight, while asleep, a miracle happens and your hopes from coming here are fulfilled, or the problems you bring here are resolved. In your sleep you don't realise this miracle has happened. When you wake up what difference in your life will you notice that tells you this miracle has begun?'.* Encouraging the client to detail as much as possible while focusing on the positive (*'How will you know that the problem is solved?'*) and the specific (*'...and when you feel happier, what difference in you will your wife notice first?'*).
- *Rate progress on scales* tailored to be generic (e.g. -`If '10' means how things will be after the miracle, where are you now on a scale of 0 to 10?'*) and specific (e.g. -`If 10 is you fully confident about speaking to your boss, where are you today?'*). The therapist may define '0' as worse than the client's present state (e.g. `0 is you avoiding being in the same room with your boss at all times'*). After the client rates herself, she is asked *'What is the evidence for your scoring so high?'.* Even if she rates herself at 1: `This is better than 0. What puts you there? What stops you getting worse? How will you know when you've reached '2' on the scale?'*. The therapist encourages searching for *small* changes (e.g. replying to the boss when he asks her something, speaking a bit louder, looking into his eyes when speaking to him, etc.).
- *Constructive feedback*: This is specific and within what the client has revealed, emphasising resources and strengths, while acknowledging the difficulties faced.

**Related procedures:** *Goal-setting,* s*ocratic questioning, well-being therapy,* *happiness interventions, problem solving* (but SFQ focuses not on the problem but on small positive changes to overcome it).

**Application:** Can be done without problem talk or as part of problem solving.

**1st use?** de Shazer (1985) at Brief Family Therapy Centre 1982, Milwaukee, USA, based on work by Milton Erickson, Gregory Bateson, Virginia Satir, Jay Haley et al.

**References:**
1. de Shazer, Steve (1994). *Words were originally Magic* W.W. Norton & Company, Inc., New York.
2. de Shazer, Steve (1985). *Keys to Solution in Brief Therapy* W.W. Norton & Company, Inc., New York.
3. George E, Iveson C, Ratner H (1999). *Problem to Solution: Brief therapy with individuals and Families - revised and expanded edition*. Brief Therapy Press, London.
4. Postma K, Rao NFS (2006). Solution-focused questioning to facilitate the process of change in CBT for neophobia in adults. *Beh & Cog Psychother*, 32, 371-5.

**Case illustration:** (Postma & Rao 2006)
John aged 18 sought help for life-long difficulties eating new foods. The therapist used solution-focused questioning to help John look for *exceptions* to his avoidance behaviour: *-Tell me about times that you did manage to eat something else?; -When was the last time you felt a bit more confident that you could overcome this difficulty?; -What about times when you refused to let this problem rule your life?* John said he had sometimes tried to eat plain white rice and fish fingers despite feeling nauseous, using willpower to counteract the fear (*self-exposure*). The therapist praised John for those experiences as proof of his own ability to help himself: `*What helped you to achieve that?; How did you deal with the difficulties you faced in doing that?; What did you learn about yourself managing to do that?* In this first, 45-minute, session John enjoyed this type of questioning and the idea of being able to help himself. His 2nd session two weeks later lasted less than 10 minutes. John had eaten a range of new foods while trying to eat something new nearly every day. Therapy time was merely used to emphasise John's courage and strength to push himself beyond his fears. Session 3, three weeks later, again lasted less than 10 minutes. He had expanded his range of tried foods and eaten what appeared on the family table and enjoyed most of it.

He had begun going out with friends and looked forward to attending Christmas festivities at his sports club a few weeks later.

# SPEECH RESTRUCTURING

**Mark ONSLOW, Ross MENZIES,** Australian Stuttering Research Centre, University of Sydney, PO Box170, Lidcombe NSW 1825 Australia; ph +61 2 9351 9061 / fax 9392

**Definition:** Procedures to reduce or eliminate stuttering by changing aspects of speech production.

**Elements:** Speech restructuring therapy trains clients to use a new speech pattern to reduce or eliminate stuttering while sounding as natural as possible. The speech pattern involves slower speech, extended vowel duration, gentle vowel onsets, continuous voicing, continuous airflow, controlled exhalation, and diaphragmatic breathing. Variants are prolonged speech, smooth speech, and fluency shaping. Programmed instruction shapes clients' speech rate or naturalness, starting slowly and moving gradually towards natural-sounding speech at a normal rate. In speech restructuring without programmed instruction the client hears and sees the therapist model speech changes in connected speech, plus video or audio examples, done slowly first and then at a natural rate. Clients who have difficulty in generalising speech improvements to everyday situations may also have exposure and/or cognitive restructuring. Typically, half of clients achieve natural-sounding speech.

**Related procedures:** *Slow speech, syllable-timed speech, metronome-aided speech, shaping, skills training, rehearsal.*

**Application:** Usually by trained speech-language pathologists/therapists, done either individually, weekly or in intensive groups which may be residential spanning days or weeks, or both, or by phone/email consultations plus high-quality web cams, in which the clinician reviews clients' recordings of their speech practice. Speech restructuring normally follows a detailed manual.

**1st use?** Goldiamond (1965).

**References:**
1. Australian Stuttering Research Centre (2003). Camperdown Program manual and speech restructuring video exemplar. Retrieved 15 Feb 08 from www3.fhs.usyd.edu.au/asrcwww/Downloads/index.htm
2. Goldiamond I (1965). Stuttering and fluency as manipulable operant response classes. In Krasner L & Ullman L (Eds.) *Research in behaviour modification*, New York, Holt, Rinehart and Winston.

3. O'Brian S, Block S, Cream A (2009). Case studies: Adults. Chapter in Onslow M, O'Brian S, Packman A, Menzies R (Eds) *The clinical trials evidence for stuttering treatments.* Austin, TX: Pro-Ed.
4. Packman A, Onslow M, Menzies R (2000). Novel speech patterns and the control of stuttering. *Disability and Rehabilitation, 22,* 65-79.

**Case illustration:** (Adapted from O'Brian et al, in preparation)
Patrick, age 47, referred himself for severe stuttering which had been present most of his life and impaired his ability to work and been the main reason he had left teaching. He reported no speech-related social anxiety. Pre-treatment, he stuttered a mean of 7% of syllables over 3 speech samples recorded outside the clinic. At the start of speech restructuring therapy, during three 1-hour weekly individual teaching sessions Patrick learned to control stuttering by speaking using restructuring Elements (see above) and rating stuttering-severity and speech-naturalness on 9-point scales. Thereafter he had one 7-hour group-practice day with 2 other patients and a clinician, aiming at stutter-free speech without programmed instruction. Patrick tried different ways of combining elements of speech restructuring to control his stuttering while sounding as natural as possible, and by the end of the day could speak with zero stuttering and natural-sounding speech. From a week later he had ten 1-hour, weekly, individual problem-solving sessions with a clinician to review progress and learn to identify and solve problems with generalising and maintaining stutter-free speech in everyday situations such as conducting interviews and giving verbal presentations at work. After 20 therapist hours (3 individual teaching hours, a 7-hour group-practice day, and 10 individual problem-solving hours), Patrick had ceased stuttering outside the clinic and his speech-naturalness was within the normal range. Patrick then had 7 maintenance sessions over 13 months, spaced at intervals of 2 weeks, 2 weeks, and 1, 1, 2, 2 and 6 months which depended on his speech samples recorded outside the clinic meeting preset criteria: stuttering below 7% of syllables and a speech naturalness score of 3 or less on a 1-9 scale. After treatment, Patrick was satisfied with his improvement. He controlled his stuttering outside the clinic most of the time, though interviews and presentations at work still proved difficult at times. To maintain gains, he still had to practise his speech regularly and to focus on controlling his stuttering much of the time.

# CLP 80

## STIMULUS CONTROL OF WORRY

Rowland FOLENSBEE, 6565 West Loop South, Suite 600, Bellaire, TX 77401, USA; ph +1 713-592-8952; & **Thomas D BORKOVEC**, Department of Psychology, Penn State University, University Park, PA 16802, USA; ph +1 814 234-6048

**Definition:** Clients are asked to 1) postpone all daily worries to one half-hour period of intense worry and 2) use this worry period to habituate by extended exposure to worrying and/or problem-solve worries over which clients have some control.

**Elements:** *Stimulus control* includes 4 instructions:
1. `Learn to detect worrisome and other thoughts that are unnecessary or unpleasant. Distinguish these from necessary or pleasant current thoughts.'
2. `Worries typically occur at various times and places; instead, confine them to a ½- hour intense-worry period at the same time and place each day.'
3. `Outside your chosen worry period, whenever you catch yourself worrying, postpone that to your worry period and attend instead to present-moment experience.'
4. `During your daily ½-hour worry period, worry as intensely as possible about your concerns and problem-solve remediable ones in order to lessen the chances of bad outcomes and develop adaptive responses'.

**Related procedures:** *Discrimination training, exposure, mindfulness, problem-solving, scheduling, thought-stopping.*

**Application:** Taught in groups or individually together with procedures like applied relaxation and cognitive restructuring to manage specific worry content.

**1st Use**? Borkovec et al (1983).

**References:**
1. Borkovec TD et al (1983). Stimulus control applications to the treatment of worry. *Behav Res Ther*, 21, 247-251.
2. Folensbee RW (1985). *Stimulus control and problem solving in the treatment of worry.* PhD dissertation, The Pennsylvania State University, PA, USA.
3. Borkovec TD, Sharpless B. (2004). In (Eds) S Hayes, V Follette, M Linehan: *Mindfulness and acceptance: Expanding the cognitive-behavioral tradition*, pp 209-242. New York: Guilford Press.

**Case illustration:** (Folensbee, unpublished)
Fay aged 25 sought treatment for chronic, debilitating worry experienced ever since she could remember. Paternal and maternal relatives had also been chronic worriers. Worrying worsened her irritable bowel syndrome. Reading worry-management books had not helped. She worried 95% of the day about actual and imagined personal, financial, and work concerns, found it very hard to stop worrying, and felt physically tense 90% of the day. After a 50-minute assessment session, Fay had four 50-minute weekly sessions done individually. She was trained to do daily practice of personalised stimulus control by engaging in present-moment focus throughout every day and postponing all her worrying to a daily, pre-selected, 30-minute worry period. Present-moment-focus instruction included four steps. 1) 'Throughout the day, catch yourself worrying as quickly as possible'. 2) 'Say to yourself, "*Stop! I'll worry about that during my worry period.*"' 3) 'Focus on your physical surroundings and describe them silently to yourself in words, e.g. describe the shape, color, and texture of something nearby'. 4) 'Return your attention to your chosen current activity such as a particular work task or recreational pastime.'

For her daily 30-minute worry period Fay was advised: 1) 'Worry in the same place separate from your daily activities in order to reduce connections between worries and your physical environment.' 2) 'Worry at the same time every day to reduce connections between worry and times of other activities'. (3) 'Throughout your daily 30-minute period of worrying, write out your worries in a free-flowing format to remain immersed in your worries and improve habituation leading to reduced worry throughout your day'.

By session 5 after 4 weeks of practising stimulus control, despite social conflicts and exposure to germs that would have triggered worrying in the past, Fay had improved markedly and felt more self-confident. By 1 month after the end of treatment she'd improved even more, worried 10% of her waking day, found it far easier to stop worrying, and felt physically tense only 5% of her waking day.

## TASK CONCENTRATION TRAINING (TCT)

Susan M BÖGELS, Department of Special Education, University of Amsterdam, PO Box 94208, Amsterdam, Netherlands; ph +31 205251580

**Definition:** TCT helps people who are too self-focussed to concentrate instead on the task in hand and other outside situations.

**Elements:** The therapist helps the client to:
1. Realise, via a rationale, discussion, keeping a diary, and short exercises, how excessive self-focus impairs feelings, thinking, and behavior, and that she can redirect attention more appropriately elsewhere. Example of an exercise: the client speaks briefly about her birthplace, first time attending mainly to her own anxiety and appearance, and a second time focussing on what she wants to say and how the public (therapist) hears that.
2. Become aware, by noting on a form after each exercise and in a diary, the % of time she focuses in problem situations on herself, on the task, and on the environment (total must be 100%), and in such situations, learn to concentrate more on the task and the environment than on herself.
3. Practise focussing on a present task and on the environment in a non-threatening situation e.g. *'walk in a forest and attend closely to what you see, hear, smell and feel, and finally to the whole experience'; 'watch the news on television while focussing all your attention on the content, and afterwards write down everything you recall.*
4. Practise focussing on a present task and on the environment in increasingly threatening situations e.g. when conversing first on the phone and later face to face, listen attentively to what the other person is saying, and then summarize that on the spot to the other person.

**Related procedures:** *Other attention-training procedures* (e.g. in sport psychology), *cognitive restructuring, exposure, mindfulness, role play.*

**Application:** Individually or in groups for adults and children with social fears of blushing, trembling, sweating and body distortions, and other problems maintained by excessive self-attention.

**1st use?** Ribordy SC, Tracy RJ, Bernotas TD (1981).

**References:**
1. Ribordy SC, Tracy RJ, Bernotas TD (1981). The effects of an attentional training procedure on the performance of high- and low test-anxious children. *Cognitive therapy and Research*, 5, 19-28.
2. Bögels SM, Mulkens S, De Jong PJ (1997). Task-concentration training

and fear of blushing. *Clinical Psychology and Psychotherapy*, 4, 251-258.
3. Mulkens S, Bögels SM, De Jong J, Louwers J (2001). Fear of blushing: Effects of task concentration training versus exposure in vivo on fear and physiology. *Journal of Anxiety Disorders*, 15, 413-432.
4. Bögels SM (2006). Task Concentration training versus Applied Relaxation for social phobic patients with fear of blushing, trembling and sweating. *Behaviour Research and Therapy*, 44, 1199-1210.

**Case illustration:** (Bögels, Mulkens, De Jong 1997)
Ann had feared blushing for decades since adolescence, when she'd been called "tomato". Before marriage she stopped working in a shop because she blushed when friends visited there. When her children reached school age, entering more social situations made her blushing fear more problematic. It stopped her taking a job. Ann had eight 50-minute sessions of task concentration training (TCT). In session 1 she said "When I blush I feel everybody looks at me, totally blocked, pre-occupied by my blushing, forget what I was saying, don't hear what people say". She was asked to keep daily diaries noting for each feared situation where and with whom she was and what was happening, her feelings and their intensity, what she attended to, and division of her attention (% self, % task, % environment), and blushing intensity. Session 2 involved listening exercises: in each the therapist told Ann one of several 3- minute stories about a holiday, first while sitting back to back with Ann (no eye contact), next while facing Ann, then with Ann being asked to focus on her blushing; finally the therapist told Ann about someone who blushed embarrassingly. Ann's task was to: a) remember each story; b) immediately after its end i) tell it back to the therapist and ii) rate attention to herself, her task and her environment and % of the story remembered. Ratings enabled her to see how self-focussing impeded listening. At session 2's end Ann was asked to do short homework tasks focussing on a) her environment in non-social situations and b) conversations in non-threatening situations (see Element 3. above), and to keep a daily diary of TCT homework tasks done throughout training. In session 3 she said "I listen better, recall more details like names and colours". In session 4 she created a hierarchy of threatening situations for TCT practice e.g. walk past people waiting at a bus stop. In sessions 5-7 she did even more frightening practice (e.g. converse about an intimate topic, speak in a group) in roleplays with the therapist (plus other staff to form a group as needed), and live during sessions and as homework. At least half of session time was spent doing TCT exercises and the rest was spent reviewing past and planning new homework. By session 8 she was less fearful, much more open, no longer blocked when blushing, disclosed her blushing problem to others, joked about it, and joined a course. She discovered not everyone looked at her nor did they act very differently if she blushed but continued her ongoing task. Blushing frequency and negative beliefs about them had reduced markedly

and fear fell slightly. Thereafter she continued using her TCT skills.

# TIME-BOUNDARY SETTING AND INTERPRETING

Jeremy HOLMES, Department of Clinical Psychology, Washington Singer Building, University of Exeter EX4 4QG

**Definition:** The analyst and client agree session times, frequency, duration (50, sometimes 45, minutes), and number, and note and work with deviations.

**Elements:** The analyst adheres firmly to the above time boundaries. At the end of sessions the analyst says *"It's time to stop"* or something similar, having occasionally, near the end, warned *"We only have a few minutes left"*. If important topics arise near the end of the session or while the patient is preparing to leave the analyst says *"Let's come back to that next time"*. The analyst notes, and uses as a prompt to interpretations, failure to attend sessions, lateness, reluctance to leave, and activity at the time boundary.

**Application:** All psychoanalytic work, whether individual, group or marital.

**Related procedures:** *Transference interpretation, countertransference, use of.*

**1st use?** Freud (1912).

**References:**
1. Freud S (1912). Recommendations to physicians practising psychoanalysis. *Standard Edition* 13, London: Hogarth.
2. Bateman A & Holmes J (1995). *Introduction to Psychoanalysis*. London: Routledge.
3. Zur O (2007). *Boundaries in Psychotherapy*. New York: APA Books.

**Case Illustrations**: (Holmes, unpublished)
*1. Maintaining a boundary in group therapy*
    John, a talented but maverick therapist, attended a weekly hour-long staff 'supervision and sensitivity group' on an acute psychiatric ward. He asked at the start of a session that the group be curtailed by 15 minutes as he and some other members of the group had to catch an early train. The therapist was tempted to comply with this request, but believing that it was important to model good boundary keeping, said *"If you choose to go early that is your decision, but I shall be here until the hour is up"*. Other group members then announced they intended to stay to the end. John also remained, and in the last 15 minutes expressed some of his difficulties and anger at having to comply with the discipline which working on the ward aroused in

him. Had he left early these would probably have been unexpressed.

2. *Missed sessions and interpreting them*

Fred began therapy when his marriage and business failed due to alcoholism and he became profoundly depressed and made a major suicide attempt. Living in a 'dry house', and having lost his driving licence and car due to a drink-driving offence, he walked 4 miles to and from therapy each week. He formed a good relationship with his therapist and by session 4 his depression had lifted, his craving for drink had lessened, and he had successfully resumed business activities and appeared robust. At session 10 the therapist 'inadvertently' double booked and had to turn Fred away when he arrived. Fred missed the next 2 sessions due to 'flu', but arrived for session 13. When examining the episode Fred first said that he understood 'these things happen', and wanted to move onto other topics. The therapist, having apologised for his inefficiency and insensitivity (and examined his 'countertransference' for possible underlying reasons, e.g. that he underestimated the patient's vulnerability), insisted that Fred consider that he had been hurt, especially given the effort needed to get to sessions, and that the subsequent missed sessions were a form of 'retaliation'. Fred then spoke of his unhappiness at age 10 when his mother had to go into hospital for several months and he suppressed his neediness and anxiety, and how such feelings may have later fuelled his cravings for drink.

# CLP 80

## TIME-IN MANAGEMENT

**Douglas H RUBEN**, Best Impressions International, 4211Okemos Road, Suite 22, Okemos, Michigan 48864, USA; ph +1 517-347-0944

**Definition:** A method of classroom and group-home management of childrens' disruptions. It improves on the "time-out-ribbon procedure" for disruptive behavior of severely retarded children, whereby the teacher gives each child the same or a different colored ribbon at the start of class to wear while doing on-task classroom behavior. The teacher also gives praise and edibles for good behavior. For bad (e.g. off-task) behavior, the teacher removes the ribbon for different lengths of time until the bad behavior stops, and is returned when good behavior reappears. In contrast, with "time-in management", when a child misbehaves removal is of the rewarding object that the child is wearing, not the child itself, so the child can learn to deal with the situation while remaining in it i.e. the child is timed in and its rewarding object is timed out. Time-in management also differs from time-out ribbon in its: use of specific short time-periods during which to change misbehavior; speeding learning by giving children many chances for good behavior; giving wearable rewards that can be earned back faster and stay valuable longer; way of teaching children to value the worn objects; use of a reward-box; reducing teachers' forgetfulness or loss of interest in the procedure. Both time-in-management and time-out ribbon differ from usual time-out by: focussing on many children, not just one at a time; giving children ways to correct misbehavior and, with time-in management, to practise this correction in quick succession over each 2-hour period.

**Elements:** The teacher or group-home parent selects a 2-hour time period during which the children misbehave, and divides this into six 20-minute intervals. At the start of the first 20-minute interval the teacher fastens onto every child an everyday object they have not worn before (e.g. piece of colored paper; bracelet, necklace, scarf etc. for girls; deputy badge, belt, hat, toy cellphone etc. for boys) by Velcro or snap-on buttons, so it can be quickly put on or removed. Objects are worn for the 2-hour period only. The object's reward value is raised by: teachers and group-home parents complimenting children wearing their object; showing the children how to compliment one another about it (e.g. "Nan, that's neat; I like it on you"); have the child compare the object worn to that worn by another child favorably or otherwise (e.g. "I wish I had your bracelet, mine is ugly;" or "I like my deputy badge more than yours"); allowing children a brief rewarding activity for a half to 2 minutes by choosing from inside a reward box a piece of paper describing the activity (e.g. "you can look at the aquarium" or "you can go on the internet for 2 minutes"). Staff scatter 2-3 reward boxes around the side/back of the room to avoid interruptions of the teacher in front of the class. Next, staff give every child the same task at the start of the first 20-minute interval (e.g. work on math problems, set the table for lunch.) If a child does forbidden things during the 20 minutes (goes off-task, makes a noise, yells, swears, threatens, etc.), the teacher immediately removes the child's object for 10 seconds and asks him/her to apologize to any peer s/he upset, before the 10 seconds expire. If the child apologises, the object is returned but the child is barred from choosing a reward activity in a box during the rest of that 20-minute period. When the next 20-minute period begins, all children start again as in the first 20-minute period.

**Related Procedures:** *Time out, time-out ribbon, contingency management, token economy, classroom behavior management.*

**Application:** For groups of 3-50 children aged 3-11 years in schools, homes, psychiatric residential facilities, youth detention and community recovery centers, rehabilitation cottages, domestic abuse and homeless shelters.

**1st Use**? As a concept, Foxx & Shapiro (1978).

**References:**
1. Foxx RM, Shapiro ST (1978). The time-out ribbon: A nonexclusionary timeout procedure. *Journal of Applied Behavior Analysis*, 11, 125-136.
2. Macciomei NR, Ruben DH (1989). *Handbook of homebound teaching.* Jefferson, NC: McFarland & Co.
3. Macciomei NR, Ruben DH (1999). *Behavioral Management in the Public Schools*: An Urban Approach. NY, Praeger Press.
4. Ruben DH (2004). Time-Out Ribbon Revisited: Revisions for Contingency Control Among Disruptive Preteen Classmates. *Behavioral Systems Monograph*, Vol 5, 1-9.

**Case illustration:** (Ruben, unpublished)
 A teacher complained to her school social worker of disruptions by her 30 seven-year-old students. They were apathetic, fooled around, and made angry remarks, especially between noon and 2pm. During this time, the teacher fastened with Velcro or snap-on buttons on each child's clothing an everyday object the children were familiar with but had not worn before (piece of colored paper; bracelet, necklace, scarf etc. for girls; deputy badge, belt, hat, toy cellphone etc. for boys). Then, the teacher gave every child the same task of working on math problems during the entire 2-hour period. The social worker rehearsed with the teacher how to compliment the children directly for on-task behavior or wearing their object e.g. "Bridget, that's a really nice scarf"; how to compare their rewarding objects with compliments e.g. having Bridget say to Melissa "Your ring is cool"; and pride without put-do-

wns, e.g. having Bridget say to Andrea "your ring is cool, though I like mine better", or making self-put-downs, e.g. "I don't like my ring as much as I like yours." The teacher also set up four reward boxes around the room's perimeter, each no bigger than a shoebox and accessible by every child. On day 1 of time-in management, each 20-minute interval from noon to 2pm included a simple cooperative task of every child doing math problems and grading a peer's answers. When Billy swore at Brad, the teacher immediately removed Billy's deputy-badge, saying "I'll return this badge to you within 10 seconds after you say sorry to Brad." Though Billy apologized very grudgingly, the teacher nevertheless returned the badge to Billy, saying in front of his classmates that he couldn't visit the reward box until the present 20-minute interval had ended and the next 20-minute interval began. Within two weeks, the class's rates of fooling around, mischievousness and showing anger to peers fell markedly. The teacher then stopped time-in management from 12 noon to 2pm, using it instead from 8am to 10am, and thereafter from 10am to 12:00 noon. By the end of 6 weeks the teacher had used the method over the entire school day and the students became cooperative with almost no classroom infractions. At 6-month follow up there were minor relapses of a couple of children talking out of turn, but no serious delinquencies warranting the re-use of time-in management.

# CLP 80

## TOKEN ECONOMY

**Isaac MARKS**, 43 Dulwich Common, London SE217EU, UK; ph+44 208 2994130

**Definition:** A form of *contingency management* to *shape* increments of behaviour towards desired goals by giving or withholding tokens that can buy privileges.

**Elements:** Staff meet together and with the patient to *problem-solve, set goals*, and decide what increments of desired behaviour will buy set numbers of tokens given with praise. As the patient improves, gradually more increments become required to earn tokens and praise, and the number of tokens needed to buy privileges is raised.

**Related procedures:** *Contingency contracting/c.management, operant therapy/operant/ instrumental/skinnerian conditioning, positive reinforcement, reward, shaping, successive approximation, behaviour modification, differential attention/reinforcement, discrimination training, prompting, time out.*

**1st Use?** Ayllon T, Azrin ND (1968) *The Token Economy: A Motivational System for Therapy and Rehabilitation.* Appleton-Century-Crofts, New York.

**Reference:** Marks IM et al (1971). Operant therapy for an abnormal personality. *Brit Med J*, 1, 647-648.

**Case illustration:** (Marks et al 1971)
Mary aged 20 had for 8 years been mostly mute, aggressive, self-neglectful, depressed, friendless, agoraphobic, and tired and did not improve with prolonged out- and inpatient care. Psychiatric ward staff and Mary set a goal of her becoming less tired and speaking again – an agreed token economy was begun to that end. She was asked to rest in bed in the ward completely undisturbed, alone without books, radio or visitors (*time out*), until her tiredness improved as shown by her talking to people. Any talking earned praise and tokens (small plastic discs) to buy time outside her room. A nurse visited Mary for 2 mins. hourly to encourage her to earn tokens by conversation. She soon began speaking for the first time in the ward. Staff reviewed progress daily and gradually raised the speech-cost of tokens from 1 to 60 secs of speech. Mary also earned tokens if she helped with ward tasks, later if she initiated tasks or did things outside the ward, and still later (after discharge was threatened), if she walked increasingly far from hospital, went on bus journeys, and took a paid job. After 7 months on the token economy Mary was discharged to a hostel. A year later she remained improved in

conversation and was working and travelling regularly and going out with friends, though she lacked spontaneity.

## TRANSFERENCE INTERPRETATION

Tirril HARRIS, Socio-Medical Research Centre, Institute of Psychiatry, St Thomas Campus, Lambeth Palace Road, London SE1 7EH, UK; ph +44 207 188 0208

**Definition:** In an *interpretation* the therapist points out hidden meanings of patients' thoughts, feelings or behaviours (often linking current with past ones) to give patients more control over them. Transference interpretations indicate how patients "transfer" expectations from past relationships onto current ones both with the therapist and with others, showing how the patient may be acting on inappropriate outdated expectations and could change to relate to others in more realistic ways.

**Elements:** By exploring together feelings linked to topics the patient has chosen to discuss, the therapist and patient identify whether, and if so how, these may concern the therapist or others. The therapist encourages the patient to explore whether these feelings relate more to past than present relationships (with the therapist and/or others), and if they do, encourages the patient to reflect on how this affects behaviour in present relationships. Experiencing support from a therapist can further correct ('work through') prior unrealistic negative expectations transferred from a past relationship.

**Related procedures:** *Cognitive restructuring, narrative exposure (imaginal), corrective emotional experience, working through.*

**Application:** In all psychoanalytic work, usually individual, sometimes with couples or groups.

**1st Use?** Freud (1895 Studies on Hysteria; elaborated 1912).

**References:**
1. Freud S (1912). The dynamics of transference. In Strachey J (1961) (Ed) *Standard Edition of the Complete Works of Sigmund Freud*, Vol.12, pp 99-108; London: Hogarth.
2. Harris TO (2004). Implications of Attachment Theory for working in Psychoanalytic Psychotherapy, *International Forum of Psychoanalysis*, 13, 1-10.
3. Hobson RP, Kapur R (2005). Working in the transference: clinical and research perspectives. *Psychology and Psychotherapy: Theory, Research & Practice*, 78, 275- 293.
4. Piper WE, Azim HFA, Joyce AS, McCallum M (1991). Transference interpretations, therapeutic alliance and outcome in short-term individual psychotherapy. *Archives General Psychiatry*, 48, 946-953.

**Case Illustrations:** (based on Harris 2004)
1. Fearful-avoidant-transference interpretation
Fiona came for therapy for depression. Questioning at intake assessment revealed that her critical mother had always preferred her talented brother, leaving her fearful of disapproval. She chose therapy on the couch; her manifest reluctance to engage in a relationship led her to avoid eye-contact. Initially she stayed silent except when the therapist unconventionally encouraged her, after which she replied briefly (e.g. "you know, in these sessions you can talk about whatever comes into your head?" "Yes ... I'm thinking about work and deadlines. But I'll just have to meet them. MORE SILENCE). In session 3 the therapist mused gently why the patient might be finding it difficult to talk free-associatively: Was it because she feared disapproval if she said something silly? Was it because she expected a rebuke for seeking too much attention and had to wait to be asked before she could volunteer something? Would she feel easier if she sat facing the therapist? If so would she like to change from the couch? If no, might she say why not? Was she reminded of any past situation, perhaps with parents? *Fiona*: Well, Mother was always comparing my "weakness" with my brother's outgoing nature. *Therapist*: So I wonder whether you feel I think you are weak for not talking? Because I don't think that. I just believe you need your own space to be ready to talk. SILENCE *Therapist*: And perhaps you think I'm going to find anything you do get round to talking about weak... or stupid? *Fiona*: Yes, that was Mother's word for me always. Stupid. Stupid. Stupid. She'd always say it three times if it was me. *Therapist*: That must have felt very undermining? *Fiona*: Yes it did *(tears in eyes)*.

ONE MINUTE PAUSE. Fiona then recounted more childhood memories, finding it easier with every comment responded to with empathy by the therapist. The therapist asked about her mother, following it up with "or does it feel a bit undermining for me to ask you this?". Fiona smiled broadly "No, not at all". In a later session Fiona said she'd felt too anxious to ask her boss if she could attend a 2-day course regarding her work. *Therapist*: Would your boss really be that fearsome about your wanting to do something so useful for your work with her? Could it be like it was with me at the beginning - that you expect her to react like your mother would have, when your boss might really not be disapproving? Fiona agreed it was possible. The therapist then explored what might **really** happen if she raised the topic with her boss.

2. Enmeshed-transference interpretation
Penny's preoccupied enmeshed attachment style meant a different transference needing a different type of interpretation. Her mother told her she'd been `spoilt', but her continuing dependency and need for attention probably came more from inconsistent care-giving from her mother and 4 older sisters as she grew up. As for many with enmeshed attachment, Penny

spoke with rambling fluency but occasionally became almost succinct – worrying whether her therapist could be trusted or was even listening. Linking these feelings with her past experiences gave relief and an incentive to continue therapy. **T:** I wonder if it's because we had to miss last week for the Bank holiday and this reminds you how your mother was often absent so you felt she didn't really care. **P:** Well sometimes she really didn't. **T:** OK, and you assume that because I wasn't here for you in the usual way I don't really care about what you want to tell me. So then you start to feel a bit clingy, even a bit fed up with me. **P:** Well no, I know you're different really, but you're right I'm sure that it's to do with missing last week. **T:** Do you remember how you felt about Mary when she was held up and you thought it was because she looked down on you? **P:** Yes it's the same isn't it? I needn't have felt like that - she's not like Mum and I know she cares really.

Towards the end of therapy Penny gave her own transference interpretation of why she felt cast down during a particular session: "I think I know why I've been feeling a bit angry and discouraged today: it's because I came here a bit early and saw the person who comes before me leaving and I thought oh yes she's blond – she's the pretty one and she'll be respected more than me. But it's the same old story isn't it? I'm bringing it from what I felt with my sisters and Mum. I don't know anything about the girl I saw leaving. Chances are she's just the same as me, no better. **T:** Yeah, chances are... **P:** PAUSE. "You know, I don't really feel so down as I did a few minutes ago".

3. Dismissive-transference interpretation

Derek was referred for psychosomatic symptoms. His dismissive attachment style reflected emotional unavailability of caregivers during his upbringing: he avoided pain by devaluing attachment needs, but respected intellectual explanations, particularly about other people. This prevented him leaving therapy after only a few sessions. Initially he was sceptical of his therapist linking a worsening of his abdominal symptoms with anything occurring in sessions ("No, with respect I don't think my pains over Easter had anything to do with there being no sessions for two weeks"), though he accepted that work conflicts might be relevant. The catalyst was a colleague's intense distress at work which he told Derek who discussed it with some amazement in his session that evening. That night he dreamed – a rare occurrence – and raised it the next week. It involved an older boy from boarding school whom he remembered "for the first time for years" as someone he had admired but had later turned against. In the dream this boy took Derek's hand but on looking again the boy seemed to have become matron, and even stranger –turned out to have the therapist's face. He woke feeling relieved about something. "The whole thing was odd, even spooky." **T:** What did you make of it? **P:** I was surprised that I felt quite fond of matron after all this time. She wasn't really my type. But was it matron or you? It definitely

197

wasn't him any more... *Briefly describes how that boy had hurt his feelings at school.* **T:** Well maybe it's telling us that you're also a bit surprised by me being another sort of matron - a person to come to about hurt feelings - and surprised by feeling a bit fond of people like that, matron and me? Perhaps you've needed to protect yourself from becoming too reliant on me, or anyone else except yourself, in case we let you down. But perhaps your dream is telling you that it's all right to relax a bit over that now. All right to let us help you?
**P:** Yes it might be. Yes ... I did feel that sort of relief, didn't I, yes.

# TRIPLE P – POSITIVE PARENTING PROGRAM

Matthew R SANDERS, Parenting and Family Support Centre, School of Psychology, University of Queensland, St Lucia, Queensland 4072, Australia; ph +61 (07) 3365 7290

**Definition:** Triple P is designed to enhance parents' knowledge, skills and confidence to prevent and manage behavioral, emotional and developmental problems in children.

**Elements include:**
1. *5 positive-parenting principles* to promote children's well being: a) Ensure a safe and engaging environment e.g. age-appropriate activities to encourage language and intellectual development; b) Positive learning environment e.g. give your child brief moments of uninterrupted positive attention; c) Use assertive discipline e.g. teach acceptable behavior, respond to misbehavior consistently, quickly and decisively; d) Realistic expectations e.g. choose goals that are developmentally appropriate for the child and realistic for you; e) Also care for your own needs e.g. take time to ensure you are relaxed.
2. *Strategies to enhance relationship with child*: a) Spend quality time and talk with them; praise good behavior, give non-verbal attention like a wink or hug; b) Teach new skills by *Ask, Say, Do* e.g. *Ask*: `What do we do just before we go to sleep?' *Say*: `That's right, we brush our teeth'. *Do*: `Brushing is hard, I'll help you put the toothpaste on the brush'; c) Incidental teaching e.g. if your child shows you a collage they've done, ask about colors, shapes and textures to prompt learning; d) To manage misbehavior: i) planned ignoring of minor problems - neutral position and expression without eye contact; ii) logical consequences e.g. remove a troublesome toy for a few minutes; iii) quiet time e.g. if child is misbehaving have them sit quietly in a section of the room for a minute, or time out e.g. if child is continuing to misbehave after using quiet time take child to a separate room to be quiet for a few minutes. Combine these strategies to prevent problems in high-risk situations e.g. while shopping give the child their own shopping list or allow them to bring their favorite toy, plan how to manage misbehavior e.g. if they misbehave with a favorite toy while shopping, then remove it.
3. *Level of intervention* depends on severity of the child's problem: a) media to educate all parents about positive parenting e.g. radio/television shows, public-service announcements, newspaper columns; b) & c) brief primary care consultations for mild-moderate problems; d) more intensive family work for more severe problems. Levels b) to d) can include group, individual, phone or self-directed sessions. Level e) involves working with families whose difficulty continues after levels a)-d).
4. *Multi-disciplinary*: involve required service providers e.g. health visitors,

community child health nurses, family doctors, paediatricians, teachers, social workers, family support workers, psychologists, psychiatrists, counsellors, parent educators, police officers.
5. *Self regulation*: Promote parents' self-management skills e.g. problem solve, identify causes of child's or own behavior, set own goals, self-monitor own performance, manage parental tasks confidently.

**Related procedures:** *Behavioral family therapy, behavior rehearsal, contingency management, parent training, skills training.*

**Application:** In appropriate settings: the media (3 a. above); at work; with parents of children in day care, pre-school and school; in primary care e.g. general practitioners, nurses, phone counselling; mental health service e.g. intensive group and individual programs. For parents of children from birth to age 16, one facilitator runs up to 5 sessions 90-120 minutes long over 8 weeks with 10-12 parents in a group or just 1-2 parents in an individual setting, and uses slides, DVD, workbook activities e.g. `identify behaviors to praise your child for', and role play of positive-parenting strategies (2. above), followed by 3 individual 15- to 30-minute phone discussions of topics the parents choose. Brief Triple P programs (3 b and d above) may take just 1-4 sessions 30-60 minutes long. Triple P *variants* are for parents of children age 0-12 years (*Group, Standard*), age 12-16 (*Teen*), age 0-12 who are developmentally disabled (*Stepping Stones*) or age 5-10 who are overweight (*Lifestyle*), and for parents who are working (*Workplace*) or divorced/separated (*Family Transitions*).

**References:**
1. Sanders MR (2007). The Triple P-Positive Parenting Program: A public health approach to parenting. In JM Briesmeister & CE Schaefer (Eds.), *Handbook of parent training: Helping parents prevent and solve problem behaviors* (3rd ed.), pp. 203-233. Hoboken, NJ: John Wiley & Sons Inc.
2. Sanders MR (2008). The Triple P-Positive Parenting Program as a public health approach to strengthening parenting. *Journal of Family Psychology*, 22(4), 506-517.

**Case illustration:** (Sanders 2007)
    Jane and Tom sought help for severe problems with their son Jamie aged 3. He had tantrums at home and in public, hitting, kicking, and head butting them and his sister, swore, and had bedtime problems. He ransacked his room and destroyed toys when rebuked or denied his wishes. His behavior meant outings were often cut short or avoided. They gave him little presents daily when he behaved badly, to calm him and allow Jane some peace. Jane and Tom felt stressed, tired, out of control, and ruled by Jamie.
    At intake the therapist interviewed the family in the clinic for 50 minu-

tes, and observed parent-child interactions at home for 20 minutes. Over 8 weeks, Jane and Tom joined 8 other parents in 5 Triple-P 2-hour group sessions led by a therapist in the clinic, and also had 3 individual phone consultations on a speaker phone. Advice about Jamie included: a) give praise, attention, and frequent brief one-on-one contact to increase desirable behavior, and tell him what is and is not acceptable, especially at bedtime; b) when he misbehaves, give Jamie clear and calm instructions, logical consequences e.g. remove his toys when he's damaging them, ignore him or use quiet time when he doesn't follow instructions. Jamie's parents role-played how to give clear calm instructions and to use quiet time, and were encouraged to discuss Triple-P with staff when Jamie attended daycare.

At 8 weeks there was marked improvement in Jamie's behavior, Jane's depression (Tom's mood was normal throughout) and parental stress. Jamie was now rewarded for good behavior and his bedtime problems decreased. The family went out more, and people commented on Jamie's good behavior. The bond strengthened between Jamie and his parents, who had become firm, decisive, calm, and consistent.

## TWO-CHAIR TECHNIQUE

Leslie S GREENBERG, Department of Psychology, York University, Toronto, M3J 1P3, Canada; ph +1 416 736 2100, fax 66111

**Definition:** Encouraging a client to dialogue between two aspects of the self, one aspect expressed while sitting in one chair and the other expressed while sitting in the other chair, switching as needed from one chair to the other.

**Elements:** After a relationship has been established, on noticing that a client has expressed a split into two opposed parts of the self, one of which is expressed in a harshly critical voice ("inner Critic") e.g. `I'm such a loser` or `... too stupid, ... fat, ... ugly, ... needy, ... selfish`, the therapist may prompt a client to start a two-chair dialogue. When sitting in the Critic's chair the client speaks from that perspective, often using the unquestioned language of a parent or society as a whole e.g. `I guess it's "You don't live up to what I wish/expect, to your potential, I know there could be so much more but you don't allow it.`' Seated in the Experiencing/Self chair the client expresses how it feels to be criticized e.g. `Yeah (crying), I can't find anything to hold onto, can't see where I've ever been able to do it, be effective, I don't have any confidence at all`. The client might switch, often in mid-sentence, from sitting in one chair speaking from one self to sitting in the other chair speaking from the other self. When perceiving switches in an aspect of the self during the dialogue the therapist may prompt the client to switch chairs as required. Contempt expressed from the Critic's chair e.g. `You're pathetic` might first evoke hopelessness and then shame expressed from the Experiencing chair e.g. `I feel so worthless, like curling up into a ball and hiding` and later more adaptive feelings such as anger and sadness and then self-assertion e.g. `Leave me alone. Stop attacking me like that`. Resolution of the split might be seen with the Critic softening into compassion e.g.: `I don't want to make you suffer, I do care about you` or the two sides negotiating a solution e.g. `I understand you need my support, I'll be right behind as you go out and apply for a job` or more often integrating into self-acceptance and better self-esteem e.g. `I feel stronger, more confident`.

In a "self-interruptive split" one part of a client may interrupt feelings of another part e.g. `I close off my feelings, don't allow myself to feel`. In two-chair dialogue the interrupting part is expressed in one chair e.g. `Don't feel it, it's too dangerous, hold your breath, distract` and the interrupted part is eventually expressed in the other chair e.g. `It's like being in a cage, let me out`.

By the end of therapy a client may have engaged in many dialogues each lasting 10 to 50 minutes, usually in alternate sessions.

**Related procedures:** *"Hot seat"* & *Gestalt therapy* of Fritz Perls, *psychodrama, role reversal.*

**Application:** In individuals and groups, especially for self-critical depression and for catastrophising in anxiety disorders.

**1st use?** Carstenson (1955).

**References:**
1. Carstenson B (1955). The auxiliary chair technique – a case study. *Group Psychotherapy, 8*, 50-56.
2. Greenberg LS (2002). *Emotion-focused therapy: Coaching clients to work through their feelings.* Washington, DC: American Psychological Association.
3. Greenberg LS, Rice LN, Elliot R (1993). *Facilitating Emotional Change: The Moment by Moment Process.* NY: Guilford Press.
4. Perls FS (1969). *Gestalt Therapy Verbatim.* Lafayette, California: Real People Press.

**Case illustration:** (Greenberg, unpublished)
Mid-life Eva tearfully reported feeling down and unresolved family issues. She criticised her failure in family relationships: `My sisters are all married and successful. I've been the black sheep'.` One treatment goal was to resolve her self-critical conflict split.

In session 4, the therapist encouraged Eva to start a self-critical two-chair dialogue by pulling up a third chair and saying *"Let's try something. You seem to have two voices, one critical and the other reacting to it. You can dialogue between them, expressing the critical voice while sitting in that third chair and switching to sit in your present chair when answering that voice.* Eva connected her bad feelings to parental criticism, saying in her parent voice: `You've never amounted to anything. You didn't complete University. Look at you - you wear rags'.` During her dialogue her critical voice when sitting in the third chair eventually softened and on switching to sit in the other chair her answering voice showed a sense of worth emerging: `Even though mom and dad didn't love me or show me love, it wasn't because I was unlovable, it was just because they were incapable of feeling or showing love. They still don't know how to love'.` Eva now felt less hopeless.

In sessions 5 & 6 Eva's dialogue worked on her feeling bad about her father's physical and verbal abuse via emotional exploration aided by the therapist's empathic responding and Eva's using other two-chair dialogues. In session 7, Eva and the therapist identified how Eva interrupted and protected against the pain of not having her needs met by laughing whenever she was sad. In session 9 in the "interrupter" chair she said "*You're wasting your time feeling bad because you want them, and they're not there. So it's best to shut your feelings off and not need them. That's what I do. When people hurt me enough I get to a point where I literally cut them out of my life like I did with my mother."*

Eva engaged in self-critical and self-interruptive two-chair dialogues in 4 of her 14 sessions and each lasted about 40 minutes. Other sessions involved empathic exploration and other types of two-chair dialogues. By the end of therapy the hopelessness that was so dominant in early sessions had virtually gone. Her voice wanting love and acceptance became stronger and the critic's voice softened to express acceptance of this part of her.

## VALIDATION OF FEELINGS

**Rosario ESPOSITO**, Scuola di Psicoterapia Cognitiva, Napoli, Italia; ph +39 347 7858036

**Definition:** Communication to a sufferer that what s/he feels is right (valid), worthy and important in her current situation.

**Elements:** Show understanding of what people say, empathy with what they feel, confirmation that it is valid, legitimate and important.

**Related procedures:** *Showing empathy or compassion, paradoxical intention.*

**Application:** Individually or in groups for distressed people, especially those with low self-esteem, at any age. Can be used as part of many therapies.

**1st Use?** Linehan (1993).

**References:**
1. Linehan M (1993). *Cognitive-Behavioral Treatment of Borderline Personality Disorder*. New York: Guilford Press.
2. Gilbert P (2005). *Compassion: Conceptualisations, Research and use in Psychotherapy*, pp 195-217. Hove, UK: Routledge.
3. Leahy RL (2005). A Social-Cognitive Model of Validation. In Gilbert P (Ed.) *Compassion: Conceptualisations, Research and use in Psychotherapy*, pp 195-217. Hove, UK: Routledge.
4. Mahoney MJ, Arnkoff DB (1978). Cognitive and self-control in therapies. In Garfield SL, Bergin AE (Eds.), *Handbook of Psychotherapy and Behaviour Change: An Empirical Analysis* (2nd ed., pp 689-722). New York: Wiley.

**Case illustration:** (Esposito, unpublished)
After his relationship had ended a year earlier, Pat, a very insecure man, became depressed, failed to improve with medication and cognitive restructuring from 3 therapists, and seriously overdosed on antidepressants. When Pat said "I'm bad, depressed, can't sleep, cry, don't enjoy eating or doing other things I liked before", his new therapist replied "I understand what you're saying. It's important, normal and natural. Go home, stay in bed, and don't eat if you don't want to, just do as you feel" in order to empathise with and validate what Pat felt and referred to despite Pat's sense of being worthless. Pat did not answer but looked surprised and calmer, and went home and did as the therapist suggested. Pat phoned two days later saying

he felt better. In another session Pat said "I did everything wrong, am useless with people, she was right to leave me". The therapist answered: "I understand why you say that, and agree with you". Pat again stayed silent and seemed surprised, and at the next session said he felt better.

The therapist applied such validation repeatedly plus cognitive restructuring and skills training during 1-hour sessions given weekly for a year, then fortnightly for 6 months. Pat improved and continued so to 3-year follow-up. Antidepressants had continued to 6-month follow-up.

## VALUES EXPLORATION AND CONSTRUCTION

John T BLACKLEDGE, Morehead State University, Kentucky 40351, USA, ph +1 606-783-2982; & Association for Contextual Behavioral Science Board of Directors

**Definition:** Helping clients to explore and choose values to strive for by ongoing, evolving patterns of activity that are rewarding in themselves.

**Elements:** In discussion with the therapist clients look at and select life-long directions of behavior that the clients value for their own sake and can sustain indefinitely by a stream of satisfying activities. Examples of valued ongoing pursuits are: education, which is unending, unlike getting a degree; being a loving spouse, which involves continuing support that is never complete, unlike a short-term reconciliation; being a caring parent, which might include regularly assisting children with homework, helping them think through problems, attending their sports events. Clients are encouraged to choose values to strive for that are personally meaningful, not lip service to prevailing norms, in interactions arising in a session (Case illustration 1 below) or by structured experiential exercises (Case illustration 2 below). Clients are also helped to uncover and devise ways of overcoming barriers to pursuing valued directions such as feeling inadequate when seeking long-term intimacy with a partner, or finishing professional training to engage in valued work with colleagues to care for other people.

**Related procedures:** *Motivational interviewing, goal-setting, guided imagery.*

**Application:** In individual - or group ACT (acceptance and commitment therapy).

**1st Use?** Hayes & Wilson (1994) in ACT, long preceded by related procedures in other therapies.

**References:**
1. Hayes SC, Strosahl KD, Wilson KG (1999). *Acceptance and commitment therapy: An experiential approach to behavior change.* New York: Guilford.
2. Hayes SC, Wilson KG (1994). Acceptance and commitment therapy: Altering the verbal support for experiential avoidance. *The Behavior Analyst*, 17, 289-303.
3. Luoma JB, Hayes SC, Walser RD (2007). *Learning ACT: An Acceptance and commitment therapy skills-training manual for therapists.* Oakland, CA: New Harbinger.

4. Wilson KG, Murrell AR (2004). Values work in acceptance and commitment therapy: Setting a course for behavioral treatment (pp 120-151). In S Hayes, V Follette, M Linehan (Eds.), *Mindfulness and acceptance: Expanding the cognitive-behavioral tradition.* New York: Guilford.

**Case Illustration 1:** (Blackledge, unpublished)
Therapist: *"When you talk about time with your daughter Ava you get excited, animated. She's very important to you, isn't she?"* Client John: "Yes, she's everything to me." Therapist: *"One thing jumps out when you talk about her - you really want to be 'there' for her. Is that right?"* John: "Yeah ..., I really do." Therapist: *" What kind of father do you really want to be to her?"* Long pause: "I want her to know how much I love her, support her in what she's doing, make her feel cared for, secure." *"You want to be a loving, supportive, caring father, and give her a safe, secure home. Is that right?"* John nods enthusiastically. *"You're so animated as you talk about your relationship with Ava, it strikes me we've hit on one of your values. But to be sure - if no one else ever knew you valued doing these things for her... your wife, parents, friends, neighbors, me... would you still do these things for her?"* Pause: "Yes... I would." *Therapist (to elicit specific actions according with this value): "What exactly could you do today to show her how much you love her, just one thing consistent with that value?* John: "Well, usually when I get home from work, I just eat dinner, relax, and let my wife take care of Ava. Tonight, I could get down on the floor and play with Ava, and pull her up on my lap and read a book to her".

**Case Illustration 2:** (Blackledge, unpublished)
Therapist: *"Let's do an exercise to figure out what's crucial to you as a person. Sit comfortably and close your eyes.* [Client settles and becomes aware of her breathing and other sensations] *Think of your best-ever memory about anything that's happened to you. Scroll back through the best moments of your life. Raise a finger when you have your best, or almost-best, memory of something in mind ... "Now focus on every detail of that memory ... pull it into the room with you now. Picture where you were then, everything around you, who was with you, their faces, what you and others were doing and saying ... what you were feeling and thinking ... Let that memory's events play themselves out in front of you now, from start to end... Attend especially to what you were doing back then, how you were behaving toward others, toward the world?...What kind of person were you being? ...".*

The therapist focused on aspects of the client's memory that made her animated and open. These concerned being loving to her husband and children and helping them do something important. Asked if she'd like to have more such moments with them, her answer was a resounding "Yes!", that they made her feel "alive", showing that a core value had been identified.

## WELL-BEING THERAPY (WBT)

**Giovanni FAVA**, Dipartimento di Psicologia, University of Bologna, Viale Berti Pichat 5, 40127 Bologna, Italy; ph +39-051-2091339

**Definition:** WBT tries to enhance patients' sense of well-being by: 1) enhancing their awareness of positive moments; 2) discussing and changing negative thoughts which disrupt episodes of well being; 3) improving patients' impairments in 6 well-being areas - autonomy, environmental mastery, personal growth, positive relations, purpose in life, self-acceptance.

**Elements:** In up to 8 sessions the therapist asks the patient to record in a structured diary current episodes of well-being and thoughts which truncated them, re-interpret those thoughts viewed from an observer's standpoint (*cognitive restructuring*), and use re- interpretations to increase a sense of well being in any of the 6 areas which might be impaired. WBT includes:
- *cognitive restructuring*: change from negative to positive thoughts which interrupt periods of feeling well.
- *scheduling of pleasant activities:* negotiate with patients enjoyable activities they will carry out each day, e.g. go for a walk, listen to music.
- *graded tasks:* e.g. to improve positive relations, encourage a patient to phone a friend, invite that friend out for dinner, spend further time with that friend.
- *assertiveness training* – see that entry
- *problem solving* to improve patients' autonomy and environmental mastery, e.g. (*help another patient deal with everyday activities;* ask for a promotion at work etc.).

**Related procedures:** *Cognitive restructuring, distancing, rational-emotive therapy procedures, fostering positive thinking, homework, happiness intervention.*

**Application:** Taught individually or in small groups to adults or adolescents, in clinical or other settings.

**1st Use?** Fava et al (1998).

**References:**
1. Fava GA, Rafanelli C, Cazzaro M, Conti S, Grandi S (1998). Well-being therapy. A novel psychotherapeutic approach for residual symptoms of affective disorders. *Psychol Med*, 28, 475-480.
2. Fava GA (1999). Well-being therapy. *Psychother Psychosom*, 68, 171-178.

3. Ryff CD, Singer BH (1996). Psychological well-being: meaning, measurement, and implications for psychotherapy research. *Psychother Psychosom* 65, 14-23.

**Case illustration:**

Tom, a student aged 23, had severe obsessive-compulsive disorder (OCD) for a year. It was refractory to SRI medication and cognitive behavior therapy. In well-being sessions 1 and 2 he was asked to record in a structured daily diary his episodes of well- being and feelings related to them and thoughts which interrupted them. By such self- observation he found that a sense of well-being (e.g. `Maybe I'm getting better and my life will change') was terminated by an unpleasant thought (`A terrible crisis is on its way') and an obsession ("My girlfriend will soon find a better boyfriend and I will be alone again"). He was asked to add an observer's interpretation to his diary (what someone else might think in the same situation). This helped him see that obsessions could be prevented by practising a thought different to the pre-obsessive thoughts that a sense of well-being had brought on (e.g. `To acknowledge progress does not mean asking for trouble'; (the patient starts recognizing well-being may be the result of previous work). He was persuaded to schedule pleasant activities (e.g. walking on the beach) which he had hitherto avoided as he felt he didn't deserve them and activities such as attending lectures and taking exams, and to record in his diary whenever he carried out these graded tasks. He was made aware of similarities between situations he had successfully coped with in the past (e.g. previous exams) and those he had to deal with now or in future (e.g. new exams) (transfer of experiences). He was taught to problem-solve everyday difficulties (e.g. combining work and leisure). Over eight 2- weekly sessions the intensity and perceived importance of his obsessions fell to sub- clinical levels. Tom felt much better and finished his studies, and at 4-year follow-up had no OCD.

*Notes:*

# CLP 80